THE GHOST VARIATIONS

THE GHOST VARIATIONS

Damian Lanigan

WEATHERGLASS BOOKS

For my dad

THE GHOST
VARIATIONS

NEW YORK

1

I finish practice at midnight. My hands and arms are warm and loose, the rest of me needs human contact. I'm taking a break from having played piano all day to play piano for most of the night. There are four or five bars in Upper Manhattan with instruments I can use, a rust belt of these old machines, remnants of a world becoming derelict. I ghost around town until the early hours trying to prove that there's still something to be said for this world: there's nothing that improves a room more than the sound of a well-played piano.

Tonight I choose Kinsale on the West Side in the 70s: Irish tricolours in the rafters, corny framed mottos, horse brasses, a heavy mahogany bar, even more fake-Irish than me. The place is a dive, but they have a piano in their lounge in the back, and in this lounge there are often girls. The idea is not to go home alone until that's the only possible course of action.

I know the bartender, Sandrine, a small, intense Parisienne who has angel wings tattooed across her chest and a verse from *Les Fleurs du mal* on her neck. She spends her days teaching French to Upper East Side wives who quit after the fourth lesson, and her nights fending off drunks with dark sarcasm.

Sandrine's a singer. I've accompanied her many times: Françoise Hardy, Birkin, Cole Porter, Carole King. On her night job she can seem gloomy: I suppose she's miles from home and not at all sure why and it's after midnight and she's trapped in a cave with a pack of drunks. But when she sings she is transformed into a joyful little demon.

'Oban, Declan?'

She has to stand on a little footstool to reach the good Scotch. I see she has a silver stud in each one of her sacral pits.

'You playing tonight?'

'I don't know yet.' But I do, of course. 'It's fine, isn't it?'

'You don't know?'

'I need your approval.'

'Am I your priest or your mother or what?'

I give her twenty dollars and she looks at me kindly, which is all I needed.

'Do you think anyone would have sex with me if I wasn't good at the piano?'

'Why not find out one night?' She gives me her hand to kiss then passes me the tumbler of Scotch. 'Good luck out there.'

I look at my glass. There's no doubt that I'm an alcoholic (the single family heirloom), and understanding this, I never have more than two drinks. It used to be a torment: every night this tedious internal dialogue between the disease and the part of me that loathed it. But now I know that if you can face something down for long enough it loses its desire to fight back. Never drinking would mean I'd lost, and that the thing that got my ancestors had got me too. This way, I know I have mastery: never more than two, not once. Also, you can acquire a habit that's less harmful than the one it replaces. In my case, it's practising for hours a day. Sometimes I go through the night, into the next day, all time awareness gone, ten hours maybe, more and more: a complete bender. When I go to bed, the room spins.

Today, though, I needed this break. My body is still humming with Beethoven, my mind with thoughts of something else.

The front part of Kinsale is not for me: it's always a little too cold in summer, too warm in winter. Flat screens show live sports till the games are over, then sports highlights till closing. The whole place smells of beer and toilet cakes. The crowd is Young Upper

2

West Siders dressed sharper than their surroundings, from the new towers west of 10th, the unconverted tenements on the avenues: it's transactional and restless, no one really wants to be there.

But the lounge is different. It's low-ceilinged, almost pitch-black, no TVs or Irishry, just big shabby Chesterfields and a few lamps with velvet bobbles hanging from their shades, like the parlour of an old bordello. I slip through the heavy velvet curtain, sensitive and expectant: I can feel the ice cubes kiss in the whisky glass.

Not many people around tonight: a few, boozy, tie-loosened men inclined towards dubious girls, a low male-voice murmuring.

Then there it is, alone in the corner, with its dumb toothy grimace, ignored and needing attention: a piano. Tonight, even after the day's work, I feel brimful of music. But before I get to play, I have to do some persuading.

It took me a while to figure this out, but you should always ask the women first: they never say no. Maybe it's because they're more polite, or maybe they're always in some sense trying to get away from their date. Anyway, what's clear is that women are curious about gifted men, and upon this fact I continue to rely.

I walk across to the first couple, stoop and speak softly, trying for what I imagine is a 007 vibe.

'Excuse me, so sorry to interrupt, but would you mind if I played the piano a little? I'll be quiet. And I'll be good. I'll be quietly good.'

The woman is immediately interested, sits up a little straighter, lifts her chin in playful defiance: 'Ooh, quietly good?'

Her date looks away. I see at once that she's bored by him. She's pale, the nearly black glow of Kinsale hardly warming her skin tone at all. Her face is small and alert, her eyes are dark and skilful: they've no doubt had a lot of work to do at night in New York City. Close up I notice a faint spray of freckles, another one of these lovely, slim, dark-haired New York girls: Italian, Russian, Chinese, Jewish, sometimes all of the above. She's wearing a tight, pale blue blouse, cigarette pants, neat patent shoes: a together, going-places look. She probably does a lot of meetings, has complicated real-world ambitions. I have nothing to do with all of that, which, in this place, is clearly to my advantage.

'I'll let you decide.'

She widens her eyes as she nods. Her date stares at the side of her face with ruined lust.

'OK then. Thank you.'

I move to the piano, and, still standing, play one soft G major chord. I look around: people re-settle in their seats, one or two gesture at me to go ahead.

The instrument is a noble American upright with a bit of age on it. The owner keeps it tuned for their Monday music nights, the ones where I humbly accompany Sandrine's torch songs. It has a sweet upper register, a thin, metallic bass, but I'm not critical.

'A piano has characteristics, not flaws.'

'You cannot win a fight when your opponent has nothing to lose.'

These are from my teacher, Sasha Tal, who, being old and Russian, gave out a lot of such wisdom. He would sit off my right shoulder as I played, whisper 'Oh, Declan' at every moment of cowardice, awkwardness or schmaltz, then say something like:

'Let the piano play you.'

'The right hand is a fairy, the left a tyrant.'

'The piano is in its heart a percussion instrument.'

Is any of this true? Perhaps. Do I know what they mean? I do not.

But then:

'To play the piano well, Declan, you must completely disappear.'

4

And I always knew the precise meaning of this.

I take my seat, and glance at the girl with the pale skin: already – surely not! – a look of hope, or interest at least. So quick, alarming and absolutely thrilling, the thought of music, the thought of her, instantly present and combined.

I place my glass on top of the piano, take one quiet breath and start to play: Chopin's 'Butterfly' Étude, at a rapid tempo, almost inaudibly. I close my eyes, imagine the ditzy erratic beast careering around the flower heads. It's something I started when I was very small and still do every day: play a piece all the way through as quietly as possible. The idea was to learn fineness of touch. Playing quickly and quietly is like whispering while running. Slow and loud is easy. Slow and quiet is easy. Loud and fast is easy. Fast and quiet: very, very difficult. But here I am, doing it, and doing it without effort.

I open my eyes once I'm in the swing, and look into the whisky glass. I can see tiny see-sawing oscillations in the surface of the liquid. It's reassuring to see the effects of my actions on the physical world. I stare into the whisky, playing a little louder now, leaning into the piece's giddy ragtime, watching the whisky dance along. My playing is so lucid tonight, it's just flowing out of me: I can do whatever I want.

As soon as I have this thought, Tal's voice brings me down: 'If it sounds so easy, Mister Byrnie, then why should we take you seriously?'

I face him down, though, and move straight into the 'Harp' Étude, curious, as I'm playing so well, what a love song would sound like.

Like this, I guess.

I begin to disappear into it, but not so completely that I don't sense her movement behind me. I feel elated and only the tiniest bit ashamed. I don't extend the final chord, almost kill it at birth.

I take a sip of Chopin-infused whisky to stop me from emitting a groan of musical ecstasy. She moves from behind me and is now standing an uncertain distance away. I glance quickly at her companion on the couch. He is circling an empty beer glass in his hand, looking pretty much trounced.

'He's no one.'

'Are you sure?'

'Tinder trash. *Literally* no one.'

She's small and holds herself like a dancer, something about her head, held a little in profile, the position of her feet, the deep gymnastic arch of her lower back.

'You *are* pretty good.'

'Yes. Especially tonight, for some reason.'

'Such humility.'

'Sorry. I can't take any credit. I never asked for it.'

'It was beautiful. You're so talented.'

I like being told this and I don't like being told this.

'I practise a lot.'

'Are you going to play something else?'

'Must I?'

She laughs. 'Probably not, but I'd like you to.'

She draws a chair up, sits just within my peripheral vision. I think for a second or two and exhale softly. I play Debussy's 'Reverie', very quietly again but this time at a perfect natural speed. Soon I'm under the spell and so, I can sense, is she. What I do, this close up, looks and sounds like a miracle.

When I finish we talk a little on the couch, me with my second and final Scotch, her with a vodka soda. Her date is long gone. She is funny and tactile and smart and her name is Penny. She had indeed been a dancer but is now in commercial real estate. Her tone becomes darker when I ask why she quit her ballet: something to do with a discouraging father and also, in truth,

6

her fear/knowledge that she was never going to be good enough. At any rate, it was obviously something serious for her.

'It looks so pretty, but it's a kind of murder really. Of your body and your mind. It was for me. I loved it, though.'

'I can sympathize.'

'Really? It looks so easy for you.'

'It absolutely isn't.'

In the subsequent pause, I reach out to her, and she accepts my hand, her eyes bright and grateful.

———

We're out of there before one. I catch Sandrine's eye as we leave and she blows me a kiss.

Penny holds on to my arm too tightly as we walk across town. The city is warm and quiet. Something within me makes me come to a stop. I feel this something press to the surface:

'I'm so sorry.'

She turns to look at me.

'Don't say sorry. I'm doing great. Are you OK?'

I look back at her, and can't stop myself:

'Penny, I realize this might sound a bit strange, but I was talking to my wife.'

2

So now it's the morning after. I'm walking down to Midtown playing through a nuanced little suite of anxieties. It's almost fun to toy with them, like practising something tricky you know you're soon going to master. It should be said that for me everything is like practice in some way: I don't do much else, so my range of analogies is small.

Firstly, the prospect of seeing my agent. He is encouraging and critical, a combination of two bad parents who think they're good ones. He represents duty and responsibility and money and The World, and who can stand all that?

Secondly: Penny. She left me, got straight into a cab. I didn't attempt to explain, didn't even want to. Did I say it involuntarily? Maybe not, because I was happy to see her go. But why now?

There's no time to figure it out because of the third anxiety, the ever-present: I absolutely need to practise and am terrified something will prevent me from doing so.

I slept late this morning, and now I won't be able to get to a piano until noon, maybe later. I make an involuntary growl and look up into the glinting high-rises. I play back some of yesterday's session in my head: the bloopers ricochet around the steel and glass. Fuck, why am I such a terrible pianist? So many things that need fixing, and quick. I enter my usual panic, and the panic leads to my urgent desire to be seated at a piano and all this makes me walk slightly more quickly down 57th. If I speed up I'll be done with this awful meeting sooner and back to my longed-for slavery, and all other thoughts will be gone.

I'm in the elevator now and have to organize my mind for my agent's friendly questions that make me feel I'm being checked up on, his polite requests that feel like commands. I think about doing a runner but don't.

—

Peter Barlow is now part of a large agency called, with maximal obviousness, Sonata Management. When I won the Leeds sixteen years ago he was one of many who pursued me, and he got the gig because he was obviously a better human being than the others: kind, musical and extremely suave. He also brought with him a classy letterhead, attractive financial projections and a contract. The legal apparatus was decisive for my parents: it meant that they, who had reached middle age never having seen a contract, could for once participate in the serious, complicated world that had always been beyond them: our Declan's got a *lawyer*!

Then, once he got hold of me, he set about creating me. He started with an idea you can roughly characterize as 'Declan Byrnie: Slum Prodigy'. We had the evidence we needed to back this up: I was indeed brought up in a council house, and I was even more indeed pretty damn good at the piano. And then, I have to shamefacedly admit, there was what he called the 'glamour element'. Peter persuaded me to grow my hair. Over one summer I became a High Art Jim Morrison. And so it was, when dolled up and photographed with enough shadowy sleight of hand, I looked like an Italian princelet or dashing young snooker player: pale, supercilious, overdressed. Even in this century being a Hot Slum Prodigy gets you on TV: I played 'La Campanella' at the BRITs and the nation got all hot and bothered, even though they probably thought it went on a bit long.

Then I needed to develop a repertoire. Here Barlow's contribution was to suggest that I learn pretty much the entire piano literature, and mine was that I went away and learned it. At the same time, he built up my schedule, which quickly became tightly packed and multinational (London, New York, Berlin, Lucerne, Sydney, Tokyo, Seoul, São Paolo, Tel Aviv, Helsinki). Gradually and then extremely rapidly I was in a career that was going fantastically well, over which I had precisely zero control and which consisted of airports, grand pianos, adulation and some rich women and quite a few rich men making passes at me backstage. I was always in motion, always in demand, made up almost entirely of jet lag, nerves and hotel breakfasts.

Of course, since Esther, there has been no career, no schedule, not even much of an idea: another type of disappearance. In the weeks and months after she died, Barlow was as good at being sympathetic as one would expect. Then, after a beautifully judged period of time, he tried to coax me out. He failed. He tried again a while later, but gave up just as he sensed me getting angry. Three years ago, I went completely dark on him and he finally left me alone.

Then, two weeks ago, I sent him a one-line email: *I need to play again.* He replied within minutes – *Lovely! Leave it with me* – and instantly reverted to his mode of stylish enterprise. He has no doubt been working on some new Idea. I'm curious: where do you go after 'Hot Slum Prodigy Who Can Play Every Damn Thing'?

And actually it was never a 'slum'. Our house was in Burnage, a sarcastic, low-built suburb on the main road into Manchester; a little red-brick semi, in a neat cul-de-sac, perfectly fine for three. All the neighbours voted Labour but bought their houses the minute they could. Once they were property owners, the first in family history to own a little piece of the planet, they competed earnestly with each other over gardens and Christmas decorations: clumps of pansies planted three feet apart in the borders around the tightly mown front lawns, box hedges round the perimeter, a Rudolph made of fairy lights on the porch roof when the time came, more lights festooning the windows. Most put in Downing Street-style front doors but painted them red or blue because black looked too much like the undertaker's; then hanging baskets either side spilling over with pink, red and purple blooms every spring. They bought second-hand foreign cars and, sometimes, mocking their own fanciness, bottles of white wine. Not us, though, with the wine: Mum drank Bailey's, which she liked because it was proof that the Irish could be posh and that posh could taste nice; my dad was beer and whisky all the way.

I'm not sure what they'd make of Sonata's reception area: cool, grey, overlit, two of those low European couches with nowhere to put your arms. The receptionist brings me a fizzy water in a ribbed plastic cup before returning to behind her glass and oak rampart. She sorts her hair and starts to tippy-tap on her keyboard, a tinny little harpsichord. The space is hung with artist portraits: low-lit mugshots of haughty conductors, or them with arms outspread in vainglory before the orchestra; pianists caught in secret rapture over the fabulousness of their own phrasing. The singers: the men smiling dashingly in cashmere V-necks, the women eroticized in regal fashion, airbrushed creamy skin, highly structured hairdos and glossy lips. The images as hackneyed as the bios in the concert programmes: 'astonishing… genius… wedding technical mastery to artistic feeling… finest of their generation… intelligent, lyrical and fresh…' The fact that none of it is quite untrue doesn't make it any less embarrassing.

I'm shown through to Barlow, who has seemingly come up in the world. His old office was a cubicle at the back of a second-rate literary agency on 44th and Broadway. It consisted of a worryingly empty desk and him behind it, small and immaculate on his squeaky rotating throne. There were two drab office chairs and a ficus in the corner. On the wall there was a photograph of me as a spidery seventeen-year-old clutching a prize. Over the years, the ficus grew over it, so eventually I looked like some treetop monkey with a piece of stolen treasure. Now he's fully corporatized: he has the same belittling chair, and also his very own uncomfortable couch, a coffee table bearing copies of *Gramophone*, *Pianist* and *Opera*, a bowl of clovey potpourri and a view down the avenue. There are many client headshots on his wall, but none of me.

'This is all very plausible.'

'Isn't it just.'

He doesn't get up to shake hands. Our relationship has a gratifying continuity: I haven't seen him for four years, but we pick up where we left off, even down to the conversational topic.

'Declan, have you eaten since I last saw you?'

'Not really.'

'You should.'

'Huh.'

'You've been practising though?'

'Oh God yes. Like a maniac.'

'Bloody marvellous.'

He pours me some water from the decanter on his desk with a strangely contented look on his face. Maybe he's pleased to see me. All resentment fades when I'm in Barlow's presence. I notice that I love him: a good, clever, interesting man.

'Shall I call in some tea?'

'*Call in some tea?*'

'I can do that now.'

Anglophilia penetrates deep into his personality: he subscribes to *Majesty* magazine and has an MGB at his house in the Berkshires. This should be some kind of phoniness, but he's absolutely for real. He holidays in Suffolk and is an authority on Gothic Revival churches, which is to say that he presents as an episcopalian celibate but is clearly a Catholic homosexual. He plays the piano quite nicely, but his ear is his real gift. He's a better judge of a pianist than me, and certainly of singers: the female voice is his passion, and they can emotionally dismember him. He is comical and utterly wicked in company, rarely flat-out nasty. The fact that he reads either poetry or detective fiction of the most gruesome kind is perfectly indicative of his balance of grace and darkness. He drinks.

'Any other news?'

'Not really. Well, I've been doing this thing where I go into bars and I play the piano and it sort of… gets me women.'

'Why are you whispering?'

'I don't know.'

'I see no problem. Frankly, why else would anyone play the piano?'

'It feels wrong. Is it wrong?'

'Why is it wrong? If that's the extent of your sexual misbehaviour, Declan, then you're at the very bottom of the musician list. The things I could tell you about some of these people. It's like Roman times out there.'

I feel somewhat absolved and study him while he allows me to study him.

'Are you wearing *make-up*?'

'Piss off.'

The face is still pristine and slightly pink, the hair an almost translucent silver, but his jawline is getting indistinct. His neck is starkly cabled, and his pale brown eyes have become watery, yet he still has his quickness. He's wearing a navy chalk stripe English suit with a plenitude of tabs, pockets and flaps.

'I hope you don't mind me saying, Peter, but your nose is getting wider.'

'Oh, I know. Not one I was anticipating.' He pinches it briefly between finger and thumb and hums wistfully.

'Am I here for a reason?'

'A very good reason. Let me grab the boss.'

He goes out, ruffling my hair as he passes. It's possible he loved me once and never let on. He has long claimed that his libido is theoretical, and that he prefers it that way. Still the same scent in his wake: figs, but dry, not sweet. He is so highly detailed.

While he's out, I confirm that there are indeed no pictures of me in the room. I recognize pretty much everyone: Dmitri Kazan, my friend who, for shame, has gone crossover; Deborah Bennett, an alcoholic bluestocking who is acknowledged as a superb player of French music everywhere but France; Smyslov, an ancient Russian who taught me for a week before declaring me 'too flashy' and now does a slow, eternal circuit of Old Europe playing Beethoven at quarter speed. A few people I don't know: a beautiful young violinist who looks Japanese, her lips so thick with red gloss they almost reflect, her skin the colour of mist. I wonder which one has the most Roman love life. Deborah, for sure.

I'm interrupted by Peter re-entering with Melissa Gore, a complicated, big-boned woman who smells of rosewater and cigarettes.

'Oh, Declan, we're so happy to have you back, I can't tell you!'

I half get up to kiss her, but she's unmanageable with all her bags and folders and coffee cups. She flops onto the couch, strewing a sheaf of paper beside her, and flicks away a sprig of hair with the back of her big pink hand. Her wedding ring's off and she's breathing hard.

'You remember Melissa?'

'Of course.'

Melissa is Sonata's CEO. She was number two at Carnegie Hall for years, a manager at Deutsche Grammophon before that. She's pretty much tone-deaf but has vast reserves of a kind of Tory energy, and an eye for the 'narrative' thing. Barlow regains his seat and tips himself back, making way for her proposition, kissing his pyramid of fingertips.

'We're just so *excited*, Dec. But more I'm just so glad, you know, that you're back. It's been such an *awful* time for you.'

It seems weird in terms of the power relation that I'm higher than she is, and she feels it too, so she shuffles herself to perch on the edge of the sofa: pounce position.

'I've been good, actually. Much better. I've been playing a lot, and also… well, not really much else, just playing.'

'Have you? Of course you have. *Wonderful.* It's honestly *thrilling* that we have you back. That everyone has you back. It's insane, really, how long you've been gone. We've missed you *terribly.*'

'I feel ready. To start thinking about it, at least.'

Her energy flattens the life out of me, but it's reassuring that someone in our world has such a good solid chunk of it.

'We are so, so *thrilled*. Let me just get clear on your schedule, again, next few days?'

'I fixed up a small thing at Quine College early next week, then a house party in Connecticut. That's it, just little tiddlers really. But afterwards I should know how I feel.'

'That seems so perfect as a first step. But listen – and this is amazing – you know Semyon Kozar?'

'Of course.'

Kozar is an ancient Russian plutocrat who has his own concert series in Boston: not more than ten pianists per season, always the most famous old European man or the newest, hottest Asian girl. A vanity project with oligarchic fees.

'He called me. Next week, Reti has cancelled and they need someone, and I mentioned you.'

I have a miniature white-out. 'Oh no.'

A brief silence and Barlow says: 'What kind of "oh no" is that?'

'I'm stalling for time.'

So this is why I'm here. My intention was to creep slowly

into the world, to judge the temperature and the threat levels like some early tetrapod. This is not that. I look out into the wall of Midtown windows and have a premonition: me, the house lights dimming over the audience in his perfected concert space, me and the piano in our ball of light, that silence I could choose to maintain, the wave of music about to break. Once you start, there's no way back. The tightrope walker, the tumbler spreading their arms in readiness in the corner of the mat, everyone gazing intently, envious, waiting to be amazed. I close my eyes in refusal.

'What's wrong with Reti?'

'He's dying.'

'Oh God, I liked him.'

'Everyone did.'

I look at Peter, who is trying to judge my state of mind. He moves through all the stations of mild discomfort before he settles on a light grip of his lower face.

'Dec, we know it's a lot to take on.'

Melissa bursts in. 'I've been talking about this a lot to many, many people. So much excitement around it. If it goes well we're back at the races, it's a triumph and so on, and you're easily a major artist for us again. Just *easily*.'

'Poor Reti. He was such a great player.'

Melissa is still breathing heavily and trying to get me to look at her. I avoid her smoky thick-lashed eyes and look down. Her plump unpedicured feet are crammed higgledy-piggledy into strappy gold sandals.

Now I look out the window. No eye contact yet.

Melissa again: 'And, in a sense, he's doing us a favour, obviously.'

That's a mistake, and the artist's righteous anger surfaces: '*Is* he doing me a favour? I'm also doing him a favour, right? It's a deal, not a favour.'

'You know, with you not having played for a while.'

I watch her recalibrate a little, but it's only really the tone that alters, not the intention. 'Sorry, Declan, obviously, but Semyon is huge for us, he really is. And Barlow and I thought you could play the *Hammerklavier* again, and this is what closed it for him. He does so few concerts a year, only the very best people, the best promotion, the biggest fees. He likes to have a hook. He's sort of trying to corner the market up there, and he's doing it so *beautifully.* He's such a great admirer of yours. And you are fortunate, being one of the few after all this time: let's be clear about that.'

I look again at Barlow, who has faintly but perceptibly winced at the Speaking of the Name. I try to keep quiet for a bit to regain the attention of the room. It doesn't work; it's a fait accompli.

'Hold on, Melissa. We've committed to the *Hammerklavier*? Before I committed to playing at all? What is it? A week's time?'

Peter leans in. 'No one's committed anyone to anything, Dec. It was *mentioned.*'

'He gets to do the programme as well?'

'He likes to make suggestions.'

'He *really* wants you to play it, darling.'

I ignore Melissa and look directly at Barlow. 'Come on, Peter. Jesus. This is a fucking ambush.'

'We took a call and had a conversation.'

'And what was your side of it?'

Melissa is still charging at me hard, like some commercial hippopotamus. 'Think of it this way: the brilliant young man and so on, away for so long, returns with the piece that first blazed him across the scene. Triumphing over what's happened.'

'Oh, Melissa, that's *awful.*'

Barlow leans forward now, cautiously rearranging his mouth

before he says anything. Then: 'It was me, Declan, who mooted putting it in front of you. I thought it through quite a lot and it really is, I think, the best way to go. He will do his bit perfectly, and we should rise to meet that.'

I inspect him for flecks of bullshit. He inspects me in return, for signs of fear or doubt. It's clear he's doing this because he thinks it's the right thing to do. I decide to make them sweat.

'You know I can't.'

Barlow looks completely unpanicked. Presumably because he knows I'm lying.

'Declan, really. We want you to do what you want to do. We want the best for you, of course we do. And let's be honest, you always said you wanted to play it again. And we mentioned that to Semyon, and he was delighted. In fact, he was overwhelmed. And we've reached out to the *Times*, who are on board, even some TV people: PBS in Boston. The power of the story and so on. Nothing's confirmed, but there's interest.'

'The power of the *what*?'

Barlow re-grips his jaw. I dimly remember that face-touching is some kind of primate shame gesture.

I'm disoriented; what am I really being asked to do, and why am I resisting? This is something to work through. The analogy, of course, is a page of new music: it's easy to grasp the overall picture, but this clearly is unhelpful when you start to read it through. Music is some sort of totality, but is mainly about how to get through the next two bars.

So: of course I want to play the *Hammerklavier*. I've not looked at it in years, but I think about it daily. I recorded it fifteen years ago, straight after winning Leeds, driven to do so by Peter. An eighteen-year-old Englishman, with a name like a sitcom leprechaun, taking on the Great Monument. The enterprise sent the critical class into something of a flutter:

'The impudence of it', 'Surely an ill-advised venture', 'Way too soon'. But then the little scally pulled it off: 'A bravura performance!', 'What power, what delicacy!', 'What technique!', 'What vision!' All that nonsense. But because of it I was suddenly in the world.

I listen back to the record occasionally: the notes were played in the correct order, and that's about it. The Steinway I used wasn't right: such an opaque, glutinous tone. The Fugue was all church organ, the Adagio molasses, the first movement drums and trombones. It made me think of some vintage Bugatti, a vast, oily wheezing engine, cluttered with bells and horns, chromium exhaust pipes gleaming, chugging through the Black Forest at twilight, some mad-eyed old sausage-eater grimly manning the controls.

'The *Hammerklavier* is of course much better on paper than it is played out loud.'

Tal.

The CD cover had me looking out over my right shoulder, black tux, black shirt open at the neck, my hair in its curly Morrisonian/snooker boy pomp, not far into daily shaving, forehead smooth as glass. Fancy little bogtrotter. Jesus. How did I get away with it? *Hammerklavier* is for old people becoming familiar with deafness, ugliness and the dark. In short, His Nibs wrote it for His Nibs, and no one else should have to listen to it ever again.

Barlow is looking at his clean fingernails. Melissa has tilted her head like a little dog, for God's sake.

'Give me a minute. Where's the bathroom?'

They can wait a little longer.

Back into the monochrome thrum, people watch me pass by their little cubes, a girl at a photocopier wearing a headset and staring at the slow mechanical juddering, two older women conferring over a beige folder. The administration is there to administer the music, the music must generate sufficient funds to pay for the administration, which ensures the continuance of the music. Is that how it works?

The toilet is more monochrome. The electricity which runs the hand dryer must be paid for. So too the thin, stooped cleaner who waits outside in grey overalls, his red and white embroidered name tag reading FELIX. I nod thanks to him on my way out and hold the door open, but he doesn't respond, just kicks his wheeled bucket through on to the tiles.

I understand Kozar's motivations: he's certainly committed to the music, and maybe he's thinking about the musical world bragging rights over my comeback. But the media, the *TV*, for God's sake? That's something else. That's 'the power of the story', which clearly derives from the death of my wife.

My relevance, my ability to still pique public interest, the interview with the *Times*, the TV, the accompanying photo shoot, the heroical way they light me, the trappings of dark romance and hints at redemption, my enigmatic facial expression, the ticket sales at Kozar's concert, and almost certainly the respectful tone of the reviews, all proceed from the fact that my beautiful young wife died, and that I haven't played in the four years since this event, and now I'm back, and people want to know what happened. Her death is the instigation of this new phase of my career, its endorsement, almost its entire meaning. How does *that* feel?

I walk back to Barlow's office. He and Melissa look at me expectantly. I retake my seat and make them wait a few seconds more.

And then another few.

'Yes, I'm sorry. Obviously it's fine. It might even do me good.'
Barlow is quizzical. 'What?'

'Talking about Esther.'

'We'd never insist on it.'

'I'd have to though. That's why they're interested, isn't it?'

Melissa looks surprised but eager. 'Well, it would help. It really would.'

'And of course I'll do Kozar.'

I become aware that Melissa has started to sob a little. She is looking at her hands, which are clasped tightly around her knees. 'My lovely Dec.'

Don't call me that.

I feel sympathy for her more than anything. She's not a bad person, just a scary one because her job is to speak the truth.

'Give me a day or so to decide what I'll play. But of course I'll do it. I'm a pianist, for God's sake.'

They both half-whisper 'Yes, of course,' as an amen. I feel a responsibility to change the tone.

'Why the hell is Kazan putting out records called *Romantic Nights*?'

Melissa is forced to emerge from her prayers into defensiveness. 'That was a joint decision.'

'Never do that to me. I mean never even try it. *The Star Wars Album* or *Broadway Byrnie* or some other fucking travesty.'

Melissa has briskly shed her widow's weeds and clapped on combat gear. 'That changed his career, Declan.'

'Honestly, Melissa, I'll literally debase myself in all ways possible before I do that. *Journey Into Chopin* like I'm tuberculosis or the clap.' My hostility is surfacing in unusual places, like a beach ball with Tourette's.

'It's actually a very fine album.' Peter, despite having got everything he wanted, is still impatient.

'Oh, don't, please, Peter. Forget it. I can raise it with him, if he hasn't ended his own life.'

And now, sort of unbelievably, Melissa is consulting her phone and, thinking it's mission accomplished, is ready to move on. 'I'll let you two talk. We're so grateful, Declan. It's *sooo* lovely. It's *absolutely* the right thing to do.'

She leaves in a slightly overdone flurry of purposefulness, and Barlow tips back on his chair with one big creak. 'She's right. I think this will be great for you.'

'Clearly. A week, did you say?'

'Yes.'

Now I really need a piano.

Peter inhales and makes a bid. 'Odds on *Hammerklavier*?'

'Peter, really. You've got me, and you've got my wife. Give me a day or two, OK?'

He nods, because he knows.

3

I practise in many places, though rarely at my apartment. There's a Steinway there, but I don't like to play it because its near-perfection is distracting: I continually sense that I'm glimpsing some kind of ideal sound and keep trying to make up the tiny difference, and the closer I get, the further away it becomes, some kind of musical Zeno's Paradox. I just want to practise. I'm not after some transcendence or beauty: practice is about my hands, not my soul.

Today, feeling the nagging arousal of time pressure, I decide on Greene-Fairley on 44th, and walk down 6th with impatience. They have a collection of good upright Yamahas, always perfectly tuned. As I ascend in the rickety elevator, I can hear the first broken chord in my mind.

I check in and instantly feel at home. It's an audition and rehearsal space for all types of performing artists, so the corridors and waiting areas are always teeming with nervous actors and dancers, moods of optimism and despair in some tight-knit DNA spiral. The mood of neurotic kinship is pervasive and comforting.

'Mr Byrnie, you can go through.'

They've given me my second-favourite room: at the end of a narrow corridor, small, no mirror, one window with a flimsy dark green curtain that nonetheless keeps out most of the light. Light is the enemy of sound: a steady, unchanging gloom is the ideal condition. Also, the acoustic is very dead: there's no colour in it to distract me from listening to my playing.

The piano is pushed tightly into the corner: damn it. This means I have to roll it away from the wall and into the middle of the room; I must have air behind the instrument so the music has space to breathe, a quirk I've acquired and can't get rid of. I'm flustered as I pull and push. Another quirk: I can only start to practise on the precise stroke of the hour. If I miss, then I have to leave the room, get a drink, beat myself up and stare into space until the time comes around. I can't even read. Reading causes thought, which is the enemy of disappearance.

Too much pushing, too much pulling! I hurriedly get myself straight on the stool and place my iPad, 100% charged, on the stand, open at the Liszt exercises, set my metronome to 100. I check: 12.59 and a bit.

Made it.

To start, always the same, the following words as familiar to me as my own name: *'Slowly, with a quiet hand, with high finger action and with full strength. After full control is gained, repeat the exercise following the given dynamics with utmost care.'*

I repeat it until the slight twitch in my right middle finger (caused, I guess, by a nervous reaction to Melissa Gore) subsides, about seven or eight minutes in. Then, once the tremor is extinguished, I start on another exercise, always the last before I start to play actual music:

'*Different figurations of chords and inversions in octaves. Use forearm lateral action. At first this action should be made very rapidly, pausing over the key before striking it. When aim is secured, play as rapidly as possible. Continue in all keys in chromatic succession.*'

First through at half speed, then three-quarter speed, then at speed, then speed and a half, then double speed, and this until disappearance and the real practice can begin.

And so, several thousand notes later, here I am but for some reason not quite ready. There's a distraction that is initially hard to identify. Maybe it's the fly trapped between the curtain and the window dying drowsily on the sill, or dust spindrifting in a slant of light, or semi-conscious thoughts of what I've taken on. I consider ending the fly for good.

But it's not the fly or the dust or Kozar.

I never say her name. I write it occasionally; I think it often. I don't say it, though. Why would I? I don't see people we knew any more. I don't tell the women in the bars about her, or even that I was married. There's no conscious effort to suppress it, there's no superstition around it. I just don't say it. But today I said it out loud. What was the phrase? 'Talking about Esther.' Like the name of a bad novel, in which Esther would undoubtedly be dead or die in front of our eyes. This is the distraction: not the thought of the dead wife, which I have every day, but the knowledge that I will now have to hear myself say her name much more often.

I walk to the window, draw back the curtain, watch the fly slowly whirring its way towards death. I brush it to the floor and step on it. The tiniest crackle.

I stand still for a moment and look at the piano: the iPad's screen has dimmed.

I say out loud: 'Esther.' It needed to be done.

I practise for a very long time.

4

Peter called: 'Do you know Clara McLellan?'

'I do not.'

'Influential piano blogger.'

'I hope you're scare-quoting that.'

'The people we care about read her. She asked about you. Talk to her. Good practice for you. A safe place to be, and she's very sympathetic. To you getting back out there. Kozar and all that.'

So here I am, in a coffee shop in the Village, with a certain eagerness now there's no backing out.

Clara is a slight, dark girl, with severe bangs and an oversized black sweater. My first feeling with these tiny young women is always how they manage in New York at all: the vast weight of concrete, glass and steel seems inimical to their smallness. But she seems very good at being here, gives the impression that she likes what she does, has the life force. She is cross-legged on the coffee shop banquette, hand only just poking out from a wizard-y mohair sleeve, pale and bright, fingering the touch-pad of her laptop with a look of comical despair.

'Oh God, oh God, these questions I wrote are *awful*.'

'We could just talk.'

'Yeah, I guess. Yeah, okey-dokey.'

She's still scrolling.

'Sorry. I use Anglo. When I'm with Anglos. It's a tic.'

'No problem, dude.'

'Oh, by the way, did you know you're a meme?'

'I'm a what?'

'Look.'

She spins her laptop towards me and I stare ultra-quizzically.

'What's this?'

I know what it is: it's me, or more precisely, a painting of me done when I was eleven years old. I'd been interviewed on Manchester radio as a local superstar. A while later some apparently famous portraitist got in touch through the school and came to the house for a day to 'do' me. Mum, Dad, the piano and him and all his gear sweltering in our front room, the adults chain-smoking, me like a little kipper in the middle. I'm standing up straight, dressed in a red turtleneck and bright green trousers, looking directly out of the canvas, one hand reaching out towards and just touching the piano. My parents stand close together way off to the side, gazing at their elf nerd with what looks to me now like extreme confusion. Someone has superimposed WHAT HAVE WE DONE in white block text.

'That's you, right?'

'It is. Where did it come from?'

'Oh, I don't think anyone knows where they come from.'

'What have we done? Is it really that bad?'

Clara looks uneasy and spins her laptop away from me. 'I'm sorry, I shouldn't have shown you that. Stupid really.'

And because she seems so awkward about it, I let it drop. What have we done?!

She's pawing away at her touchpad again, obviously wondering how to begin. I help her out.

'You spoke to Barlow, right? You know you can ask me about my wife.'

'Really?'

'Within reason. You can ask me stuff within reason. And I'll just say no if I don't want to go there.'

'I get it. That's more than fine.' She runs finger and thumb over the top edge of her laptop screen in some kabuki cleaning regimen. 'Was it four years ago?'

Wow, that was quick.

'Yes. Bit more than that. The thirtieth of May 2014. That's when she died. I'd played my last concert of a tour four days before. And the last recording I made was about a month before that, but I asked them not to put it out.'

'What was on it?' She's recording me on her iPhone and typing at the same time, very professional.

'It was an odd record really. I was interested at the time in sequential things: pieces that would be related in surprising ways. Or some kind of way. In this case it was children. They were on my mind. I felt that I was ready to have them. I really wasn't. But anyway, I chose some Bach from the Anna Magdalena book, Schumann pieces – from *Jugend*, not *Kinderszenen* – then piano transcriptions of *Kindertotenlieder*, and *Children's Corner*, and then a couple of Britten things. What to say about it? How to bring out a record about your future children the year their mother dies, thus rendering them, you know, no longer your future children. Don't use that. The "no longer future children" thing.'

'Of course not.'

Half her face is behind that sleeve now, her eyes trapped between her bangs and the mohair. Just a little mascara, a little eyeliner. She opens her blueish eyes wide to encourage me, which only puts me off. Enthusiasm has always unsettled me.

'It's a shame that record never came out.'

'No, it's fine. It wasn't good really. I don't know, maybe it was.

27

But I didn't want it to come out, for reasons outlined above. It felt like an effort: the cover photo, doing my own notes. Talking about kids at that point: not the right time. I hate that word, by the way – kids – but if you say "children" you sound like some old duchess or something. Would you mind if this didn't go in? Any of the child stuff. I haven't talked about it much. It's all new thoughts to me, and I don't know what I feel about it. Fuck, I'm all over the place, sorry.'

She seems to flinch a little, maybe because she interprets the catch in my voice as tearfulness, though it's actually something else.

'Of course. Is there anything you're OK with? We don't have to do this at all really, if you don't want to.'

'That sounds so good to me.'

'Of course. I'm sorry. I can't imagine how difficult this must be for you.' The pain in her face as she says this is an index of her kindness.

'I'm sorry, I'm not being fair. I made a deal. Ask me a question, but make it an easy one.'

She shifts on her chair, swiftly re-energized. 'We could try this questionnaire thing I do? It's just fun, trivial stuff really.'

'Maybe that? Or maybe I'll just talk for a bit?'

'Either.'

This isn't going well. Maybe it's the place. These New York coffee houses are even pokier than English tea shops: you can never find your own space, and you come out reeking as if you've been steeped in latte for a week. Our table is the size of a manhole cover: the Splenda dust, a forlorn stirrer, made to be used once for about two seconds then immediately discarded (little Beckettian lives!), a puddle of dirty foam in the saucer, everyone too close together, no one ever comfortable except for people the size of Clara. Maybe this is how NYC works for her, the vast space of the buildings infinitely subdivided into niches: she fits in beautifully, like a sleek little pigeon.

'Shall I just say something?'

'That would help.'

'OK, here goes. I live here now. 79th, between Columbus and the park. It's not my apartment. It belongs to an old friend – a patron I guess you'd say. A finance guy, lives in Greenwich, Tom Gilpin. A hedge fund sort of thing I think? Although I don't really know what that means, so maybe not. Their house in Connecticut is just obscene, frankly. Just the two of them, no children. They have two swimming pools, for instance: no possible explanation for it. Anyway, his wife's a pianophile, but she doesn't just like the music and the concerts, she has to be *involved*. She saw my first concert here when I was nineteen. If you're on the piano scene you'll know her: Merry Strasser Gilpin, Meredith Gilpin.'

'I know *of* Meredith.'

'They've been very generous, in lots of ways. They're very good friends and they have this place, so they just sort of gave it to me after my wife died. I needed to get out of London. I pay them rent, don't worry. Again, maybe don't use all this. It might embarrass them in some way. And I don't want to come across as some dauphin.'

'Of course.'

She mouths the word 'dauphin' while she types and looks at me. She seems natural, benign, keen to do well.

'Specifically – I'm guessing you know what happened to me? After she died?'

She seems to tense a little, resettles on her haunches, once more runs her finger and thumb along the edge of her screen. 'I googled around a little.'

'It was a mess. One of the papers even had a photographer

29

stationed right outside the flat for a while. It was driving me slightly mad. And her family. Specifically her brother.'

'I didn't see that.'

'His name's Bobby. He was beside himself. He was never well anyway. Paranoid schizophrenic, sort of over in that territory. Functioning to an extent. Medicated. He didn't work, but he wasn't in a facility or whatever, not all the time at any rate. So he was devastated, as you'd expect, and went over the edge and a newspaper got hold of him.'

'What kinds of things was he saying?'

'Didn't you see when you did your googling?'

'Some of it, I guess.'

'"The Mystery of The Pianist's Wife", the subtext pretty apparent.'

'I'm so sorry.'

And she does in fact look it.

'You can see why I needed to get out of England. And I had people I knew over here. Barlow was here. The Gilpins. That was probably it, actually.'

'Thank you so much for all this.'

'Not at all. Thanks for listening. Can't be too interesting for you.'

'Oh God, are you kidding? You're being very generous.'

'Ask me anything. But we have to be quick.'

I'm eleven and a half hours away from my last practice. But equally, I realize, she's someone to talk to.

'Or you could come and listen to me play?'

—

We're at the Geddes School, with access to the concert grand in their best rehearsal room. I spent yesterday practising

Hammerklavier on an upright that was in no way up to the task: it's time to hear it on a big rack.

'Do you mind if I write about your practice ritual?'

'It'll make me look like a madman. Let me think about it.'

The practice room has a small plump couch, and she's curled up neatly on it with all her accoutrements. Such a sweet, competent person.

'This is so amazing for me. Thanks, Declan.'

'No, you're here for a reason. I want to play you something. Once I've warmed up.'

Neither of us do much as I wait for the stroke of noon to come around.

'You could write general stuff about this maybe? "Exercises, from the book he's used since he was a child," something like that?'

'It's OK, I can do my thing!'

'Of course you can. Sorry.'

Noon.

'*Slowly, with a quiet hand, with high finger action and with full strength. After full control is gained, repeat the exercise following the given dynamics with utmost care.*'

The first notes, the usual suffusion of great pleasure.

'Ask me your questions while I warm up.'

'Are pianists born or made?'

'Oh God, I don't know.'

'Pick one.'

In a Slavic accent: 'They are born, and then they are made. That's like something Tal would say.'

'Was he as great as they say?'

'In a word: no. Don't write that either.'

She thinks this is funny.

I'm doing some double-speed things, peacocking a bit. In fact a lot. I watch myself with something bordering on contempt. This awful conjunction: this thing I regard as somehow separate from myself is the means by which I try to make others admire me – love me, even. Come on, Declan, there's surely a way of doing this that isn't needy or gross.

'Wow, you can play the piano really well.'

'I know, it's weird, isn't it? Tal once said to me, "He was a peasant, so tries too hard to gain our acceptance." At a master-class, in front of two hundred people.'

'You don't seem like a peasant.'

'He meant "a working-class Catholic". He met my parents, obviously. He heard my mum's accent. And saw that my dad was wearing a leather bomber jacket over his shirt and tie. That was an important detail. I'm called Declan Byrnie, for God's sake. The didicoi element was very apparent.'

I'm keeping things rapid for her. If you do a trill fast enough it sounds like a constant ringing. It's why Beethoven used them so much once he'd gone deaf: he wanted us to suffer too.

Then into some fast, light octaves.

'Wow. You can really play the piano well.'

'You just said that.'

'Can I put the peasant thing in?'

'No. He's still alive. He might see it. He's omniscient, just not a very good piano teacher. Listen: there's a bit in a Schumann score where it says "play as fast as possible" and then a few bars later he writes "faster!". That's what I'm going to do now.'

Double speed, then almost double again; I'm perfect today, so '*play quick and softly*' way ahead of schedule.

'Oh my God, that's a conjuring trick.'

'"Trick" is about right.'

She can see that I'm easily discouraged, so attempts a pep talk: 'When did you know you were gifted?'

'Oh God, not that one. I really don't know. I think my real gift was that I practised a lot. That I absolutely loved practising. In fact, they had to tear me away to eat. And I'm not much different now, to be honest. Right: I'll play slow and quiet for a bit now. It takes me forever to warm up.'

'We're still on question one, by the way.'

'Well, I'm going to be here a while.'

'OK, second question: Debussy or Ravel?'

I look at her, attempting to convey no ulterior meaning. She looks back in kind. I hope she can't see how happy I am with all this.

'Hold on. I've not finished with the first one yet. The question is: we – you and me – were both equally bad pianists before we'd ever played a note, OK? So the question is, did I have something that meant I got better more quickly than you? Super-functioning forearm muscles or some neurological bug where my brain speaks to my hands in a certain way? Maybe that's all it is, some tiny advantage in the body. No one knows. So, if you'd done the same amount of practice as me, would you be as good as me?'

'I would say no.'

'And I'd probably agree, but we'll never know. Did you ever play?'

'The violin. Robust amateur.'

We should play together, I think. I say: 'Listen, I like this.' I move into a transcription of 'Feelin' Groovy', which turns it into a miniature copy of a Diabelli variation. It's another private party kind of thing. It's funny and brilliant. Maybe I should just play this in Boston. But then I'd be finished: it would be too much fun and everyone would get confused and boo me off.

I can't bear the idea that the interview will end. She has

to be here, because I'm going to speak the whole thing out. Instead of it being an unwanted visitation in a dream, or as often happens, when I'm falling asleep at the apartment and its horror jolts me awake and leaves me breathless and appalled and keening and wet through, I'm going to say it out loud.

I have no interest in the psychological ramifications, what it meant to me then or means to me now. I don't want to talk about grief or dealing with grief. I don't want to talk about *my wife*. I want to tell the story of that day. Not even *want* but *need*. Maybe to this person right now. Why not?

I finish a passage of vast chords and find myself exclaiming: 'Goddammit!'

'What's up?'

'Nothing. I'm fine.'

She looks taken aback, pauses for a second, then presses on. 'OK. Question two: what is your greatest regret?'

'You must be kidding!'

'Sorry. Make up something, maybe?'

'I regret not playing professional football. Soccer. You can use that.'

'That's good.'

'You said you wanted me to hear something.'

I look at her again. I want to be her friend. I cannot be her friend.

'Yes. You know the *Hammerklavier*, obviously?'

'Of course.'

'I have to play the damn thing next week. And last night I had an idea about how to play the Fugue. Because my theory is that once you've made it through the Adagio, everyone, including me, just wants to go home. You don't want to sit through this bristling warthog of death.'

'I don't remember it *that* well.'

'Exactly, no one wants to listen to it. Beethoven reserved all his most horrendous stuff for fugues. It's like at the end of a superhero movie when he has to fight his nemesis at the end, and there's half an hour of hanging from bridges and crashing through windows, then he realizes that the nemesis is actually his dad. But in Beethoven's case it's not his dad, it's academic counterpoint. Or maybe Bach, or Christ. Or a combo. And maybe his dad's in there too actually.'

'OK, I think I'm following.'

'So anyway, I'm not even sure I should play it at all. The *Hammerklavier*. Help me out.'

'I'm not sure I'm the right person for that.'

'You absolutely are!' I thunder out a run in the bass.

If I try hard enough, maybe one day I could play the piano with no ulterior motive. Not yet, though. I want her to be around forever, so I'll try to make that happen.

'Come to Boston. Hear how it all pans out.'

'I might well do that.'

I look at her: she awkwardly reconsults her notepad. She's not coming, and that's that. How did I screw this one up? Pure weirdness, I suppose.

'You may not enjoy this, but that's OK, because I don't think you're supposed to.'

And I play the Fugue freely and well.

5

In what turned out to be her last month, I wrote to Esther every day. I remember the broad shape of what I said, but not the specifics. And now, for some reason, idling around the apartment, a bag of nerves, I need to remind myself of these specifics. As Barlow said, I'm in control of what happens now. I can take a look and nothing bad will come of it.

May 10th 2014

Sweet Esther

In Cincinnati, from the Latin meaning 'can I leave yet?'. Oh God, maybe it's not so bad; the people are kind, the hall is gracious, I'm sold out and the fee is of solid Midwestern stock. I guess this is most of America: some vast, complicated existence unfolding without anyone knowing or caring. (As you no doubt sense, the contrast with Bolzano could not be more stark.)

For some reason I got taken to a Bengals game (American football) by one of the boosters. The atmosphere had a certain Englishness to it, i.e. it was permeated by a kind of cheerful defeat. I think this is mainly because the team is apparently very bad, and this is compounded by the fact that they have tiger stripes on their helmets and trouser-things: what was once a great force is now pathetic, like the Royal Navy or France or something. And this, for an Englishman, is highly reassuring.

I played very well and got a couple of standing Os. I gave 'em three encore pieces, including a well-received 'Harp' Étude, during which I clearly thought of you and nothing else. Strange in a way that that piece can never be anything other than you. Even the fragments of it I come across in other pieces – maybe the same intervals here and there, something harmonic, a tiny scrap of rhythm – that's you too, of course. In fact, you are every corridor and chamber of the palace of Western Art music, this palace in which I must eternally roam, peering from its mullioned windows, this gilded prison, this metaphor, which now, I realize, has to stop extending itself pretty much immediately.

I'll soon be on the way to something called Northern Kentucky Airport: I'm playing Berkeley tomorrow, if you remember. I have acquired a tiger-striped acrylic scarf to which you are most welcome.

A little more than two weeks now and I'll be with you. There's no need to write a full report, but a few lines would be welcome for us poor souls imprisoned over here deep in the hull of HMS *Schedule*.

Professions of love and so on.

Dec

PS 'Mullioned'?

Bolzano: I didn't really want to be reminded of that. Esther once read something online, a list of the best places to live in Europe, and Bolzano was at the top. We'd never heard of it. Who has? An Alpine city in northern Italy, somewhere not far from Austria, no great art or fancy castles or art-stuffed duomo. But she loved the idea of small cities, some safe, finite place where you could lead a peacefully profuse life.

Then it became our thing, a game with an array of rules and in-jokes. For instance, we weren't allowed to visit Bolzano until we were forty years old. Why this age in particular? I don't remember, but ruthlessly enforcing the rules was most of the fun. We wouldn't read about or look at pictures of Bolzano: it had to remain an imaginary place so we were responsible for its entire existence.

We'd make up stories, farcical idylls: in every one there would be many, many Byrnies bilingually running around the meadows and we would be happy there; for ever, no less. Bolzano. A secret, perfect place.

My mind turns away.

Clara posted the interview the night after it was done. I read it through three times. I come across as a complete idiot, of course, and not because she'd been unfair. I remember making an effort to be a normal, interesting person you might like to get to know, but I did not pull that off. Although I remember saying these things, I have no idea why I said them.

At one point, she asked me how pianists can get better and I said, 'To quote Busoni, if I may, "BACH BACH BACH".' Then I added: 'I think all my concerts are an attempt to say "listen very closely". I think it's obvious we're close to losing all this stuff, which would be a tragedy – or more accurately a disgrace. We wouldn't stand by and do nothing if St Paul's Cathedral were being dismantled before our eyes. If the Uffizi were on fire, someone would try to put it out. Maybe I'm too gloomy, but I genuinely believe the piano repertoire is one of the chief glories of the world, and that it's all under threat. It's better than pop music. It just is. Why should I feel embarrassed to say that there are things superior to entertainment? It's OK to *prefer* entertainment, just admit that it's worse.'

Ugh. Declan Byrnie, Defeatist Elitist. Then: 'I think I'm asking people to trust my expertise. The player gets the special insight, the intimacy with the architecture of it all, and I can tell you, objectively, that the best piano music is insanely well-made and fantastically clever. It's objectively beautiful. Ob.

Jectively. It's the finest expression of some of mankind's best brains or spirits or what have you. And of course it asks things of you, but then it repays you vastly. It's demanding and generous. Instruction and delight. To hear what it's saying, though, you have to *listen*.'

All very painful. And this was me trying to be her pal.

Then she writes about my practice methods in the general terms we agreed: 'There's no trick: do your scales, do your exercises, read the piece through that you're learning, keep doing that until you can play it well. Think about music all the time. Listen to the great players. And Bach, Bach, Bach.'

No mention of Esther other than 'Byrnie lost his wife four years ago in a climbing accident in Cumbria, England,' which was the form of words we agreed on, although I'd said the Lake District.

I find myself holding my iPad up to my face, looking closely at the portrait Clara has chosen of herself: that pale face against dark green foliage, the severe yet sweet geometry of her pageboy, the clear light brown eyes, just a trace of eyeliner and mascara. What would happen if I wrote to her? The iPad lets me make the picture as big as her real-life face, and I once again lament the fact that she will not come to Boston. Needy and gross. And flashy. And just very odd.

The article has a picture of me she took with her iPhone. I realize with a gentle shock that it's the first one I've seen in years. Clearly someone in their thirties, all the photo-shoot pomp subtracted, white as a sheet, my hair now chastely trimmed back, dressed in my drab urban uniform of blue button-down and black jeans: a reduced, humdrum version of my former self.

I click away from Clara's page. I could easily write to her: I could thank her for putting me back into the world, or for making me look good (even though she didn't). But instead I write to Barlow:

Dear Big Nose

Herewith the programme for Kozar:

Bach: French Suite Number 4

Chopin: B minor Scherzo

Interval

LvB: *Hammerklav.*

So there it is: you've got your White Whale.

As for the programme as a whole, there's an idea about ambiguity somewhere, e.g. the Chopin: Liszt said it was a piece for governesses, Schumann said it was 'Byronic'. So there you have it: no one can decide if something is for little old ladies or ravening satyrs.

And then, of course, there's the ambiguity about whether *Hklav* is a piano sonata or an attempt to recreate the sound of a triceratops being fed through a threshing machine.

Pip pip.

DB

I reread it once, don't bother refining, click send.

6

It's the day before I leave the city, so I go to get my car: I can't do things at the last minute, it's a distinguishing trait.

I pay $450 a month to keep it in a garage in East Harlem and barely ever take it out. But I have to have it: car ownership is important in my family. My dad had a vintage Jensen Interceptor that he could in no way afford. It had a black vinyl roof, which he pronounced 'Black Vinyl Roof'. It was his life's delight, along with Manchester United, my mother and me, and the lads at the Star. He washed it every Saturday, through the drastic hangovers of which I was never aware. He'd get down on hands and knees to do the hubs, fingering a rag deep into the rims, then stretch balletically across the bonnet, one leg in the air, toes pointing, with the soapy bucket at his feet, vigorously sponging the bonnet in wide circles then hosing it down, his thumb half across the opening, making the water batter at all the glass and metal. The thing looked somehow alive once he'd washed it, as if it had emerged from bubbling lakes of foam on the drive. The wipers stuck out from the base of the window, wavering like bug antennae. He'd call me out from practice.

'Hey, Dec! Come and have a look at her.'

He'd be standing there, smoking a post-coital Dunhill, gazing at the car's blue metallic bodywork and crystalline glass in a kind of amazement: Stendhal Syndrome on his driveway every Saturday morning before he met the gang for a drink and went up to the match.

He was born in the real slums of Manchester: outside khazi, tin bath in the parlour once a month, his mum telling him to go and beg the pork butcher for a trotter on Saturday, all that stuff; the idea that a person like him could own a car was a ludicrous dream. But now he had one. And it wasn't just a car, it was a Jensen Interceptor with a seven-point-two-litre engine and a Black Vinyl Roof. I loved my dad.

The parking garage is under a tenement, opposite a vacant

lot around which there are now construction fences. Condos on East 128th Street? Looks that way.

Brinslow, the boss of the place, is always there, either hanging out in his tatty kiosk or shooting the shit with the neighbourhood boys who sit around on metal folding chairs playing a bit of dice. He is old and thin and Jamaican, mendaciously attired in black slacks, dress shirt and narrow tie, his hair chalk dust and rat-tails, his ageless granitic face fitted with a miscellany of yellowing teeth.

'Ah, piano man! I'll get her right up for you!'

There are always numerous extra charges levied, for invisible favours rendered at distant points in time that cost him effort and occasioned some heroic interventions on behalf of me and my Volvo. A couple of hundred dollars usually takes care of it.

It's way beneath Brinslow's pay grade to get the car himself. He summons his amanuensis, a lively Latino man he calls 'Clonky' or 'Clanky', who trots down the ramp to his diesel-scented cavern.

'You takin' the beauty out?'

'I'm touring. Well, kind of.'

'Back on the road again!'

Brinslow laughs at his own jokes, possibly because only he is able to determine that they are in fact jokes.

'Yes. And then I'm going to leave the city.' I don't know where this comes from, but when I say it, it seems as true as anything else.

'Ah well, we cleaned her up for you really nice. We did the oil and the water and the tyres. She's shipshape!'

'Thanks, Brinslow. That's very kind.'

He fingers the wad of twenties I handed over. 'You're welcome. Where you going, young man?'

'I don't know. My wife wants me to leave.'

This perks him up considerably. 'Ah yes! The missus get what she want. That's important!'

'Are you married?'

'Naaah, boy!'

This is apparently as funny a joke as he's ever made. Clonky slides up alongside in my old Volvo wagon. It is indeed pristine.

'You should settle down one day.'

'Too late for me, Mister Byrnie.'

'It's New York, Brinslow. Anything can happen.'

'Thirty-five years in New York, and it's still Brinslow from the parking place. Oh dear.' He exhales with an unexpected weight of sadness.

'You all right?'

'I'm fine. I need to go fishing, that's all. You look after yourself, piano man.'

'Thanks. I didn't know you fished.'

'I don't! Don't have the patience for it.'

And he laughs again, this time almost wildly. Clonky darts around the vehicle doing last-second checks and primps, noiseless in his matronly black sneakers, a red rag hanging from the back pocket of his well-pressed boiler suit. All Brinslow's guys are parking-garage-natty. The driver's side door is open and the radio's playing a Latino station: this 2/4 thing with a lot of syncopated brass, everything crammed together in one over-bright, clashy torrent, tinfoil between the teeth. Once he's happy with the exterior, Clonky smiles at me and holds his forefinger aloft, slips into the passenger seat and changes the radio back to WQXR.

They're playing Mahler 4: we're at the long and winding slow movement which leads into that gorgeous child song at the end. I need to get in and listen. Clonky smiles at me and

43

jumps out, does a mock bow. Brinslow, now in his kiosk, is consulting one of his calendars, cool and stultified, the great, grey palms of hair moving slowly around the glass box, sheaves of yellow official paper stuffed into butterfly clips, the worthless, unthrowawayable detritus of his daily deal. Clonky jogs back down the narrow ramp and into the unvisited lower levels, the rag dancing at his hip.

—

She's with me. Esther is with me, or she can see me, or she's looking out for me. It's hard to explain, but it's certainly true. Talk to us, the bereaved, and you'll find out: it's about the only gift death gives you. We sometimes talk to each other. She's forgiving if sarcastic about the women I meet in bars. She wants me to play in public again just once or twice, to see how I feel about it. I think she wants me to do Kozar.

I have a bad brown study thing: when I'm in one you can't get me out, and it's usually because she's there, on the edge of my vision. When I turn around to look she's always gone, just the sense of her body, her hair in the style it was around the time she died (she'd let it grow long that spring, it was unmanageable and she couldn't find a way to tie it back, but neither of us wanted her to cut it). Her face isn't really visible, or at best it's indistinct, but there's a sense of a smile around her, like a blessing, a musical glow, and her head is tipped in benediction, her hands open towards me, not speaking but knowing. She's with me now. We listen.

The song from Mahler 4 is short, for Mahler. It's a feast in heaven, a hymn to music, at this tempo which only he really does: walking pace but implying some effortless ascent, the body freed from the mechanics of bones and limbs, headed towards some radiance, the Apostate Jew finding himself in some Christian garden of plenty, a few thousand virgins around and about, vegetables strewn in profusion across the fertile lawns, the saints amassed in happy trivial tasks, running, fishing in a stream. A lamb is slaughtered – the poem is German, after all – and eventually it all dies away into a series of quiet pleasantries, the end almost comedy, three or four little parps of contentment. As I nudge down 125th it's hard to say if this music is the opposite of New York or its mirror. It seems to work today.

Left at the park. Never go in there any more. Don't go out much at all, apart from the rehearsal rooms, Lincoln Center, Zankel sometimes, the bars at night. I don't go to parties in case my wife shows up too. Esther isn't in heaven nor, clearly, in hell, but I also know she's not solely in my mind's eye. For instance, here she is again as I turn onto 79th and there's a parking space not more than fifty yards from the door of my apartment building. Am I saying she shooed away the previous occupant a moment before I made the turn (no space is empty for more than seven seconds around here), or that she instructed Clonky to take the time to hop back in and tune the radio to Mahler so my arrival was crucially delayed? Possibly not, but possibly also.

'Thanks, Esther.'

The Perry, where I live, isn't ostentatious, just deeply, quietly expensive. The lobby is underlit, beige and pink marble, twisted pilasters guarding the entry to the elevator bank, dark art deco mirrors adding a sepia dignity to your reflection. I still assume American things have European precedents: maybe there's an attempt to recreate the gloomy Masonic feeling of a London club or a Parisian mansion block in the 5th. It's certainly designed to keep New York out, though: the brief but uncompromising series of doors, the doorman himself, then the lobby's tone of arid gloom an airlock between the inhabitants and the world.

In the mailbox, amongst the usual slew of minatory finance bumf, there's a letter addressed as follows:

Urgent
Declan Byrnie (The Pianist)
W 79th Street
NY, NY
10024

The handwriting is small and apparently heavily scored into the envelope, which is very thin. Maybe only one page, precisely folded.

I'm clearly in a crazy fan situation. There's always a glow of satisfaction that derives from being adored, no matter how near mental collapse the adorer. There was an Italian woman who sent me watercolour flowers painted partly in her own blood, notionally inspired by my Chopin *Nocturnes* recording, which is easily the worst thing I ever did. Barlow said, 'Good job it was lousy, Deco, otherwise she'd have FedExed you a lung.' There's a man in Leicester, England who sent me a sixty-page analysis of the liner notes to my *Goldberg Variations*, his thesis stating that I'd missed out the obvious feature of this music: that it foretold the precise date of the return of Christ Our Lord and the Harrowing of Hell: 19th December 2008. He went quiet in 2009. Still, at least someone's paying close attention, if only to completely the wrong thing.

What's this, though? Why 'urgent'?

When I get to my apartment I smooth it out on the kitchen table. No return address. I wonder how they got mine. Then I open my laptop and read my interview with Clara again: I gave out my damn address. A mistake caused by running my mouth because I wanted Clara to be impressed. The persistent flaw: desperately wanting to be loved. I need to get rid of it, and quick.

I take the envelope over to the vast couch in the alcove. This is where I spend a lot of time: a kind of plushly upholstered mausoleum just off the main living area. It's about fifteen feet square, bookcases from floor to ceiling, much of the space filled with Merry's collection of unconsulted art books. My iPad and I can loll on this sofa for hours and peacefully drowse through any number of things (stimulus or anaesthetic, you tell me), while I wait for my practice craving to kick in. It's been a no-resistance kind of life: the piano, seeing concerts here and there, the bars, the sexual trivia, this bed of velvet and tight-packed goose down, a comfortable place to spin the clock out. The piano is hard, though: you could fall and smash your teeth on it, cut your head open, crush your fingers in the slamming lid, get stuck beneath it somehow. It's a death trap, that thing.

Fan letters masquerade as offerings but are always some form of demand. I open the envelope. An immediate shock: it's from Esther's brother. I don't have to read it to know its contents, but I can't avoid the first sentence:

'Now all preliminary preparation is complete, I have a team of first-rate lawyers who are ready to take my case against you to its inevitable conclusion.'

Of course. The moment I left my suspended animation all kinds of things were bound to happen. But this? I put the letter back in the envelope then tear it in two and bury it deep in the bin.

To the piano. Block everything out.

Practise.

Most of my music is stored on the iPad, but one or two

paper scores still hang about the place like vast Jurassic moths. My score of *Hammerklavier* is one of these: an ancient weather-beaten specimen with stringy binding and seemingly millions of my precise markings. Tal taught me the art of score annotation, and starting from an already neat and tidy base, he quickly got me to a place where someone looking at my marks would assume I was a particularly assiduous android. For once I decide to work at the apartment: going out again feels somehow risky.

My exercises don't go well for a while, I'm variously disturbed: the content of the letter, of course, but then also the greater doubt about leaving the city, the concerts, and all the people ahead of me I have to be nice to, or at least tolerate. Life kicking up again after I'd so successfully put it to sleep: a bad feeling. Barlow, Kozar, Clara, Beethoven, Esther, team of lawyers…

So it takes a good while, but my hands finally overpower my mind, and I find myself right in the middle of it: *Hammerklavier*, the Greatest Piano Sonata Ever Written. Certainly the one that's trying hardest to be.

And it just doesn't *work*: I play through the first few pages of score, pretty much every bar an assembly of crimes against humanity, false oppositions, straw men and obvious clangers, the precision of my notes seemingly a rebuke of the roiling clusterfuck to which they earnestly refer. I don't know what instrument it was written for, but it wasn't the piano. If you were going to rework this material for anything, then just possibly the first movement is a symphony by a relatively un-talented person attempting to write a mockery of a symphony by Beethoven; the second is a transcription of the first for a cretin's barrel organ, and the Fugue is written for a pachinko machine the size of a traction engine.

I start again, and this time I somehow make the first move-ment jaunty: everything pompous is a heartbeat from absurdity and doing it like this almost makes me laugh. It's like a North Korean military parade: funny on the surface, but underpinned by a vast infrastructure of pain.

Let's be honest, though: I can play it like nobody's business. Certainly well enough to see that despite the fact that it's one of the most remarkably sustained aural catastrophes in history, it doesn't lack for interest. It's not *bad* exactly, just *atrocious*.

I fool around a bit: first too quick, then too slow. If I played Beethoven in my favoured fashion, I would never have had a career in the first place: you have to obey the rules, then start to undermine them from within. Unless you're Glenn Gould, who valued no audience but himself, and so was more free but also more imprisoned, humming along to his internal tune, like my mum when she hung out the washing. Gould couldn't play Beethoven anyway, because he was too conscious of what he was doing. 'How would Gould play Beethoven?' asked Gould. 'Like this,' Gould replied.

I stop all the thinking, start again, and all of a sudden the first movement is playable. With my new lightness, the Scherzo becomes a true musical joke. Then the Fugue: I run through it trying to find the dance that's in there somewhere and largely succeed.

So, OK, what about the Adagio? Not yet. Nothing slow today, nothing with silences – silence is the enemy of disappearance, and in any case there's plenty of time, a week or so until the Kozar concert for a piece I could play tonight if I wanted. So there: enough *Hammerklavier* for one day.

I play through the 4th French Suite as a detox, and then a bit of Schumann I'm learning. I read that in the middle of composing it he tried to kill himself by jumping in the river, and it shows. I am consoled by the fact that I never got to that point, and know I never will. Bit more Bach: God, he's good.

49

Peace enough achieved that I allow myself to stop.

I pack for my trip with something approaching excitement.

7

Farewell to Kinsale tonight. I want to play a song with Sandrine before I go. On arrival I get the full multiple *bisou* treatment: 'I thought you'd gone without saying goodbye, you loser.'

'I would never do that. What are you going to sing?'

'I sent you a link.'

'Cool. I'll listen when I'm in the back.'

This is how it goes: she finds a song she wants to do, she sends it to me, I listen to it and then I accompany her. People think it's some kind of genius trick, but it really isn't hard at all. Usually I just arpeggiate in the left hand and push out little chord complexes with the right, making sure they don't get in the way of Sandrine, whose voice is ragged, beautiful and brave. I try to keep the tempo up, because she tends to drag the melody a little, ruefully in love with her own injured loveliness and showing off to Steve, her fortunate yet melancholy boyfriend.

I get a Talisker and move through to the lounge. As usual fifteen, maybe twenty performers are gathered for the music night. Most are talented, without doubt: its reputation for quality keeps the duffers out. Tonight, I recognize some of them: two pale elfin girls with cheap guitars and sweet, bluegrass sopranos, and a couple of intense young men getting ready to thrash it all out.

I stand at a ledge with the whisky, watching the mutely cheerful crowd slowly accumulating in the red-lit gloom. This is it, this is what my 'gift' and the life that followed forced me to surrender: the easy geniality of the modern way. I was studying when other adolescents were stumbling into each other at parties and bus stops; I was being reprimanded by Tal when they were clubbing in town. Not drinking either. It was Manchester: if you're a non-drinker you're a Dalit. Of course I went to parties now and then, but by nine o'clock I was the sober loser, longing for the piano while everyone else was crapulent on two tins of Special Brew, snogging toothily then weeping or puking in the garden.

This crowd are engaged in a slower, more decorous version, hanging in their little motley groups, quietly proving their love by validating each other's hairdos and career choices, buying each other drinks and complimenting each other's sneakers.

For a while I rarely thought about it, the loneliness of it all: I had Esther and the music, a place in London just sufficient to call a home. But my life was more accurately represented on a Google calendar originating in Barlow's PA's computer: cab, airport, flight, Strasbourg, airport, cab, concert. Then cab, airport, flight, cab, Stockholm, cab, airport, flight, airport, cab, Amsterdam, then the flat for a day or two, a glimpse of Esther, some practice then cab, airport and so on.

She never came with me: she hated flying, concerts, me when on tour. In fact, The Schedule was her mortal enemy, enshrining the things she disliked the most: that is, my absence, a continual reminder of her relegation to second place, and my absolute commitment to this absence.

Esther was also quite friendless, but never seemed bothered by it. She didn't need much to keep her happy. She liked to walk around London for hours on end taking photographs. Occasionally, she would hesitantly describe herself as a photographer, afraid perhaps that she might appear absurd in front of me. That's a painful thought now. Was she actually a photographer? She never made money out of it, nor attempted to. It seemed to me that she was constantly engaged in retaking the same picture: a cityscape, always black and white, someone caught in the lower corner about to walk out of frame, occasionally a passing car, a dog looking stupidly into the lens. She taught herself how to use a darkroom (always film, never digital) and would spend hours at a studio nearby quietly shifting the trays and liquids and wet paper around. She certainly, I would say, became a connoisseur: at exhibitions she would stand close to certain photos and gaze intently at things I couldn't see from where I was. She would be sweetly outraged by bad printing, at times the images themselves seemingly irrelevant to her judgement:

'He's hopeless, Dec, why can't people *see*?'

She wanted me to look closely, but when I did I saw even less.

'I quite like it though?'

And she'd be annoyed, maybe shake her head a little and walk away, dumbstruck by my blindness.

She liked yoga, too, though she never got very good. I don't think that's a yoga idea – that you get 'good' – but she could never do the crazy pretzel things, legs reaching out sideways, threaded through arms, eyes straight ahead, all that. She was content with her beautifully still tree pose and neat, rock-steady boat.

And she wrote poems she never showed me, and which I never asked to read.

She had her one friend, Kristen. They would watch TV together, talk in some sort of coded language about things I knew nothing about, get a little drunk and burst out laughing every so often – jerking around on the couch, spilling red wine all over the place, incapable of speech except in breathless falsetto, the kind of laughing women reserve for other women. I'd be envious sometimes; I couldn't make her laugh like that. Maybe I didn't try. Can that be true?

Who *was* she anyway? This thought emerges more and more often. Getting married was an uncharacteristically impulsive act for both of us. I can explain my side of it: I'd lost my parents, was out there completely alone, with only a grand piano for an anchor. She was beautiful and kind and made me feel less frightened. But what was Esther thinking? The first few months of our relationship, we barely saw anyone else. There was no intensity, rather a simple, friendly, gentle, domestic ease. She was happy at home, the world outside was a little complicated for her, too forthright in its expectations. I learned quickly that her vagueness, her vulnerability, concealed a subtle yet determined intelligence. Also concealed: her absolute inability to know what she wanted. Not quite true: like me, she had a longing to care for someone but didn't really know how. We cooked badly for each other, tried to find things we liked doing together and largely failed. And even when the conflict over The Schedule started to arise, we always had this thing: when we were together at home, even in our different worlds, we needed the other person to be there.

Kristen asked to read at the memorial service – something from Christina Rossetti, which struck me as bizarre. She was never like that, was she? Secretly yearning, lachrymose, an Ophelia complex? If she was, I hardly knew her at all, and this thought came as a wave of terror. But in any case, when the time came, Kristen wasn't able to give the reading, and I've not seen her since.

—

The lounge at Kinsale is about as full as it's going to get. I put my headphones in. Sandrine has sent me 'The Man I Love', a song I know well. I'll talk to her about tempo: we should move through it steadily, play quietly but with some insistence so it doesn't dawdle and remain merely pretty. She'll sing 'Ze man I laarv', me building up a subtle crescendo, until we end the song with her staring at the ceiling, gripping the mic cord, haloed in spotlight, and me surrounding her in a gorgeously messy E flat. We should act surprised that we got there.

I walk back to the bar. An intensely busy Sandrine is moving her tattooed arms quickly, fuelled by the adrenaline of the upcoming show.

'OK, Declan, what do you think?'

'Follow my tempo. It moves or it's dead.'

'*Oui, monsieur!*'

A salute of fake deference, but she knows I make her look good.

I go back to my Talisker, push it to my lips, just let it rest there, and listen to the song again in my headphones. The Scotch is camphorous and briny, hard to love until you do. This poison took my father. Look at it: an inch-thick bronze coin of liquid at the bottom of the glass. You could tip it away in an instant and walk away. Anyone could, surely? Not at all. I may only ever have two, but I always drain the glass entirely. I would never *dream* of not finishing it. I upend the glass so the final drop runs to the rim, stalls, then pools on my tongue.

We need to do the song, and then I need to get out. Not much longer: the two girls singing like nightingales about love by a lake are about to wind up. I try to hold on to the fast-receding taste of whisky.

Sandrine steps lightly onto the stage, the spotlight cartooning her bright red lips and winged eyes. 'Declan, stop daydreaming, *viens!*'

I go up, bow devoutly at the little mess of applause, and take my seat. Sandrine and I look at each other wide-eyed, open-mouthed for a moment, then we're off.

She sings it just right, picking up my idea. The urgency should increase as the dream becomes more distant, the reality of what the singer wants should never be in doubt. Like all great songs, it's both just what it appears to be and something else much more interesting. And she has it, she has it completely, the steady rise in intensity, the mad insistence, the absolute need for sexual love. I notice Steve is in the front row, the urban lumberjack in his pale jeans, clogs and red plaid shirt, an air of sylvan solitude. I watch him as we reach our wild and adamant conclusion — *who would, would you, and so all else above, I'm dreaming of the man I love* — and when we're done he hammers his paws together, chews the bearded bottom lip as his glasses fill with tears. Sandrine skips to him, grabs his head and kisses his upturned clueless face.

Also there, I notice: Penny. I catch her eye, and she waves in a friendly, no-hard-feelings fashion.

Everything's settled.

I go home for what I now know is the last time.

UPSTATE / CT

1

The first stop on the Dead Wife Tour: Quine College, forty miles up the Hudson, a sprawl of verdant civilization next to a collapsed, no-account town. Kozar, Boston and *Hammerklavier* just a few days away, coming at me very fast.

I park in the appointed place and there's a guy who's to help me. He's preppy, relaxed and has a somewhat fatherly handshake for one so young.

'Hey, I'm Tyler, Tyler Schwalbe, and I'm gonna get you settled in.'

There's the normal slight fuss over which room I'm in and where I should be and who I'm supposed to meet. These little logistical kerfuffles are almost pleasant; you get them a lot when you tour. Minor confusions: I think I have the wrong key, no, I think he's coming at two now, so he said to just make yourself comfortable, and so on. The Arrangements that are the inevitable consequence of The Schedule.

Tyler comes to help me unpack the car. He's even scored himself a little fat-wheeled dolly for the purpose. He wrestles my keyboard case out of the Volvo and leans it on said dolly. 'A little unwieldy.'

'It's my Clavinova. A keyboard. When I'm touring around I bring it with me.'

'Sweet. We're headed over yonder.'

He loads the rest of the gear onto the dolly and moves ahead at a fair clip, apparently thoroughly enjoying himself, the dolly squeaking and making a comforting trundling noise. He talks over his shoulder.

'You playing tonight?'

'Yeah. The Gerson.'

'Amazing.'

'Come along. It's free.'

'I would, but you know.'

'It's right here though.'

'I know. Not my thing. I'm anthropology.'

'Oh, there'll be plenty of anthropology if you know where to look.'

'No, yes, sure. I just meant I'm here over the summer working on my thesis.'

'Right. It's only going to be an hour.'

'Yeah, but the music though. No offence.'

'It's pretty good music.'

'Meh.'

'Oh dear.'

'Yah, I know. Anyway, here it is.'

I'm staying in one of a row of beautiful little cottages set in their own deep green park, the high gabled roof of the Gerson Performance Center visible through the beeches. My room is on the ground floor: a study, then a bedroom with a solid double, bathroom with a claw-foot tub. The linens are Quakerish: white, pale blue stripe. There's a coffee machine, room for me to set up my Clav, leafy sunlight abounding. These places make it easy for you.

Tyler smiles at me with a bit of school pride. 'I love these rooms. Anything you want, I'm in the library.'

And he leaves me to my rising anxiety: I'd almost forgotten this feeling, not stage fright exactly, more stage fury. I try to subdue it by unpacking the Clav, pretending to be on top of everything.

After Esther died I taught at Quine for a while. But how could I have been expected to teach in such a state of futility?

Although I turned up to all my classes, it was like watching someone else. I tried to seem solemn rather than defeated, but beneath the priestly air I was a profane mess. I couldn't concentrate, was absolutely no good to anyone. I slunk back to the Upper West Side before the end of the winter term.

I chose this place for my first concert in over four years because I needed it to be in a friendly, forgiving place. Garry Klain, the head of the music faculty, offers both friendship and forgiveness. He's a vigorous, boyish Brooklyner in his sixties, who's definitely on my side. He's a solid (i.e. lousy) pianist who specializes in American twentieth-century repertoire to insulate himself from both competition and audiences. But he's a great musician, a warrior for the cause, and a good conductor – he keeps up the tempo and brings out the tune, which is all you can ask for in my book. When I emailed him he quickly, almost joyfully, agreed to my plan, obviously thrilled to be the starting point for whatever I choose to do next. I asked if I could make a 'lateish decision' on the programme, and he agreed immediately. He's a good friend, Garry, and, let's be honest, a pushover.

All set up now, chair positioned at the Clav, the stirrings of the fury become more present. I need to shut them down.

Practise.

I do my exercises, then play through the Schumann piece. Why did he chuck himself into the river? It was either the syphilis or the syphilis medicine. Back then, it was a case of if one doesn't get you then the other one will.

It's called Ghost Variations. Seems a little on the nose to play undead music on the Dead Wife Tour? I don't know, but it sounds right today. I play through. Fine, not many fluffs, a bit studied – the adrenaline of performance should sort that out.

Then the French Suite. I'm no Bach pianist. I don't think I'm sufficiently grown up, or don't have the patience or subtlety. I always want to press, show off a little bit. The dynamics are so difficult to get right. It needs to be utterly precise yet swing like mad – every moment is a dance, after all – but everything I try today is either gawky or precious. Lots of facility, no damn talent. Bach is such a lie detector. Ecch. It'll come. If I don't find the truth I'll fake it plausibly. I do more exercises to smooth me out, and go back to the 'Allemande'. Better already, but something makes me stop, could be any number of things. I need a lie-down.

—

I'm on the edge of sleep, gasping for air in some skydiving Esther dream, when Garry wakes me with a rhythmical knock and walks straight in.

'Hey, Declan, sorry, man.'

He gives me a muscular hug as I dizzily get up. His round belly is tight and feels harder than it looks, and his large head is planted with shoots of crazy white hair.

'It's OK.'

'Hey, look.'

He gives me some baked good in a squishy cling-filmed package. I give it a squeeze. Garry nods at me.

'Judy said it was your thing. Treacle cake.'

'Wow. That's so nice of her.'

He looks at me, then sits at the Clav and starts to noodle. 'This is cool!'

'Yeah, it's good.'

'Hey, man. So you're playing again. That's so great.'

'It's time.'

Everything I say that relates to The Death or The Tour sounds like it's from a movie trailer. He's got his ear to the speaker while he plays a few Hanons. I remember he was always a Hanonophile, a love no doubt hammered into his soul by some unsmiling maniac during those long evenings of lost childhood all musicians know.

'I'm going deaf, which is fun!'

'Oh damn. That's rough.'

'It'll be fine. I'm getting a thing. Visible though. Which is shitty. In terms of the ladies.'

'Just when you were on a roll, too.'

He's been married to Judy for forty-two years. He tries another exercise, humming along a little.

'You all OK here? Sweet room, right? We save it up for the good ones.'

I suddenly have an intense desire to be Garry: the energy, the fun, the steady job, Judy, sufficient talent, all the excellent children.

'Yeah. Couldn't be better. I'm meeting the tech at four, then I'll practise onstage for a bit. On at seven thirty, right?'

The Arrangements.

Garry stops playing. 'Perfect. I'll leave you to it. Just so you know, though, they made me put something for the programme, so I said "Selections from Beethoven and Chopin". I just thought you could throw in a bagatelle or a mazurka or something. An étude, Declan? Can I get an étude?'

'Of course. Maybe even an impromptu.'

'I would love an impromptu.' He stands and looks at me, and I get a little scared. 'Judy wrote a few times, Dec.'

'Yes. I'm sorry, I'm hopeless.'

'OK. I get it. But you could have answered. Just leaving us, us not knowing all that time.'

'Yes, I know, Garry. No excuses.'

63

He goes to leave, then pauses at the door. 'Anyway, I'm glad you're back. We'll talk after. We got catering, the whole deal. Judy's gonna be there. She can't wait, obviously. In fact, she was wondering if she could stop by this afternoon?'

'Probably best to wait till after.'

'OK, Dec, you're the boss.' He leaves, giving me an expectant or reproachful look, hard to tell.

When I started teaching here they put me in my own house, but I just couldn't take being alone. It turned out that the Klains had an apartment over their garage, and they took me in unquestioningly. I drifted around their house as I pleased, staring into the fridge in my underwear like some stray adolescent. Garry was out a lot, and Judy, who was once a flautist, gladly gave into the campus wife existence, teaching Hebrew and Italian, receiving and transmitting university gossip with clarity and delight. Their kids were already by then far-flung, sprinkled up and down the coasts in media, tech or finance. Judy liked having me around to spin out her motherhood. I initially drew the line at her doing my laundry but caved after about a week. She was hooked on detective shows: we'd watch them together while Garry was at a recital, choir practice or faculty meeting or whatever he was doing. The shows are tight little études themselves: setting you up, sending you off, giving you a few moments of doubt then bringing you home safe.

Judy looked up 'food from northern England' online and made me stew with dumplings, meat and potato pie, treacle cake: certainly overdoing it, but why would I complain? Better than Mum's fish fingers and oven chips anyway. She found Typhoo tea at some place in the city and had it sent up. I'd been drinking Typhoo since I was five, and it was the spine of my diet: a mug of tea in the morning before school; tea at half-time at football practice; a mug when you got home before piano;

tea with tea (that is, your dinner) then, before you went to bed, a nice cup of tea with a jam crust, the heel of a white sliced loaf topped with a streaky impasto of margarine and strawberry jam. To a Japanese person my entire life might have looked like a loosey-goosey tea ceremony.

My first teacher, Peter Schofield, said to me when I was twelve: 'You're getting out of here, but always hold on to a bit of Manchester. It'll come in handy.'

I think I've managed that: it pokes through like a compound fracture. I've kept my a's flat, don't smile much, don't laugh at all, my perfect weather is fifty-eight and overcast, and I have numerous misgivings about the people of Liverpool.

Judy hosted the other campus wives and her language students at excellent, brief cocktail parties, usually on Thursday nights. I played piano; they had an old Bösendorfer they kept in triple mint condition and I'd do requests, devastating the old ladies with improvs and musical jokes ('Ten Variations on the Nokia Ringtone'). Judy never let me tidy up, so I'd sit at the table in the kitchen with my mug of Typhoo as she zoomed around and talked me through academic Kremlinology or recounted the complex and surprisingly with-it hang-ups of our departed guests.

Fridays they had a semi-serious Shabbat dinner, and I'd stay in my granny flat and feel distinctly pork pie-ish.

My mother and Judy: so similar in many ways – the embarrassing lionization of the boy, said boy never permitted to lift a finger. Also the same stratospheric level of comfort around children. Slow to chide, swift to bless.

Maybe I should go over and say hi?

Now, seated at the Clavinova with my hands on my knees, I look out of the window of the darkening room. So here it is again, that half-forgotten mood, hard to name but instantly recognizable. Every day of a performance this resentment rose up from nowhere, sudden, unbidden, unfightable. I fixate on the distant roof of the Gerson and realize I have to let it happen, and then it's all over me in a moment: disgust, blame, looking for an easy escape (I'll say I'm ill, cancel it, run for the hills, nothing they can do about it, that'll show them!). I shake my head and curse under my breath: 'What *is* this garbage?'

I start stalking around the pristine cell, the voice, like a drunk winding himself up for a bar fight: the plain *stupidity* of it all. Who are these fools I'm playing for anyway? These vacuous, tin-eared, drowsy know-nothing, empty fucking jibber-jabbering tossers, the restless turkey-necked old coots waiting for the one they've heard of so they can mouth 'how brilliant!' as they applaud, thinking that playing fast is the only real measure of talent. I'll play fucking fast for them all right… the *disgrace* of it!

Out loud: 'Wankers!'

I remember I haven't decided on a programme – nor even begun to consider one. This isn't helpful. There's simply no chance I'll play *Hammerklavier*, and this isn't a Bach mood, this isn't any sort of music mood. The flat-out *ignorance* of these wankers. Don't they know? And the cell phones, the cell phones. Turn your cell phone OFF.

'TURN. YOUR. FUCKING. CELL PHONE. OFF.'

I look out of the window again, see some wind catching in the high trees, and breathe. It's like fighting the whisky: I can do it if I have to, keep the zombie under the trapdoor, even if I can still hear it thumping up against.

Come on.

I sit at the Clav and crash dementedly through the Bach again. I could play this, actually. They don't deserve it, these fidgety, half-deaf barbarians longing for a cocktail and the *Late Show*, but I could give it to them.

Thump thump thump.

I try to breathe it out, focus on the score. Just looking at it you can tell it's a thing of purest excellence. We should be all in a permanent state of religious gratitude for Bach. Every note of him is available at all times, straight into our minds from the ether: astounding. But we don't listen to him all day, every day, we listen to other things, all of which are inferior. It makes no sense.

I play two bars, badly.

'Fuck it.'

I turn from the keyboard, gazing into my near-distant fury. I'd forgotten the horror of this feeling. I remember the last concert I did: London at the Wigmore, Liszt's *Consolations*, then some Mendelssohn *Songs Without Words*, then *Davidsbündlertänze* in the second half, the Weber 'Perpetuum Mobile' as an encore. Then, for Esther (who was there, for once), 'Widmung' and the 'Harp' Étude, the only pieces in the entire repertoire that were in any sense ours – and only then because I forced them on her with a mix of wheedling and sentimental ardour. She said she had no ear, couldn't hear anything at all in it: to her, Haydn sounded identical to Debussy. Never even *listened* to *Hammerklavier*, even when I wheedled extra hard. She liked Motown, Nick Drake, Joni Mitchell and The Beatles, which were her 'out' ('I *do* like good music'). I never minded at all what she listened to: people on the whole just don't like this music, you have to accept it. But when your husband is a professional pianist, maybe you could sit through – once, for God's sake – the slow movement of *Hammerklavier*.

Just once?

Black fury.

Stop, Declan. Look at the score. Play it through in your mind. Listen to its pure excellence.

I listen for the zombie thumps.

No thumps.

Let's play some more.

And slowly the rage spins down, thanks to time and Bach. As I play the piece through again, I know I could certainly get through this tonight, and pretty well. So, OK, I'm back, this is doable, because it's what I do.

But then I suppose I have to give them Beethoven. It's rather impolite, I think, to thrust things on to people like this. Is Garry not aware I've not played in public for four years now, and clearly need some time and space to find my own way? It's just so *rude*.

And if I must give them Beethoven, then what? It's such a cliché: the piano recital that contains Beethoven, how simultaneously obvious and absurd. Here's a fun game: what's the worst Beethoven sonata? So many to choose from! Op. 90: everybody hates that one. Op. 101, maybe? Not sure I can remember it; it's been struck from my memory, that march like someone in a wheelchair falling down a flight of stairs – and I won't have a score on the piano like some old dodderer.

It's clear which is worst, of course: *Hammerklavier.* Jesus, even just seeing it in my head, like some vast dragon dying in its cave, wings slowly pounding the black earth – anything but that.

Just so *awful.*

Where can I go? New Hampshire? Quebec? Somewhere far north, an icy bay, seals barking, wheeling seabirds. Baffin Island? Everywhere sounds so good right now…

Huh.

What's outside the window? The roof of the Gerson. Thirty million to build, I heard. Gerson was some alum who made a billion in something like insurance and built a performance space to take the edge off his shame.

How has this music become 'philanthropy', duty, boredom and lies, when it consists entirely of beauty?

Here's the trade: I play you some music you don't much like, put you through a dull time in exchange for social currency or just for having got you out of the house. If you're truly *interested* in the music, you'll have recordings of the pieces anyway, all of which will be superior to mine, or even if they're not you won't be able to tell. And then what do you imagine is in it for me? I don't need the baffled adulation of people who'd rather be elsewhere. I don't need *you*. You do realize that, don't you?

Call in sick. Drive off. Labrador. Fuck them all. Nunavut.

Listen.

No thumps.

A little breathing.

Bach.

I play the first three or four bars of the Gavotte. A tiny deathless masterpiece, and that sense as ever that his incalculable nature is fractally encoded in every bar, every motif – any time there is more than one note on the page, the weight of his entire intelligence is present. But this isn't helpful: the idea of unfurling this fabulous thing for people who may find it merely pleasant starts the voices again. Bach gives me this didactic urge: I want to comment as I play, 'listen to this, just listen, it's miraculous, and now this, see what he just did? LISTEN!' Another kind of madness, constantly wanting to draw attention to one's own insights, like some placard-carrying apocalyptic in Times Square. REPENT!

'There's no truth in music, only beauty.' Tal, of course. What does it mean? I don't know, I really don't. It's just Russia, where talking nonsense is OK because things are too complicated and too horrifying to be understood by something as feeble as reason.

But somehow, unasked for, almost unwanted, the rage has gone, most likely instigated at some molecular level by the few moments of Gavotte, the truth and beauty of it, and I'm aware of a kind of gratitude dissolving into my body. I know why I'm here: for Garry, to say thank you and sorry, and to show him I can still play, even if all this vast effort has been expended merely in creating tiny movements in the most sensitive of souls – which, despite the blustery persona, he undoubtedly has. And of course I'm also doing it for Judy: I want to apologize to and thank the fine, kind, generous woman.

I remember the treacle cake. I bite off a chunk. It's perfect, and my mood is sufficiently improved that I can even eat as I play. Tal would be appalled, and this makes me happy.

—

Awaking from the dream of practice, abuzz with music, an hour to kill before the show, I check I'm calm enough for what I'm about to do and repair to the firm, white bed. I open my iPad and have the perennial thought: I could do anything now, see any image, read any poem, listen to any sound, experience anything from all recorded time. But then, when it comes to it, I always end up in the same place: the emails I wrote to Esther, and so in I go again.

The first thing that's clear is that their tone comes nowhere close to what I was feeling. A scorpion in a display case isn't much like a scorpion.

Houston
May 12th 2014

Dearest Wife

First things first: when I am the *direttore* of the Conservatory of Bolzano, and you are the beloved Mayoress, there will have to be a few changes. Firstly, we should run a campaign to have the fresco in the Conservatory chapel restored: after all, it's not every music school that has a Piero della Francesca on-site!

I realize you will be spending most of your time fine-tuning the transport system (already named as one of the finest in Italy, and awarded the Rose d'Or by the European Public Transportation Secretariat and the highest possible score by the Tram and Bus Club of Antwerp), and attracting inward investment into the Clean Energy Park, plus running the increasingly respected jazz festival and judiciously calibrating local tax rates so whilst a sense of community is instilled at the same time the rich people don't all bugger off to Verona or what have you.

HOWEVER, the fresco will be, once restored, our gift to this city which has given us so much.

Yes, I know you will have your hands full negotiating supplemental educational budgets between the regional government and the local school board system, but spare a thought for this apparently glorious pietà – and think of the extra tourist revenues when it is finally established for good that it is in fact a Piero and not a work of secondary importance by some likely lad who worked in his studio. Another triumph for the Byrnies!

A few remarks about Houston, if I may. They told me, with strange, swampy pride, that it's built on a swamp, but I'd guessed this, because it's teeming with lizards and iridescent insect life and is currently 120 degrees centigrade. The people are exquisitely polite and generous: I just shared a porterhouse steak (this is lunchtime, by the way) with the woman who is the chair of the concert hall, who has a fanatical and scabrous knowledge of all pianists on earth. She told me that Artemiev can't go on unless he's had an orgasm within five minutes of taking the stage: this would explain many things, not least his wobbly gait and underpowered octaves.

I had chips too: one of those little pewter containers, but it wasn't that little; it was like a window cleaner's bucket. My concert is in three hours and I feel like one of those snakes on the internet that has tried to eat a whole pig and now can only lie there in the depths of his shame and wait to go viral.

Write to me! I'm checking emails every day between being stung on the cock by the swan-sized mosquitoes.

Yours ever
DB

Did she respond to that one? Two lines of pablum, then the sign-off 'Miss yuo!' [sic]. I close the iPad and wait.

2

Showtime. The Gerson has a swish, corporate-style dressing room with a flat-screen TV, a leather swivel chair and a big soft couch: better than most, which are designed to help those with stage fright get out there on the grounds that any place on earth would be better than the janitor's closet in which they find themselves. I've had the Clav brought over and hurtle through a few exercises, the objective not to disappear but to bring myself to life a bit, warm the body, let the adrenaline light me up. My Brioni suit jacket is a little tight over the shoulders, which is odd, maybe age just thickens you slightly, regardless of whether you eat or not. Barlow's widening nose.

Garry leans in the door, buzzy, freshly showered, suited and red-faced, hair dancing like undersea fronds.

'Hey, brother.'

I stop playing with the faintest of sighs.

'Sorry, bud.'

'It's OK.'

His fingers are slapping out some merry ragtime on the door frame.

'We're full, even a few people standing at the back.'

'Two hundred fifty people, maybe two eighty?'

'Yep. Perfect, right? As step one?'

It's so sweet that he wants my approval, so I decide to withhold it.

'So, Garry, here's the programme.'

I give him my list, handwritten on a Post-it ten minutes ago, and he reads it back to me:

'Schumann, Ghost Variations; Chopin, 'Berceuse'; Interval – nice touch. Beethoven Op. 90, ooh, looking forward to that; fourth French Suite. Fuck. Terrific. Lots of musical notes in there. I like it. Decided against the Ham-O?'

'Yep.'

'That's cool.'

'I'm supposed to be playing it at Kozar's thing next week.'

'What? You're playing Kozar? I did not know that.'

'Nor did I till three days ago.'

'Wow, the big kahuna.'

I gesture at the Post-it. 'That's OK though, right?'

'You betcha!'

I can tell he's genuinely excited, and I get a little teary.

'Maybe I'll take requests for the encore?'

'That would be beautiful, Dex, they go nuts for that stuff up here.'

It's true: I throw it out to the crowd and they get into bazaar mode, haggling, complaining, guffawing, and I get to talk back to them. I'm allowed to enjoy my position of power, make some jokes at their expense, and the women will love it and the men will feel a bit envious.

'Two minutes now, Declan, OK? Kill us out there.' Garry gives me a wide-eyed thumbs up and goes out, pretending to pore over the Post-it note.

The Ham-O??

He's now out on the stage announcing me in words I don't hear, but I get the impression that it's all quite complimentary. The audience, still in light, throw up a good, respectful wall of applause as I walk out onto the broad stage. I see Garry hop into his seat on the second row, and there's Judy who seems to be crying while smiling, clapping in front of her face, and suddenly I remember this is the first concert I've played since my wife died. It seems I'm much more over this than Judy is.

The Schumann is a terrible place to start: the opening theme is leaden and hymnic, and the piece is almost entirely inept until the last variation, which is merely insane. You can sense old Robert dripping wet at the keyboard, insisting he has to get this down before they sedate him and drag him back to the clinic. But I'm given the benefit of the doubt, and the applause rises in a solid, rapid barrage before dying away instantly as I settle in for the 'Berceuse'.

I look poetically into the middle distance, apparently trying to summon inspiration from the murk, but in fact not wanting to start until the panicky woman in the front row finds whatever it is she's looking for in her bag. Your glasses are on your head, if that helps, madam. A bit more flustering, and she takes her phone out of the bag and double-checks that it's off. Very good!

I'm about to begin when I see the girl. She's standing way in the back of the hall, leaning against the exit door, her head inclined to her phone, the soft electronic light illuminating her face, her head tilted towards it, a silvery Madonna.

I start to play these starlit water games, and once I'm in, I fuse with the music in a way that wasn't possible with the Schumann. Once I'm up and running, I again pretend to consult the muse in the distances of the auditorium, entirely in order to gaze at her, still in the same aspect, thousands of miles away, deeply instilled in the light of her phone: I may as well not be here, and she is obviously beautiful.

I cheat the Chopin a little, using too much pedal, because I sense the dryness of the acoustic which all the warm, well-fed bodies cannot reduce. But it's OK, I've always played this delicate thing well, and I try to communicate this fact a *little*, indicate the easy mastery of *just a tiny bit*, and when it ends in sleepy rapture I try to hold them in silence for as long as possible, keeping my back straight and my hands on the keyboard until every last scintilla of sound has gone, then I soften my posture and the applause emerges slowly, before building and immersing me in its ardour, a mirror of the music. I take one bow and go back to the dressing room, in several overlaying states of contentment and one of anxiety.

Garry pokes his head round the door. 'Jesus. That Schumann, last movement, so good. And the "Berceuse" too. Wow. Huh. I'm just saying it's all good stuff, I guess.'

'I appreciate it, Garry. It felt OK. By the way, who's the girl? At the back. The usher?'

'I don't know, they sent out an email asking for volunteers. She's probably a grad student?'

'How do I find out?'

'What's up?'

'I know her. I think I met her when I was here maybe? Or in the city. I want to reconnect.'

'She'll be at the reception. The ushers are doing drinks.'

'Thank God.'

'Ah, I get it!'

He leaves me and I feel as if I'm realizing something. It seems obvious: this is what I should do, just do this as much as I can, as often as I can, all the time if possible. Just find a new Schedule I can hitch myself to, don't think about it, let the Schedule do the work. *So* obvious.

I play the second half of the concert with a facility I find slightly alarming. I can't ascribe it to the girl, it's more the way the Bach haunts the Beethoven, so when I enter the Suite there's a fantastical sense of *rightness* to it all: from Schumann's miserable bobbing in the thick brown Rhine, through Chopin's radiant morbidity, then Beethoven's lewd vigour up to Bach's intricate godliness. It turns out that this idea I produced from nowhere not two hours ago contains some kind of progress of the spirit, and I am aware as I finish the Suite that it ends in a crisp and certain E flat, and as I lift my hands from the register Sandrine, Barlow, Brinslow, Garry, Clara are all momentarily gathered into its presence, and the applause – which is sufficiently fanatical that irony or ingratitude are pointless – seems like some assent to a view of life that is substantially mine and that culminates in me being on this stage, bowing, staring at my shoelaces and only now thinking about the girl with the moon in her hands.

Once everyone settles down, I move to stand on the apron of the stage, feeling naked without my piano.

'OK. Shall I play a bit more?'

Of course I should. The first request: Schubert, from a woman who prefaces said request with a long, self-serving question about how she heard me play in Philadelphia in 2002 and knew then I was a 'genius' because of the way I played the such-and-such sonata. I make all the obligatory 'oh, surely not' hand movements and stop well short of informing her that I remember the concert, and it wasn't a sonata but the C minor Allegretto, and I feel a little spritz of fury but play it anyway.

Then Judy stands up, looking elated. Sometimes you see a kind of love in women's faces that is just not available to men.

'You know what I'm going to say, Declan. Well, firstly, we are all so delighted you chose Quine to play this concert, and we love you very much indeed. Secondly, just for me, "Variations on the Nokia Ringtone", please.'

There is a roar of hilarity, and I bow and take my position with mock seriousness, flick my imaginary tailcoat over the stool, pause with hands like tiger claws high above the keyboard, and get into it. It strikes me that it's already more out of date than the French Suite but gets a lot more laughs. Another inundation of applause, people stand up in sequence, they have no choice after the few have made their move, so another few minutes bowing and smiling like a crazy geisha, and that's enough.

—

In the dressing room I reflect on the salutary power of praise on the human mind and body. Maybe I'm quite good at this after all? Then I force myself to remember some of the flubs in the 'Berceuse' and the plentiful emergency rubato in the second movement of Op. 90 and I'm ready to acknowledge my mortality, go greet the apostles and have my two Scotches.

The lobby of the Gerson is a cool, high-ceilinged place with a plate glass front, like some new-build church. They've dimmed the lights a little, and are piping in Haydn quartets. There's maybe sixty people, and I probably have to say a word or two to all of them. I recognize quite a few from my time here, all at least relatively fondly. I have a thought that this is where I should be, where I should have stayed: it's so gentle yet all so stimulating; such intelligent accomplished people. I always avoided the intra-faculty squabbling about chairs and tenure and other people's spouses; this idyll of good conversation and respect for talent, what a perfect resting place it could be, like playing in an everlasting Haydn quartet.

The girl is here. She moves around the room, coming to rest at each little group, tray unsteadily proffered. She then states the title of the canapé in question and, before moving on, nods a little when people thank her. Closer up she's different, but no less essential to my immediate future: she's very upright yet graceful, her face roundish and sweet, her lips plump and almost a little shapeless, thick dark eyebrows, and blue eyes where brown eyes should be. She moves around slowly and a little vaguely, permanently unsure as to the optimal time to enter a group. She has tied her dark hair back in something of a tangle and a big strand keeps falling over her cheek: she often tries to blow it away when she thinks no one's looking, but it always floats back. I notice that her giant phone is only just wedged in the back pocket of her jeans. It looks as if it could fall at any moment, whereupon I would of course swoop in and restore it to her like Cinderella's slipper. She has an atmosphere: gentle, accepting, I don't know. She looks intelligent and self-critical, and maybe a little melancholy. My type?

She also looks slightly puzzled, or maybe that's just her face of concentration or boredom. Also, she's clearly not a part of all this: I am nothing to her. Maddeningly, she doesn't approach my group; instead we have a courteous, beautiful hipster guy who seems to be the boss waiter in some way and who is enthusiastic about the show, but I could really do without that at the moment.

I'm talking to Judy, Garry and a couple of others, friends from the university, one woman who teaches French and wonders why the piece is called a French Suite, is there anything particularly French about it? Every so often someone comes up and compliments me in awkward terms that bear the signs of careful preparation; a couple of small, older women in chiffon prints, smelling powerfully of citrus cologne, twitter with embarrassing candour about the extent of their appreciation, one tightly gripping my forearm all the while, bright red nail varnish on the speckled talon. Garry takes them off me a little, but now a large, untidy man with a face like a boxer's is telling me about the first time he saw Pollini, and I see my girl kissing Hipster Waiter on the cheek before leaving the lobby entirely. Panic stations.

I excuse myself from the dull heavyweight and try to follow her out, when a tall man in a velvet suit and straight black hair steps in front of me and says, quietly but distinctly, 'You're a fraud.'

'What?'

He nods with eyes closed and walks away. I watch him as he walks slowly towards a side entrance. What did he say?

I have a more pressing question: where is she?

I go outside and look around the lawn. She's there, smoking against a tree, gazing into her phone.

'Nice to be outside.'

Without looking up: 'Yeah. I got another hour in there.'

'Me too.'

She doesn't know who I am.

'It's a lot. Playing the piano for an hour, then having to socialize.'

This is very untrue: I'm wired, no fatigue anywhere in my system.

'Oh, I'm so sorry, I didn't realize.'

'Oh God, it's fine. I find the attention a bit much, to be honest.'

'You're English.'

'Yes. From Manchester.'

Trying for cool points.

'Nice.'

No cool points awarded.

Her phone rings. 'Sorry.'

She moves away as she answers, speaking softly, possibly with tenderness. I realize with shock that I'm utterly invisible to her, as a pianist, sexual prospect, Mancunian, anything. Tal would be proud of such a complete disappearance.

As I walk back to the lobby, Judy is approaching me.

'What are you up to, Declan?'

'Just catching my breath.'

She won't let me pass. 'You played so beautifully.'

'Thanks, Judy.'

'And I need to know how you are.'

'I'm doing great. Well, not really, but better than you'd expect.'

'You should stay a few days.'

I'm trying to avoid eye contact; the adolescent has returned.

'I can't do that: I have to go to Connecticut tomorrow.'

'Come after.'

'Then I'm off again. I'm doing Kozar.'

'Yes, I know. Garry mentioned.'

'Thanks for the cake.'

I see she's upset, but also a little angry.

'I'm sorry, Judy.'

'We were very surprised, let's put it like that. Garry was, and I was. You shouldn't have just left like that. We were worried, but also it was inconsiderate, Declan. It was bad behaviour. We expected a little more from you.'

She can't chasten me, chastened as I already am.

'I know, Judy, I really do. That's it, the last stage of grief: you become a horrible person.'

'Don't be silly.'

I look at the Gerson: the bright yellow glow against the dark blue night, all the good people suspended in this lantern of benign civilization. It all feels so available to me, but not really anything worth having after all, certainly when compared to the girl, or with getting the hell out of here forever.

'Let's go back in.'

A few faces turn towards us as we approach. I look for the man in the velvet suit, but he's not there.

—

I leave the party before the last few guests, claiming the artist's privilege of exhaustion, which everyone knows is in fact selfishness. It feels good to be away from the crowd, from the Klains, having tepidly agreed to have breakfast with them tomorrow. The night seems to be getting warmer if anything; the trees are stock-still. I rest on the lawn while I wait for the Clav to be brought to my room. I lie face down, close up to the sweet vegetal odour of the earth, and, Gulliver-like, feel the creepy-crawlies infiltrate my shirt.

I did some grief therapy while I lived here, at Judy's insistence. He made strenuous, untiring efforts to understand what

I felt, and to offer help; he did lots of homework on me and was an excellent, compassionate man. He was almost exactly my age, and someone who without any doubt will help many people, but to me he was useless, not least because I wanted him to be. Perhaps he was right about one thing: my work is important, it can act as a means of coping, this notion of 'burying yourself'. Using work as an avoidance strategy is one thing, but as a positive habit (I followed this one: I never take a day off) and also as a means of gratitude. It seemed so absurd then that I would ever feel gratitude again, though I do, and increasingly often and most of all tonight: the combination of the excellence of my playing, its disconcerting fluency and fire, but then also the generosity offered by the applause, which for a few moments felt boundless and filled me with guiltless bliss, and, for a brief time, no thoughts of Esther whatsoever.

I hear the squeaking wheel of the dolly and get up, spitting grass filings, expecting Tyler, but it's the girl.

'Hey.'

'Oh. Hi.'

As I say, my wife watches over me.

—

She brings the Clav into my room and it's all businesslike for a few minutes, we even mention the weather. She doesn't sit down, but there's definitely something in the way she lingers. In the light, close up, I can see she is a little older than I thought, maybe late twenties.

'Stay for a bit? I can't sleep after I've played. Just for a talk?'

'OK.'

I sit on the edge of the bed; she leans her butt and hands against the desk, it's all pleasantly nervy.

82

'I'm Elise.'

'You didn't listen to a note I played.'

'Yeah, I know. Things going on.'

'It's fine, I like it. I mean, I like it when people listen, but also when they don't.'

'You like everything.'

'Apart from the haters.'

She laughs, I do too, and everything else happens naturally and with thoughtless modern ease and she is just as nice as she looks.

—

I'm awake at six and the bed is empty. I understand, but it still hurts. I take a bath, and hear her come back in.

'Elise?'

'I went to get my stuff.'

'Really?'

I feel like a child, pinkly curled up in the tub, looking up at her, now in jean shorts and a gauzy white T.

'You're coming with me?'

'Of course I am.'

I sink back into the water, delighted if confused. 'Are you sure about this?'

'Mm-hm.'

'I don't want you neglecting your studies for the sake of pi-ano-related adventures.'

'That's exactly what you want.'

She kicks off her ballet flats and sits on the inside edge of the tub, resting her feet on my thigh.

'I knew. When I saw you in the lobby. Even when you gave me the "fuck you" out on the lawn. At least I think I knew.'

'That's creepy. And I didn't give you the fuck you. I was just under strict instructions not to mess with the talent.'

'You're flunking everything.'

'That's so true.'

I get dressed in a hurry, Elise supine on the bed, everything momentarily optimistic and cool.

'Let's do it.'

I skip Judy's breakfast, which is clearly not right, but the choice between this brand new thing and talking about the old days was easy to make. I text Garry. He says he understands. I'll write to Judy later, and try not to lie too much.

Elise and I get in the Volvo, nod to one another like we're in a getaway car, and speed off.

3

She's navigating me on her phone, quizzically pinching and zooming Google Maps. We're avoiding the traffic on some back road that dips and swerves through the dense greenery of upstate. Her window is open so the cigarette smoke whizzes out, her seat reclined, her toes clinging onto the dashboard, a chipped violet pedicure, that even light brown skin tone. Whisky killed my dad, cigarettes killed my mother, but it's a bit early for that.

'So what does a PhD entail? I'm so clueless. I was supposed to go to university, but then I never did because of the piano thing.'

She seems reluctant. 'You have to write a book. Find a subject that's worth a whole book.'

'That sounds hard.'

'Hmmm, not really. For most people.'

She looks out of the window a lot, which makes me think she's having second thoughts.

'I can drive you back. I have time.'

'No! Why would you even say that?'

Then she's silent for a while, listening to the music she's Bluetoothed into the car. She calls it 'kind of trance?' It's entirely electronic, insistent and echoing, musically empty. Then there's some slow, grinding hip-hop. Some bitch is a cocksucker, some cocksucker's a bitch, the rapper's basso profundo like the voice of a filthy-mouthed god.

'Do you have anything else?'

'Nope.'

And she looks at me with a smile that's all the sweeter because of this generally melancholy aspect. The road continues to dip and swerve.

'What's the book about?'

'Augusta Webster.'

'I've never heard of her.'

'You're not alone.'

'How long you been doing it?'

'Oh, just the three years. I'm pretty deeply in now, but I'm not going to make it.'

'What are you going to do instead?'

'Absolutely nothing.'

The trance is back and is getting a little alienating, which may even be its intention.

'Shall we have some of my music now?'

'I'd rather not. I had to sit through about ten hours of it last night.'

She seems to have said enough about her book. She texts *a lot*, phone upright, her thumbs moving at fast-forward speed, then she replaces her phone in the cup holder for ten seconds. Then she picks it up again.

'I'm taking us the long way round. I'm just kind of loving being in the car.'

'That's fine. As long as I'm there by lunchtime.' I'll need to practise by then; I'm already feeling it a little, just around the edges.

'Where are we going?'

'I thought you were in charge of that.'

'I am, honestly. There's one here: cheap.'

'That's our boy.'

Even though we could stay at the Gilpins' vast palazzo for a month and not see another person, I want to be at a motel for the night. It's three days till the concert, and the idea is to choose a programme, practise, have Elise to myself, figure it all out and then go down to Greenwich tomorrow.

'I'm worried you're going to be bored. I have to work this afternoon.'

'Oh no, I'm good. I brought a book. I could easily get through a page of that. Or I'll go to a bar and try to pick up a violinist.'

'Ha.'

She inclines her head towards her window, her hair blowing madly in strands and whorls, closes her eyes and rests her hand on my leg.

This is surely a mistake. This whole thing. No escape, she'll do me in, another thing between me and practice, me and the purpose of this enterprise, which all of a sudden, despite last night's facile triumph, is again beginning to feel doomed: Kozar and the *Hammerklavier* up ahead, some complicated un-fixable problem.

The smooth grey road, the ceaseless greenery, and every so often the road widens and there's Walmarts and Nissan dealerships, Dunkins, the yellow M, nail bars, Subways, gas stations, a tattoo parlour or yellow-signed adult store on the way out, one old truck in the lot, presumably belonging to the last man on earth without broadband or shame. Still she texts, says not much, dozes, strokes my face at one point with the back of her hand, so I can smell her smoky fingers.

'This is a hell of a long way round.'

'We're good, only eight miles now.'

The music is now fey men crooning about nature and lost love over pretty guitar figures.

Out of nowhere: 'Actually, I never really figured out why I'm doing this doctorate.'

'Don't you want to teach?'

'Well, what I do with it is one thing. But also why I'm doing it all.'

'That's a pretty common feeling.'

'I was this insanely bookish teenager. But I couldn't figure out if it was real or just because I wanted to go to Brown. Like, Brown was always my dream school. I thought about it all day and night. I knew their website by heart. I even memorized the layout, the names of the buildings. Picked out a dorm. I thought they'd want an insanely bookish kid, so I made myself into one. Then I got rejected and it fucking killed me. I was completely destroyed by it. It might sound pathetic, but it still hurts. So maybe I was doing this to prove them wrong?'

'I think that's healthy. Or at least inevitable. You need to find something to fight.'

'I don't know why I'm telling you this.'

'I like it. I'm really grateful you can talk to me.'

'I don't know anything about you.'

'Come to this party, meet my rich friends. Pretend to be my girl.'

'Pretend?'

'How far *is* this place?'

'Eight miles. Shush yourself.' And she turns the music up.

—

We're on the upper floor of a two-storey motel. I had to get the Clav up to our room myself. There's not really a spot for it with all the built-in teak cabinets and the wide sagging bed. I have to move things around while Elise sits outside and texts. It was indeed eight miles, but we took a wrong turn and she didn't realize until we were fifteen miles the wrong way. Then she needed to stop and get a coffee and 'chill for a minute' in the parking lot. Although it was all so artless and unintentional, I hated her like we were retirees on our fiftieth road trip.

Check-in was time-consuming, the geezer on the desk engaged in some low-intensity conflict with his ancient computer. By this time I was almost frantic, *Hammerklavier* eating me alive.

Once we were in the room we pulled the thin orangey curtains and fooled around and then she wanted to fuck or more precisely she wanted to come, which took longer than it really should have done (this being not even day two) but she said she's always a little slow, and it's deliberate, she likes to hold herself just off for as long as possible. I didn't have the same problem. Then she was lying half in, half out of the comforter, soft and tan, her leg and hip describing a long, sweet serpentine line, her face an image of beatification, her toes scrunched, humming to herself, eternal promise in her deep, warm shadows.

—

A nine-minute wait till the hour, and practice.

—

Elise is again curled up with her phone. The speed with which she picked it up once we'd disentangled was pretty annoying. The only place to set up the Clav was by the door to the room, facing towards the bed, so I have to watch her fiddling away, nose six inches from the screen.

I play the Liszt exercises, but I'm not making progress towards invisibility. It's more difficult to disappear with someone else in the room, especially if that person is Elise, whose body is present but whose mind is clearly not. This is maddening, as I realize I want both. I repeat the first exercise five or six times.

'How many times do you have to *do* that?'

'Another twenty or so.'

'Shit.'

'Then I start practising.'

'Jesus.'

She's still typing or scrolling.

'I'm going to be here for the next four hours, by the way. Maybe five.'

'Wow. Seems like a lot of work.'

'It is. You can go if you like. Take a walk.'

'No, it's fine.' She turns away from me, puts her earbuds in better to be elsewhere. The comforter falls over her sloppily, the T-shirt barely covering her hips, limbs so warm and brown.

'Hey.'

'What?'

'I'm a bit distracted.'

'Really? By me?'

'Yes, by you.'

She sits up. 'I get the picture. I'll leave you alone. Get coffee or something.'

'OK.'

She leaves, possibly irritated. But that's OK, because finally it's just me and the *Hammerklavier.*

4

The Gilpins live in Cos Cob, which sounds like an Anglo-Saxon mud village but is in fact some great realm of palaces. Their house is an angular multilevel series of pavilions of glass and grey stone built around a sequence of artificial Giverny lily ponds. The grounds are profusely and variously green, high swaying ferns, Lebanese cedars, firs, slender pines all in proportion, shot through with pink gravel pathways, all thought through to the *n*th – a silent triumph of deeply organized lushness and shade.

We get there late afternoon, Elise riveted to her car seat undergoing a slow-burn real estate orgasm as we cruise up the drive, the sunlight seeping through the trees creating a greenly celestial aspect. I know my way around, and we park round back and enter the kitchen, an airy white and steel hall. There is plate glass down one entire wall, a loggia beyond, then, of course, a Japanese garden. Elise and I wait by the blonde oak refectory table. She whispers: 'Wow, this is incredible.'

It's Merry who enters first, at her normal driven pace, in her normal type of outfit: tight black pants, ultra-white blouse, a solitary heavy silver bangle, her dark hair in a salon-fresh updo, Suburban Immaculate. She hugs me, feels wiry and crisp.

'My boy.' She then embraces Elise, who looks kooky, rustic and highly fucking alive standing next to her. 'Oh, darling, I've heard so much already!'

'Tom's on a call, he'll be right down. Sit down! Drinks?'

Merry must be fifty by now, the point at which there's no hiding it any more: cabled neck, slight crimping around the mouth, a sense of stiffness around the hips. She's the daughter of an Episcopal priest, brought up in New Hampshire, went to boarding school and Yale, worked in advertising for a while, but she's way too good for regular work. In her mid-twenties she quit, ski-bummed in Vail in the winters, spent her summers couch-surfing on the Cape, wrote a novel about same. She met Tom on a boat some glittering blue day off Nantucket and it became quickly apparent that if she played this right she'd never have to work again: so what if he was a little older and a little limited? She could cope. Tom's age was to be expected, given her goals, and she could work on his rough edges. He tried hard, but devoted the bulk of his cultural development to understanding Burgundy's *premiers crus*. This was OK, because he was consistently tolerant of the art openings and post-recital receptions at which he found himself, particularly with the advent of smartphones, which meant he could take his calls outside, dawdle over the Red Sox play-by-play and smoke a cigarette before re-entry.

To be fair to him, he picked up more than a little of her pianomania. And because he liked it but didn't really care, his attitude retained a pleasant knockabout quality that's unusual in the field.

'Hey, Dec, this Russian dude Trifonov: just so great.'

'He's OK, if you like that kind of thing.'

'Lays it on a bit thick? I personally love it.'

'That's entirely your choice.'

And in he comes with his friendly confidence to the fore, offering a man hug from twenty feet away, like some big brown crab: 'Hey!'

At just over sixty, his body is becoming boxy. He told me a while ago that he's been having testosterone treatment and feels twenty-five again, but he has a slight air of elderly distraction about him now – and he's severely underdressed: grey T-shirt, stretched out at the neck, old PJ pants. Merry has her dander up a little. It's lunchtime.

'I'll take Elise to your room.'

Tom waits for the girls to leave. 'Wanna swim? I've got a story for you.'

—

We're in one of the pools. Tom's got his arms along the edge, occasionally dipping to suck the surface of the water and then spit it out. I don't understand the details of this story, but its general meaning is clear: he's in big trouble.

He ducks all the way under the water; I can see his tawny sea lion form shimmer through the depths. He pops up at the far end and smooths his whitening hair back. I'm standing at chest depth, skimming my arms over the surface tension. I look into the water and consider the deep-sea whiteness of my feet.

'Did you understand any of what I just said, Declan?'

'Well, I can tell it's not good.'

'Yah. Jail is generally agreed not to be good.'

He slithers heavily out of the pool and goes to a table where he has his wine and cigarettes. He dries himself vigorously and sits on his lounger, the black towel draped over his bullish shoulders.

'I'm so fucked.'

'*Jail?*'

'Oh yeah, lots of jail. Me and Frank Brice are on the hook. Sal, Arnold and Shapiro are scot-free.'

He pours himself a lot of presumably tremendous Burgundy into a glass the size of a grapefruit, and lights a Marlboro.

'I'm going to try to bring some other assholes down with me but will probably fail. I did it. I'm guilty. So, as I said, I'm fucked.'

From what I can tell, his firm did a series of deals related to or dependent on the value of the rupee. The deal went wrong, and one of the co-investors lost a fortune. This wronged man tried to exact revenge and threw a lot of money at a private investigation. They found out that Tom and this Brice person had had a contact in the Indian finance ministry who was leaking them minutes of currency-related meetings. This sounded to me like how I assumed everything works, but is in fact illegal. There were some other complications: the Indian contact was a plant or stooge or some other thing, and it was all a set-up, the information was pretty much useless, and the interest rates went the wrong way anyway, Tom was found out, and that was that.

'Plus Merry and I. Also fucked.'

'God, Tom, I'm sorry.'

'She's got a little money they can't touch. And I gave her the apartment years ago. Your apartment, I mean. If she sells and goes somewhere smaller she'll have close to ten million.'

'That sounds like enough.'

'You never had a hundred million, did you?'

'I did not.'

'I didn't either, actually. But anyway, screw that. I've got a month or two before the real shitshow starts. And so until then I intend to drink my assets. Starting with this seventy-eight

Richebourg, which is quite staggeringly good.' He takes a large draft and pulls hard on his cigarette.

'What's up with you and Merry?'

'Oh, you know, there's a girl. A woman. Or there was. Merry found out. Nothing very original, I'm afraid. So, as I've mentioned: I'm completely and utterly fucked.' He lifts his arms high in the air. 'Look at me now, ma!'

—

The Gilpins have Josef Hofmann's piano. It's in their 'ballroom', which is on the second storey of an unused section of the house. The room is supported by its own array of columns, a glass box that juts into the garden, overhanging one of the dark lily ponds. I'm in this room, walking towards the Hofmann: it looks only just stationary on the glassily smooth parquet, ready to be pushed through the plate glass and into the black water below by some characters in a bad satire. He had small hands, so Steinway made him an instrument with slightly narrower keys. It's not much harder to play, especially as the fingers on my vast hands are super-thin anyway. Dad thought I'd be a goalie, but instead I was a left winger, flying down the touchline, never straying unless it was absolutely necessary. He said I was like that mechanical rabbit that speeds around the outer rim at the greyhound track. This was a little harsh: no rabbit that ever lived could smash crosses in from the left like me.

I sit at the piano. It's never played, and you can somehow sense it. The room is set up for tomorrow evening: forty or so chairs arrayed around the instrument, which is polished to a black mirror, lid open, a gleaming three-legged thing, half-insect, half-rhino. I play some octaves, up and down two or three times. The acoustic in the room is stupendous: spacious and resounding, metallically bright at the top, a cluster of vast growling bells down below.

They said Hofmann played with too much power. They didn't realize he was the first person to play these things to their full capacity. He proved that pianos are totally over-engineered for the music played upon them: you can't play Beethoven at the proper speed or as gently as needed on these war machines: there's just too much *sound*. Everything becomes grandiose and symphonic and the true voice is snuffed out by all the over-glorious noise. The solution: play well within its capacity, only hit the gas when absolutely forced to, and probably not even then.

I do my exercises and can't resist the temptation to play loud and fast just for a minute or two. I even start to use the pedal, create a forest fire of sound.

Then straight into the Fugue of the *Hammerklavier*. Just as the music stumbles upon its cack-handed, unfugueable theme I have a sudden moment of wild romance when I realize I'm playing Beethoven's *Hammerklavier* sonata on Josef Hofmann's piano. At that moment I start playing like a klutz, stumbling through a fog of bad phrasing and self-hatred.

'The piano is a percussion instrument, which is why you must play it as if it is not.' Tal's delicacy of touch was his greatest attribute as a pianist. He played fast and quiet much better than me, truth be told.

So I have to start again, at a very slow tempo, pay no attention to the dynamics marked in the score (maybe he was wrong, have you thought of that?). I play it as if it's Bach, tiny subtle shifts. No pedal now, just keep up the tempo, bring out the tune. As I move through it I feel a warm undertow, as if the piece is heated from deep down below somewhere and you can sense the deaf old bear rethinking everything all over again.

The *Hammerklavier* is an attempt to figure out what *music* is. What's a theme? What's a melody? What's a fugue? And how can anything be any good when it's worrying about what it is all the time?

But then the third movement, the Adagio, predicated on a tiny melodic idea of descending thirds, is a rebuke to all this, not the gloomy old idea of 'the mausoleum of humanity's deepest sorrows' but in a way all music, or at least the apotheosis of everything music can offer: an eternal consolation, an example of austere, joyful compassion, a vast, painful, entirely successful attempt at beauty, the highest expression of the value of deep thinking and hard work. Oh, Esther: why not *once*?

Still in the Fugue, I lose purpose at this thought, and soon I'm all over the place, a miserable slave hacking blindly through the thickets of meaning just begging for life to end.

Then I stop, aware of something in the periphery. I look around: Elise is in the room in one of Merry's beach robes, barefoot.

'Is that real?'

'What, the piano?'

'No, the music. It's fucking *awful*.'

I find this gravely irritating. Esther didn't like the music, but at least she knew she was wrong.

'It's not "fucking awful", Elise.'

'I'm sorry, but it's so *clangy*.'

I clang out a few bars.

'It is. Very clangy. You're right.'

'What's it called?'

'I'm not telling you, you'd just laugh.'

'Laugh?'

'The *Hammerklavier*.'

'*Hammerklangier* more like, amiright?'

'You're a philistine.'

'Thank you. You may proceed.'

'I'm done for now.'

'Thank God!' She sits cross-legged on the floor, chastely organizing the robe over herself. 'Why didn't you tell me?'

'About what?'

'Merry was telling me. What a big deal you are.'

'Oh, she's a good friend.'

'I feel intimidated.'

'Oh, please don't be.'

'I mean I'm not intimidated by *you*. Just by your world. The music world. Why haven't I heard of you?'

'It's a weird little place and most people aren't allowed in.'

'I feel bad for being so ignorant, is what I'm saying.'

'It's fine. You can't be ignorant about something you know nothing about.'

She smiles at me, then a small shade of confusion – Esther! – passes over her face. 'What?'

'It's OK. Let me play you something. Is there anything you think you might like?'

'I'm such a dunce… erm, Mozart? Did he do piano stuff?'

'Sure. Lots of things.'

I pretend to be lazily considering what to play, toss off some startlingly fast Art Tatum-style runs, just so she realizes that on this new planet she's stumbled across I probably have my own small nation. Then I do a snippet of Nintendo music, an alternative encore that passes by the sleepyheads I usually play to.

'What's *that*?'

'Elise, it's *Donkey Kong*.'

'Oh, I don't play games.'

'That's funny.'

'Bit early for the unsettling retorts?'

'Is it ever too early?'

I look out the plate glass into the still green trees outside, syrupy with heat. This glass cube is far too cold though. What a waste it all is.

Then she says: 'Why don't you talk to me?'

'That old one. I'm working up to it. I do want to talk to you, but it takes me a while.'

'I'm going to need something eventually.'

'That's fair. This is Mozart. I think he was eighteen when he wrote this.'

I want to play the first movement of one of the early sonatas: 'trivial' supposedly, a kind of nursery rhyme, but also a small, immortal act of kindness.

'Even tyrants recognize kindness, Declan. It is what drives them mad.' Tal, whose family is one fiftieth the size it should be because of these tyrants, so he has authority.

Playing it is a kind of sacrilege, though, because I recorded it and dedicated that recording to Esther. It was a *real* dedication: I gave the thing entirely to her. I close my eyes and briefly consult her.

OK, I think she's fine with it.

Firstly: E flat again; my mind must have drifted here of its own accord. Secondly: it feels very small yet very spacious after the Fugue, as if not really the same art form, but not bad at all. We follow this little silver bubble as it tries to float away. The ogre of a piano tries to rise up around it: it must be protected at all costs. I play it as gently as possible within the confines of this powerful technology. I think about overhearing it from a distant room, the player in that room involved in the… what was it? the seriousness of a child at play or something. Did Tal come up with that? I don't think so – somebody though. I know it so well I don't need to think at all: that's the key. It works out fine: exquisite, purposeless, and so very pretty, like a game of ring o' roses in the cathedral nave.

I let it die, which takes an age. I look at Elise, not needing a response or approval but getting both.

'That was beautiful.'

She looks moved for the first time since I met her. Admittedly a short time, but after two days with someone you've already seen many versions of their face, and I've not seen this one.

'And you didn't mention your wife.'

'No. I'm sorry. Sometimes I do, sometimes I don't. There's no method to it.'

'I'm sorry.'

'It's fine.'

'And I'm no good at that kind of thing anyway.'

'Don't worry, no one is. Really, from experience. Not one person is.'

Elise stands and walks towards me, retightening her robe. She's next to me, smells like candied fruit, her thighs pressed softly against the blue silk. If I encircled her it would be around her lavish hips, and the practice would be over. She strokes my head, gets a little comical.

'This is awkward.'

'What is?'

'Getting at someone when they're at the piano. They're all kind of in the wrong direction, and I can't move the thing, so how do I get at you?'

'You don't. I need to work.'

She takes my hand and leads it inside the robe: her skin seems freshly bathed, cool, a little sticky.

'Too close. I'm sorry.' I withdraw my hand at a highly reluctant pace.

'To what.'

'To Esther. We talked about her just now.'

'Huh.'

And now here's another unseen version of the face, indicating irritation. This is nastily consoling: in the sharp contention of new love I have a tiny momentary advantage, another unforeseen upside of the Dead Wife. She walks away and leans sulkily against the white wall.

I glance at the iPad: 8.58. I try to look impatient.

'I better go then.'

'Yes, thank you. I have to work. I won't be long.'

'Merry's a drunk, right?'

'No.'

'She seems to be.'

'I'm sorry. I've never seen her drunk. Not drunk drunk. Give me an hour?'

Which means two at least. She leaves the ballroom and all the colour is gone: piano black and white, white walls, black chairs, the darkening windows making a perfect mirror, my monochrome elongated reflection. But it's OK, because it feels like a perfect setting for a disappearance. Also, 8.59 on the iPad. I look at myself: my legs seem long in the slim black pants, my straight-backed posture somehow old-fashioned, a little lordly. I rest my elbow on the corner of the piano, pose my face between index finger and thumb. I speak out loud towards the distant perfected image of myself: 'Declan Byrnie, pianist.'

I wave my fingers at myself, hands so vast, white and spidery, and hear my dad's voice: 'Hands like goalie's gloves, our Declan.'

A sentence not designed to contain so much love, but doing so with ease.

Nine on the dot.

Practise.

5

Morning. Elise is leaning way out of the bedroom window, smoking, her T-shirt-clad body exquisitely angled. There was something new about her last night. Maybe the Esther moment had changed her a little, a twist that's caused complications, maybe forced her feelings. I wonder how she'd behave if she were in love with me. And what if I were in love with her? I don't know, that has only happened to me once, and this certainly isn't that.

She turns and draws her hair up into a scrunchie. 'I'm going swimming. Come watch me.'

'I have to work.'

'You sure.'

'Yes.'

She studies me for a moment. 'I'd lose this fight, wouldn't I?'

'I'm afraid so.'

She gives me a dry, ashy-scented kiss and I get a reminiscence of my mother and her forty-a-day habit. Dad, as the man, got the premium brand: Dunhills in the red and gold box, sweet-smelling and comforting to me; Mum got Dorchester 100s, which were cheaper, more loosely packed and seemed to burn down twice as fast. That extra twenty pence a pack, add in the whisky, and he died six months before she did. She didn't stop or even cut back, her constant grief forbidding intervention, and it was far too late anyway.

Elise goes into the bathroom to change. As soon as she's out of the room, I retrieve my iPad from under the bed and go back to my Esther emails. I realize I'm working through them chronologically, maybe looking for clues, but I'm not finding any.

I was quite different then, or was pretending to be.

Esto, Esti, Esta, Estate, Estuarius

I'm in Glasgow: drear, cowrin', whatever-the-hell, beastie a gogo. It's pissing down, is dark by noon, and the whole place looks like a water-damaged Lowry. The concert isn't sold out, because there was some mix-up with the publicity and they put the wrong date on the poster and the web. In addition, the woman who runs the hall has asked me to do a Q and A afterwards, and Barlow is strongly recommending that I oblige: 'When did you realize you were a genius?' (it's a daily struggle) or 'What is music *really*?' (a scam!) and then 'Celtic or Rangers?' and everyone will laugh like crazy, especially when I say 'Stenhousemuir'. In addition, I'm having to play their Number Two piano, a timid, wheezing barrel organ of a thing which sits there all ashamed like some dog that thinks it's about to be thrashed (true dat!). Their Number One is in Dundee, for reasons not clear to me.

So, Esther, my mind naturally gravitates towards Bolzano and the fine work we shall do there. It occurs to me: we should make an effort to beautify the walls, and construct a promenade around the entirety of said walls. Italians love their passeggiate, and surely there's no soul alive who doesn't like the idea of walking around a city in an afternoon on an elevated walkway, shaded by cedars, gelato vendors spaced evenly around and about with their well-priced succulent wares. I like your idea of a children's festival: the central *piazza maggiore* should be illuminated in the evenings, and the festival should definitely include opportunities to make art, dance and humiliate clowns. Just before dinner there will be a concert of Mozart, Haydn and Vivaldi by the Bolzano Sinfonietta, under my baton (natch) and we'll absolutely kill it out there, and, what's more, none of the children, not even the little ones, will get even the tiniest bit bored, even during the slightly workmanlike bits of the Haydn. Then the piazza will (or even shall) be turned into a giant outdoor seating area for families, and the food will be plentiful, various and completely free.

You, in your capacity as Mayoress, will sit at the highest table, garlanded with whatever garlands are made of, dressed in white dress of purest cotton, to denote your purity (ahem), and, yes, there will be much joyful hubbub and merry hullabalooing, and someone from the pasticceria will have my mum's recipe for trifle and be serving it in great dollops to everyone. To round it off, the tables will be cleared and there will be a kickabout, which will become slightly competitive (they are Italian after all) and I will score the winner in the last minute: a volley from the edge of the box, top left-hand corner.

Get in.

OK, the Gorbals are calling.

Write to me all the time. No, really: do.
Soonest, D x

PS Did I mention write to me?

She didn't, and three weeks later she was dead. I am momentarily staggered all over again.

Elise comes out of the bathroom in a bikini, wafty cover-up and big sunglasses. She's adapted like lightning.

'You could sit by the pool and watch me splash about. It'll be fun.'

'It probably would be.'

She does a catlike jump onto the vast bed, pads towards me on all fours. 'I'm having a weird time. But I quite like it.'

'I feel the same.'

She's over me now. I try to speak again, but she puts a finger on my mouth. 'Shhhhhhhhhh!'

I instantly push her off and get out of bed. 'Sorry. I'll explain later.'

She lies back, exasperated.

—

Merry wants to hear me play, so joins me in the ballroom. She looks somehow simplified as she pulls over a chair, dressed in baggy black pyjamas, no make-up, her face freckled and pale, her thinning lips in a permanent straitened smile.

Tom seems almost blasé about what's happening to him: not Merry. She talks as I pretend to practise, her voice low and realistic.

'I knew he used hookers for years, it was our understanding. So *sophisticated*, right? There was one who threatened to black-mail him, and he had to tell me what he'd been doing: staying in the City and all that. I could deal. But you remember he was always in San Diego? You probably don't. They have an office in La Jolla, and this one girl was based there. I got to know her a little, after the fact. A tiny little Polish girl. Not a young girl, maybe thirty? She got my email and sent me, like, hundreds of photos of them together. Sal too at the firm, they all knew. The

Polish girl wanted a million to go away, but she had no leverage: she got a hundred and fifty thousand. Tom said he'd stop with the hookers, and maybe he did, but I got this sense about two years ago, that *something*, you know? A different feeling. Maybe he actually loved this new one. The first time I felt at risk. I thought Tom always loved me, but then I wasn't sure. And it killed me when I found out how old she was: forty, you know, not twenty-five. Must be love, right? It wasn't just someone to fuck in the city or La Jolla or wherever. She was forty, divorced, two kids. *Had* to be love. They'd been seeing each other four years. He rented her a place in Sag Harbor and she moved out there with her kids. '

'Who is she?'

'She's a lawyer. I don't know, I only met her once. She asked me to meet her and I said yes. We met in the city, and it was horrible. She was so smart and nice and good, and she was such a good mother. Her first husband left her out of nowhere and went to Thailand, so we know what was going on there. She said she was so sorry, and that Tom always spoke highly of me, but she loved him and didn't know what to do. And she *was* sorry too, I never doubted that.

'And then she said Tom gave her up for me. And I thought about his calculation: the money, the pain of the divorce, the fact he never got to despise me at all like usually happens around here. You haven't seen it: the men, they have nothing but fuck-ing *contempt* for their wives, outright fascist *contempt*. He's not like that. There's no cruelty in him. Which might be why he got so screwed by the guys at the firm. He's hapless. I know it sounds dumb, but he is. And he's dumb, too. He doesn't know what men can be like. Shapiro's stuck with us, no one else.'

I remember Shapiro, a quiet, slightly awkward man with a New York Mets yarmulke bobby-pinned to his head. He's a good amateur piano player: we played a bit of the Schubert fantasy at the apartment in the Perry, and he held his own, to an extent. I think he was Tom's boss in some way, but he didn't really look it: he wore a woolly sweater under his suit, for instance. Why did he stick with them and the others not? It's all too dark for me, too adult.

Maybe I should want to understand what's been done to Tom, but I don't. Didn't he say he did something illegal? So why shouldn't he suffer the consequences? Isn't the whole firm now busted? Too much complexity. I turn back to my score: so much to do. I want Merry to go. I don't want any part of this. I have nothing to say. I still don't have any space for other people's misery, truth be told. I look over to her, and she's looking down at her intertwined fingers and mouthing something. She seems bereaved and I feel bad for my irritation, as someone who knows the feeling.

'Let me play you something?'

'Yes, of course, obviously I'd love that.'

'Let me think. I'll just noodle around for a bit.'

'I should have done something with my life, shouldn't I, Declan? Then I'd be OK.'

'You've done a lot.'

'We should have adopted, but I was scared the money would fuck them up, or I would.'

'Oh, Merry.'

'I know.'

I get to the end of my exercise but hold the pedal down so the last chord surrounds us, a bright and cold glow in this glassy acoustic.

'I don't want to stop you practising.'

'No, it's fine. If it helps even the smallest amount I'll do it.'

Merry has such an astounding ear, such a deep sense of music, like no other non-musician I've ever met. It's a gift in its own right. I never once doubted that she loved my playing, she is incapable of phoniness on this topic: falseness would be a kind of sacrilege. She has no ideology, no ranking of Ten Greatest this or that, no effortful contrarianism, no seventy-five recordings of the Chopin ballades, none of the miserable analytical trappings of connoisseurship, all that pretending to despise what you love. Just passionate understanding, deep knowledge and a perfect ear. I'd happily play for her every day.

'How's the piano?'

'It's fantastic.'

I prove it with some oceanic Lisztian scales, then noodle for a moment or two more, think about a run through *Hammerklavier*, but conclude that she's in no state to be trampled by a mastodon.

'You should have it.'

'The piano?'

'Yes. They'll take it from us, no doubt. Then sell it to some Chinese people or whatever.'

'I can't really—'

'Take it. Play it, sell it, whatever. We'd rather you have it than anyone.'

I don't even fight. 'Well, thank you. I don't know—'

She waves me away. 'Play me something.'

'OK, what about this?'

I start to play the last Schubert sonata, serious yet sweet, wanting to please her. I don't even play it well: I'm too slow, so it drags, and when I speed up I'm throwing it away, and my left hand is a little heavy and it's stodgy despite the piano's clarity, but after a while I feel I'm managing the slow tumbling journey through *harmonie paradies*. She listens perched on the edge of her chair for a while, then moves softly to the floor and lies with her head resting on hands arranged into a prayer formation, a bony little orphan with nothing but ten million dollars to her name.

6

It's an hour or two before the concert. Elise and Merry went off a while ago expressing their desire to spend three hours bathing, drinking and getting dressed up, so Tom and I go to the terrace. He's working his way through another plutocratic Burgundy, rolling an unlit cigar around in his fingers, talking current affairs. He sounds like a conservative but describes himself as 'James Baker Democrat', which apparently is a good joke in certain circles. I hate politics because when politics and art collide, art always gets hospitalized and politics barrels on regardless.

Tom has that high-handed rich guy metapolitical thing: 'The *reality* is… such and such and such and such… *the Fed* such and such and such and such… what Trump *really* wants' and so on and so on.

I hate politicians even more than politics, they're all, by definition, bad people. They just want power, and we'll never understand them because we *don't* want it, and they despise us for this. They're a different species, animated solely by an overwhelming desire to have dominion over others, so fuck them. And this new one, this fetid oversized Oompa-Loompa of misery, lies and shame: fuck him in particular. Imagine, for one thing, the sheer *scale* of his indifference to Bach.

'Dec, the markets want stability, and this world is a madhouse. That's the tension. If everybody would just sit still and obey the rules then we'd all be rich.'

'Even the prisoners.'

'Oh, OK, that hurt.' He goes quiet for a moment, then: 'Merry told you everything, right?'

'Pretty much.'

'You know the biggest mistake I made? Persuading myself I loved anyone else. You find the one, Declan, and that's the one you gotta stick with.'

'I did try that.'

'Oh God, I'm so sorry.'

'It's OK. I forget about it myself sometimes.'

'What a fucking mess.' He puts the unlit cigar in his mouth and stares at the ground. He starts to nod, the dreadful realization presumably rising inside him again.

'I should get ready.'

We go back into the house to change. I shower and look for Elise, but she's in some distant wing. I put on the Brioni: it's a tiny bit rank from Quine. Work clothes, what do you expect?

I head back to the kitchen. Tom is now more sprightly, dressed in his Connecticut uniform of navy blazer, blue dress shirt and grey slacks. Rita, their housekeeper, is teasing him about his gut while mixing him a G and T. He points at himself. 'I'm putting on a good act, right, Dec?'

'You're killing it.'

He takes the mixing straw out of his glass, exclaims, '*An die Musik!*' and downs his drink in one.

The girls enter the kitchen together at full sail, glamour-pussed half to death. Elise is curvier than Merry (as is an ironing board), which means she fills the perfect scarlet minidress almost too gorgeously. Merry is in all white, her hair swept back, proudly mounted on four-inch heels. Elise does a semi-curtsy.

'Merry lent me this. What do you think?'

'I really like it.'

'It's Givenchy you know.'

'I really, really like it. You know what, I need to change. This shirt is pretty gross by now. Come up and help me choose one.'

We go up to our room at some speed, and for the first time I feel like more than someone she picked up, and she's affectionate and endlessly sweet.

Afterwards, we can't think of anything else to do except hold on to each other.

Elise whispers: 'I got you in the end.'

And holds on tighter for a while.

Eventually we get ourselves sorted in the Dubai-level bathroom, and enshrined in the mirror, we look pretty good together.

Elise is putting on make-up with an unexpected level of precision.

'I love Merry.'

'Yes, she's my other mother. Not like my real one at all. My anti-mother. And Tom's my uncle-father.'

'And she *is* a drunk.'

'No way.'

'And look.' Elise dips two fingers into her bra, pulls out a tiny see-through bag of white powder and waggles it gleefully.

'What's that?'

'Cocaine, idiot.'

'Oh no, that's bad.'

'Why?'

'Because I don't like the idea of making love on drugs. It ruins it.'

She's exasperated or defensive. 'I did one line, Declan.'

'I don't even know what that means.'

'It means "hardly any". Look, OK, I'll get rid of it. I'll give it back.'

'Is she a cokehead?'

'I don't know, but she has a *lot*. She says all the girls do it on the weekends, after yoga.'

'I hate this now.'

'It's fine.' Elise looks at the bag for a moment, then slips it back into her bra.

'So you're not giving it back to her?'

For the first time, another face: defiance. 'Are you telling me to?'

'Of course not.'

'Good.'

———

There's a pre-drinks, and it becomes clear that the audience will be small, maybe twenty people. I've been to the Gilpins' parties with hundreds of guests, all with the high burnish of money, arrayed around the terraces and mezzanines of the house in a filmic display of social plenty. I've played concerts here too: sixty, seventy people, a solid contented gathering. I guess it relates to Tom's fall, but wouldn't people then rally round? I know zero about how this place works: America's subtle and brutal encodings are completely invisible to me. When something bad happens where I'm from, the women come over and the houses are filled with steaming kettles, sponge cakes, cigarette smoke and savage irony at the expense of men. The boys make the mess, the girls clean it up.

Tonight's group is clustered nervily around the entrance to the ballroom looking mismatched and not quite there. Merry and Elise are wildly overdressed and tower like orchids over the shuffling band, Merry talking a little too loudly: trying to gin people up or hopped up on cocaine, I have no idea. Elise is clearly trapped by Barbara Lefferts, an old hand at these nights, who must be not far off ninety, whose hair is too long and straight for someone her age and who's holding on to Elise, her mouth red-lipped and gaping, wearing old plaid slippers with her dress pants. What do feet look like when you're ninety? The Fugue from *Hammerklavier*, no doubt.

I'm with Tom and a bore called Jeff DiPaolo.

'It was always my backhand that was stronger. Single-handed: me and Federer, the last of that line.'

'Interesting.'

'I was good. I know what it's like to have talent. It's not easy. It puts that pressure on you, you know? It's rough.'

'Oh, *were* you good?'

'I was, I was pretty good. State level, as a junior.'

'Wow, that's amazing.'

'Thanks.'

'Ever think about being a pro?'

'I definitely had the talent. But it's the commitment, right? I mean I *had* the commitment, but I was accepted by Yale, so then it was tennis, Yale, Yale, tennis.' He weighs them up with his hands, keeping his vodka tonic nicely balanced.

'Yes, you do have to be very committed to things nowadays.'

'Maybe I could have done both? But I kept myself pretty busy at Yale. Got involved with a club here and there.' Although he wants me to follow up, I can see the bait on the hook and skulk off downriver.

'Right.'

Then, a tiny bit impatiently: 'The Skull and Bones, you know it?'

Of course I don't know it. Some dress-up thing?

'Yes, wonderful.' I try to sound as bored as possible.

Tom's drunk, but not blind: 'Hey Jeff, Declan's gotta prep a little. Let's go say hi to Merry, I know she misses you.'

I do a tiny bow and think about what I'm going to play, but having seen the crowd there's no adrenaline, hence there is no rage. This is not a preparation for Boston, this is a wake for Merry and Tom's previous life. I go to sit at the piano, and people slowly follow, unsure of what to do with their drinks. Motley, a little indifferent, ironically reminiscent of the guests at a sad, hastily arranged wedding, they don't even fill the front two rows.

Merry stands next to me and clinks a ring against her glass, which is unnecessary.

'We all know why we're here: we have a pianist in our midst.'

The tiniest of ripples, people clapping with cocktails in one hand.

'And he's going to play for us. Which is, let's be honest, quite amazing, to have someone like Declan in our home, and we're all so grateful. And I just want him to know that we're also very proud of him tonight. He knows why. He's a fine pianist but he's also a very, very good friend.'

Only 'fine'?

She seems to become upset, but gathers herself quickly.

'Anyway, you all know what music is to me and always will be. If it's the only thing we've got left, then it's all worth it. Seriously. What else is there that only gives and never takes, that expects nothing of us? Just listening and loving and appreciating blah blah. Shuddup and siddown, Merry! OK, I get it. Do we want to listen to me or Beethoven? Right? So, ladies and gentlemen: Declan Byrnie.'

She takes her seat next to Barbara in the front row, nods at me with a slightly drunken jerkiness and takes a sip of her drink. Elise is way over at the other end of the row, sitting next to a little girl I only now notice. Elise and I will be looking at each other throughout the performance, which is bad for both of us: I should have told her I don't mind if she yawns, and that

I hope she doesn't mind my facial expressions, which I try to control but often cannot: it looks like all kinds of awful things are happening to me.

I have to say something, but as the artist you can get away with a lot, as everyone assumes you know what you're doing.

'Thank you, Merry. Thank you for this wonderful little gathering. And thank you for letting me play this piano, which is one of my favourites in the entire world – and I've played a lot of pianos: at least' – I pretend to count in my head – 'nine. I'm not going to talk any more and I won't play for long, don't worry. This is a piece by Chopin that my dad liked.'

I play the 'Berceuse' again, really shouldn't start with it, and my dad didn't like it much either, although he pretended he did.

It took me a long time to realize, but he was frightened of me: I'd sometimes catch him looking at me, seemingly wondering who this strange person was in his house. He never talked to me much; I was my mother's boy. Also, I didn't see much of him: he was still working on the buses and he often worked nights for the extra money. He didn't like those night buses: fewer people, and the ones that were on them were drunk or weird or eating kebabs or punchy. But there was that car he'd bought on the never-never, so it had to be done. They eventually moved him to an admin job he loathed: in the office at the depot, scheduling maintenance and organizing shifts, bored to death. The new job meant he was home every night by six. He'd have his tea, watch *Corrie* and then he was off to the Star and his little gang of mates. I can see them all now: Terry Fay, John Maguire, Bill Navarro, Tony Powell – boozy, jovial fuckers, all proud of their drinking chops and scared stiff of women. I wondered what they talked about all night, or, some days, all day and all night? Man United?

Possibly. I couldn't imagine them talking about their families. Then Navarro told me at the funeral that my dad talked about me and nothing else all the time, every night, and they always had to tell him to shut it.

He would come and watch me play football, but not often. Nothing in it: just the way he was. Once he'd settled that I'd never play for United (his grandest, most astounding dream) he came less often. Same with most of the dads from round there: Saturday morning they were hung-over, back in the pub or the bookies, working on the car in the garage, watching *Grandstand* – that was about the range of options.

Then, when I got to twelve or thirteen, his interest in me picked up. On the way back from church, he'd ask me questions about the girls we'd seen with their Sunday-best slap on.

I realized later that this new concern was entirely driven by his terror that, because I played piano, I was probably gay. Sometimes I'd catch him watching me closely, mystified or at least wary. The only child is a giant in his own home: every move I made was observed, mulled over and, I presume, analysed once I went to bed. I was small for my age, had a girlish voice, was seemingly only interested in playing this ancient, effeminate music or being curled up under Mum's wing watching soaps, wearing a pair of green trousers. What more evidence did he need?

He was in a state of high tension for a couple of years, I guess. Then at fifteen I started going out with Anne-Marie Duffy, and he visibly relaxed. Anne-Marie, with her early-flowering body and sweet, compliant nature, was regarded as a great prize around our way. But she quickly chucked me for Fintan Slade. He was two years older than us and knew it. He didn't practise the 'Appassionata', or watch videos about Sviatoslav Richter. He took her to the pictures or bought her Malibu and Cokes at the pubs where no one checked your age. In addition, and the clincher, he'd passed his driving test (first time, as he often made us aware) and had access to his mother's Vauxhall Nova. Even I had to concede that that was a big deal indeed. I was overmatched, and it was all quite amicable.

Anne-Marie transitioned fast. Within a month or two she was out of her flouncy old-fashioned skirts and breast-en-hancing blouses that made her the undisputed beauty queen of Burnage. She was now in drab grey coats, stringy T-shirts and black jeans, her chestnut hair now dyed purply-black, the virginity I negotiated for with such ingenuity now safely ensconced in Slade's crowded trophy cabinet. She was at my mum's funeral a few years later: conventional-looking, almost mumsy, worked in WHSmith's and training to be a nurse. She was gorgeous and kind and seemed to care that she'd once lost me, but thought that where I'd gone she couldn't follow. Correct.

Why all this now? I don't know. The 'Berceuse' closes with me barely breathing on those last two chords, but I can't pre-vent them ringing out, all the dissonances and fractional tonal infelicities mixing in the dead cool air refusing to go to sleep.

Applause, tiny, but I am gratified at how heartfelt. I take a brief look around as I nod and smile and try to think of what to play next: the little girl is clapping evenly, a serious distant look on her face; Barbara, open-mouthed again, is sloppily moving her jaw; Jeff DiPaolo is looking at me with surpris-ing intensity, and I incline my head towards him in a genuine attempt at grace. Maybe this is his first time so near to the action, maybe ever at a recital. I used to get it whenever I saw anyone at close quarters: it's impossible not to be amazed and maybe slightly alarmed at the vast power and range of noises these monsters can create. It's nothing like listening to a CD, which elides everything into a seamless lie of perfection. A piano performance consists of a body that can never get quite comfortable, possessing an insufficient number of hands and a sucking vortex mind. The poor frightened beast must assert his control over this bizarre Heath Robinson mechanism: strings and hammers and wood and steel and felt and glue stretched in and around a misshapen coffin that weighs about nine tons, has the temperament of a prima ballerina and the capacity of a nuclear power station. Done well, it's quite a thing. When humanity puts its mind to make something beautiful, then achieves it, then attempts to improve on it, paints on more and more layers, each admittedly most likely thinner than the last, each improvement more infinitesimal, then you might get something that may even be an excess of beauty, but you get beauty nonetheless. This is Hofmann's Steinway: though it may not look like it, this is about as good as humans can do.

Next.

'This is Beethoven. Opus 28, the "Pastoral" Sonata.'

I probably know this piece better than any other. It's not necessarily pastoral to me, but rather amicable in the best sense: gentle, equable, easy-going, which sounds so bland but is a great virtue in someone, something I aspire to. I'd like to live in a genial world: heaven on earth would be recognizably earth and not heavenly at all, people bumping knees with each other in a country pub or on a journey somewhere nice, with people they love and who make good jokes and this music would play often, a line from a poem I dimly remember from school, 'an air of great friendliness also', attractive for someone who never had the gift for friends.

Yes, who are these friends? Merry, Tom, the Klains, Barlow, Sandrine perhaps, Dmitri Kazan, whom I never see. Could I have had Fintan Slade's life? I googled him once: he works in

IT for Manchester City Council. His profile picture is him pudgy in a green cagoule, arms encircling two little boys, the only vestige of the dirty glamour of his teenage self a small gold earring.

I catch Elise's eye; she's plainly not having much fun, and looks as if she's been caught out. She's simply immune, like Esther, and I have a moment's impatience but find it funny more than anything. This is all I've got, girl. So what is it you like about me? What are the bits left over once you take the pianist away? Some old-fashioned, friendless person with no money and nowhere to live. What else? Good sense of humour, hates animals, wants children, non-smoker preferred. Maybe it's the Volvo.

The slow movement of the 'Pastoral', like someone merrily humming a death march. I look around mistily and Barbara is fast asleep, silver head in supplication, long thin hair splaying over her skinny little torso. I just hope she's not dead. And then back over to DiPaolo, and he's rapt. In the row behind him Tom is surreptitiously, fiercely involved with his phone; a representative tableau, some mildly entertained, some longing to be elsewhere, some in their own dreamworld, one or two enchanted, a single fatality: I don't ask for much more.

Esther really didn't like coming to see me play live, and I tried not to see her for at least four or five hours before a show; her nervousness was contagious, The Fury always fighting to be heard, and we'd bicker, which we never usually did:

'You're not helping.'

'I'm not trying to help.'

'Can you at least stop pacing?'

'When I sat down you told me to stop wobbling my leg.'

'Yes, because it was fucking annoying.'

'Thanks.'

'You're welcome.'

If she did come I'd seat her somewhere way in the back, but I would pick her out instantly when I came on and did my bow at the start of the performance: her erect, vigilant, anxious, sweet-faced presence amidst the crowd, like a deer in the trees.

I played well when Esther was present but also made more mistakes, so she always must have thought I was fluff-prone, which I'm not. She almost certainly didn't notice, though, and certainly never mentioned it. That was another of Esther's great attributes: she was extremely polite.

So now I'm playing the Debussy *Suite Bergamasque*, which again means I have to fight the piano/acoustic alliance, because I like to play it with maximum lack of intensity: Debussy will never love you as much as you love him. It must be effortless, lots of things unspoken, dreamed, maybe even anaesthetized – this piano's such a drama queen. I am presumably pulling a face that reflects this struggle, and catch Elise's eye again as she's reaching her fingers into her bra, to check her cocaine is still in place. She's so bored, sitting there so shockingly beautiful, her wet blue eyes, her mouth, pouty and mobile, that I momentarily ascend into thoughts of its hot slitheriness and see in extreme close-up her fingers trail over her soft golden breast, very slightly losing my musical thread, but luxuriating in her mouth and the tension between my sensual thought and the quiet intricate network of memories in the lizard brain where the *Bergamasque* is stored, the pressure somewhere else that impels the thoughts to ignite the music-making and force an involuntary groan, and will myself to close my eyes and make my way over to contemplate the music's silver tracery.

When I finish there is a small, shambolic standing ovation, and it feels all right.

—

After the concert, DiPaolo, Shapiro, a woman called Claudia who is Merry's yoga partner, Tom, Merry, Elise and I are around the brazier on the terrace, the girls with woollens around their shoulders, smoking a lot, talking confidently but seeming physically jittery, the boys deep into another bottle, or even the one after that. Tom is now on to a fat, foot-long cigar which he smokes like a cigarette, drawing on it for grim death. Shapiro sits quietly, possibly studying me a little. DiPaolo's a newborn Byrnie fanatic.

'So you did ten thousand hours, right? That's how you get good?'

'I've never counted.'

Elise is off back inside again, seemingly for the fifth time in an hour; she's sloppy and taut at the same time, her mouth now has some weird twitch to it, every so often her lower lip pulls away revealing her lower teeth, some side effect of the drugs, I guess.

DiPaolo won't stop. 'Let's do it now: so how many hours a week?'

'Depends. If you were to even it out, I'd say fifty?'

'A week? Practising?'

'Yep. I never miss a day, never do less than three hours, usually do six or seven, sometimes nine. I don't think I've done more than twelve very often.'

'So that's... twenty-eight hundred hours a year. So four years, is, what, ten thousand hours, and you've been doing that for twenty years?'

'More: twenty-five years?'

'That's sixty... eight thousand hours. That's... let me do this... around twenty-eight hundred days, so that's not far off eight years.'

'Feels like longer.'

I get a laugh. DiPaolo is clearly expecting some word on his mental arithmetic skills, but no thank you.

'So are you saying that's why I'm a good piano player?'

'Well, it's gotta be related.'

'What about the people I'm not as good as?'

'Maybe they practise more. And maybe you're as good anyway.'

'It's possible. So if you'd played all that time when you were a kid, you'd be as good as I was?'

DiPaolo leans back, preparing his kicker. 'Maybe. It's very mechanical.'

'Playing the piano?'

'Yeah: it's fine motor skills. You're just kind of typing out what other people set down.'

One of the women says 'Stop!' but I'm OK with this.

'In a sense.'

'And the trick is you coordinate your hands. I bet anyone could do one hand, right? With a little practice. But what you do is you can play with both hands: that's your skill.'

Shapiro re-settles himself on his chair and looks at me sympathetically.

'Maybe.'

'I'm not demeaning it, by the way.'

'I understand.'

'But that's what your skill is, essentially.'

Shapiro is tentative, can't look at DiPaolo or me as he says into the night sky: 'I guess there's interpretation. Choosing how to play? I think that's how most people decide who's any good or not. Am I right, Declan?'

'I think so.'

'Nah. It's just still fine motor skills. Interpretation: play faster or slower or whatever, it's the same, fine motor skills. It's not like being able to write a melody, right? Creating something out of thin air. That's genius.'

'No, certainly not. I don't pretend to be a genius. In fact, I don't know what the word means.'

'It's not hard. Gershwin's a genius. Mozart's a genius. Lennon and McCartney: melody is genius, basically. Sondheim, right? Sondheim's a genius.'

'I don't know much of his work.'

'It's great music: maybe you should.'

Don't bother, they're here.

DiPaolo clears his throat in a conclusive fashion. Shapiro now looks a little concerned. He is quietly spoken, his voice a little high, very sweet.

'There are types of genius, I think.'

I feel pressured into being The Artist and saying something True and Wise: 'As I say, I don't know, Jonathan. I'm not being difficult, I don't know what genius is. Mozart, Schubert, obviously. Wagner, I suppose. Bach. I don't really know what they have in common.'

When I lift my glass of Scotch, I let a little of it rest on my lips so I don't swallow more than a trace. We're all silent. I don't know why Shapiro's still here, sober and next to the mega-doofus DiPaolo, and then it occurs to me that it's because of me, so I change the subject.

'Who's the melodist of tennis?'

DiPaolo, without thinking: 'Federer. McEnroe at his peak.'

'Isn't it just motor skills too?'

'You clearly don't know tennis if you think that.' He seems annoyed and gets up and goes inside.

Tom's been listening all the while, paying great attention to the embers of his cigar, gulping down his Burgundy. He's barefoot and in shorts now, his brown ankle crossed over knee, his thick white-soled foot oscillating at a steady speed.

'Jeff's an asshole.'

'I don't know. Maybe he's right.'

Shapiro looks at me and risks a joke. 'I personally thought "typing" was a little harsh.'

'And then I think about it for a minute and it's sort of *true*.'

Tom waves me off. 'He told me up there that he thought you were fucking amazing. He doesn't say that about people. He's bitter. He cashed out too early a few years ago, and now his buddies are all sitting on a billion each.'

'I don't understand that. A billion? Why would you get pissed off if you don't have a *billion*. How can that even be?'

'Isn't everybody pissed off they don't have a billion?'

Merry scoffs. 'Oh, screw money talk. Come, ladies, let's go play dress-up.'

And the women leave, a gleeful little squad.

Tom looks at the ground. 'What do I know?' Now he gets up, not dealing with his chair very well, and walks off on to the lawn to get his head straight.

Shapiro hesitates a little and then says: 'Can I just say, I thought you played beautifully. I know you probably hear it a lot, but I did want to say that I was very moved. I have all your recordings, and I play them to my daughter. My grandfather was a pianist, he recorded quite often, but was never, you know, first-rate, so I've been around the music a lot. I played for many years, very badly. It's so much of my life, frankly. And you give me so much pleasure. Joy, really.'

This is usually the kind of thing women say, and coming from a man it has a powerful, not entirely pleasant effect.

'Thank you, Jonathan. That's very kind, obviously. I'm finding it difficult to react to how kind that was. I sit there and play, really. That's all.'

Shapiro nods devoutly as Tom rejoins us.

'I'm better now. A little headspin. I'll be good if I just watch the fire.'

As we all do for a minute or two.

The women return, stumbling and guffawing, all wearing zany ski hats. Merry's in a coat, carrying an ice bucket with three bottles in it.

'Hey boys, we're back.'

'DiPaolo left!'

Merry's cocaine grin looks insane on her bony firelit face. 'He's so fucking *sensitive,* little Jiffy-Jeff.'

Her tone is suddenly truculent:

'Why didn't you stand up for Declan, Tom?'

Tom doesn't say anything, breathes smoke on his ember. Merry is agitated.

'Tommy's lost his tongue!'

'I was talking to Declan.'

'Declan doesn't want to hear all your tales of *triumph*. Getting financial advice? Why ask Tommy about money? What does Tommy know?'

Elise is half-crazy on the drugs too: she pours slapdash amounts of wine for the other women then perches hunched forwards on her chair, smoking intensely, her mouth now seemingly wholly out of her control, jerking open, like Merry's, her lip pulled down and to the right as if drawn by an invisible needle and thread. I put my hand on her thigh and can feel it pumping up and down. She looks at me and stage-whispers, 'Wow, sorry I'm so fucked.'

'It's OK. Want to go and lie down?'

'Are you kidding? I'm not sleeping till Tuesday.'

'Sorry, I'm lost. Why do you keep doing more?'

'Jesus, I'm fine, fuck off. I'll be fine, I just need some wine.

The coke is completely *insane*. It's like they brought it here from the Seventies.'

'I'm sorry, I'm now totally confused.'

'Stop saying sorry, I'm fine. Wow. These two old bitches are hardcore.'

Merry comes to sit next to me, clearly with something on her mind. 'You were so brilliant, Declan. It's a crime.'

'What's a crime?'

'They never gave you the respect you deserved.'

'I think they did.'

'No they didn't. You're a little English white boy.'

'That's true.'

'You should have changed your name to Muskovitz, what about that? Hey, Jonathan: Yehudi Muskovitz, whaddya think? The super-virtuoso! Pull your pants up to your chest and look like you're fresh out the autism clinic. Then it's the great Muskovitz!'

'That really wouldn't have worked. I did fine.'

She breathes in hard and takes a go at the wine, some of which slops on to her chin. 'Little Yehudi. Then the boosters would have *really* gotten a hold of you.'

'That's not how it works, Merry, honestly. It's the same for everyone.'

'Nah, I've seen it. I know what's going on. The novelists and these guys and the pianists, the *boosters* come in and the guy's a fucking genius. They know what they're doing. Looking after themselves. "Ooh, look at me, I'm such a schlub." You think we'd be sick of that bullshit by now. Well, I am.'

Tom, quietly in the darkness: 'Merry, shut up.'

'You fucking shut up. You know what's going on. He fucked it up, right? They all did. But who's going to jail? Who's losing everything? Not fucking Jonathan Shapiro. Not Arnold. Look at little Johnny. You're not doing any time, right, Jonathan? Twenty years of his life, of our lives. "Bye bye, Tommy, you made us rich, now we're letting you hang, you fucking patsy. You fucking goy."'

'Merry, shut up now.'

'What? So when there's other people around you don't want to tell the truth. Every night for the last year, "those fucking Jews". Not now. Not in front of the kiddies, right? Not in front of the kiddies, Tommy.'

She drops her head and puts her glass on the floor, scratching her scalp madly with both hands, and then tries to drink some more wine but the glass is empty. She throws it down: it bounces, which makes her laugh. Then she gets a bag of cocaine from her purse, wets her finger, pokes it in the drugs and rubs it all around her teeth and lips. Shapiro stares up into the dark. Merry tries to make herself cry, but can't.

7

I'm not awake till ten. Elise isn't there, so I open up my iPad, looking for Esther again.

May 12th 2014

Dearest E

Helsinki in May: nippy. I love the people up here, although they mention Sibelius a *lot*. I actually took the trouble to learn a piece of his this morning, and will play it as an encore: I anticipate that the ladies will be exceedingly excited by this and that my performance will be met with a great festooning of fisherman sweaters and undergarments made from various bits of reindeer.

This is, of course, unfair: Finnish culture has much more to it than Sibelius, knitwear and antlers. For instance… I'll get back to you.

What a contrast with Bolzano! Where, as we know, the weather is never too warm nor too cold, and the precipitation is sufficient to surround the city with plains of protuberant fertility, and the culture is not only 'vibrant' but that perfect marriage of tradition and modernity, whereby the old ways are refreshed and invigorated by the new, extending the deep connection with the past far into the future, and the salads taste like pizza, and the pizzas are as healthy as salad and the wine doesn't give you hangovers, and coffee and buns are totally free by mayoral decree.

Which brings me to mottos… how about:

'Oh, fair city!'

I guess in Italian that would be 'O bella citta!', which I like for its simplicity and which puts me in mind of an anthem of some sort:

Oh fair city, in which we reside
You are unmatched in qualities
Graceful and free
Your turrets so lovely
And trams so on time
Your piazzas so sunlit
Your parking so ample
And your toilet facilities so clean

Maintained, as they are, by Marco
Who is cheerful in his work
And not depressed at all
Despite the fact he cleans the toilets
For a living.
Your tourism is manageable
And brings wealth, not congestion
And people bake you a *torta*
At the faintest suggestion

Look, it's a first draft.

I can't believe that The Schedule has granted me ten whole days off when I get back from the US. It feels like an impossible luxury. I was thinking of one place I'd like to take you: Langdale, in the Lake District. I know you've never been up there, and we must. It's pure nostalgia for me, and I'll be very proud to show you the places I know. I used to go twice a year when I was small – once with school, once with my Uncle Joe, who was a primary school teacher up there and a real Man of the Fells. My parents used to put me on the train every July and he'd meet me at the other end and greet me with some incomprehensible shepherd phrases, feed me on bread and cheese and take me tramping around the Lakes. Listen: Dungeon Ghyll, Pike o' Stickle, Thorn Crag, Eagle Crag, The Lion and the Lamb, Great Gable, Glaramara, Blencathra.

You sort of met him. He came to the wedding but left before the reception. He was taciturn, as is apt, and I imagine he was nursing some terrifying dark secrets and so on, and my mum once told me, thrillingly, that he shared a woman in the village with another man, but then one day he said to her 'him or me' and she chose the other bloke. Hence his sadness!

His house was pretty masculine: the bed I slept on was seemingly made of pig iron, and the furniture was neo-spartan: his 'divan' was a slender margin away from being a girder. The first few years he had no TV, then he caved when I was about fifteen, and he'd make me tea and let me watch the kids' programmes till six, when it went off for the night and he'd make me a chop with cabbage, boiled cod or scouse, which is a stew they make in Liverpool that has everything in it: pork nostril, eye of newt, rhubarb, human hair, essence of Ringo, whatever's lying around.

And he had two rooms downstairs: the one where we ate and watched TV, and the other which was his library and had his reading chair in it, the only concession made to comfort in the whole place, a plush, dark green recliner which had a sweet, dog-y smell and held you gently aloft, like a hand. He let me sit in this when I was up there, and always had a reading list for me. *Swallows and Amazons* to start (I still love Susan, of course), then Hardy (Tess in the garden! One else-forgotten wind-torn Lakeland evening, July rain drumming on the windows, the boy wriggles gently in his big plush chair, changed forever) and one time he went madly Continental and made me read Kafka and Camus, although they never got me like they got to some other Northern boys. Too much abstraction: I wasn't interested in 'oh, woe is mankind', I wanted to know 'what did they have for dinner?' and 'what happened next?'. *Billy Liar* too: that was Uncle Joe. I know you didn't like it, because you wanted him to get on the train at the end, but that's why I love it. I *did* get on the train. I proved that there's a universe in which Billy can leave home and make art and money with his gumption alone. I am a Capitalist Running Dog, it's the truth.

Anyway, back in Helsinki... going to meet the tech. They have an astounding piano that sounds like the extra-virgin quintessence of seventy-five Rolls-Royces. I'm looking forward to my programme so much I don't have my audience-loathing yet, Prokofiev 7, although maybe Russian things are somewhat tricky here what with it breathing down their necks all day and all night. What ho! Then a cleansing Mozart sonata (the one you like) and then Chopin 3, which I'm playing really well at the moment: I accept with equanimity the endless succession of gifts it offers.

OK, looking forward madly to seeing your face. I'm annoyed at my own jokes because they don't reflect what I really feel, which is that I miss you absolutely horribly.
DB

I close the laptop and do the maths: nineteen days later, she was gone.

—

Elise is in the bathroom again: apparently her hangovers are like typhus. She's showered and sits on a chair in the corner of the room, hair dripping, pale, eyes puffy and sore.

'Ouch.'

A question lies ahead: does she get the train back to Quine, or come with me to Boston? I hated her drugged-up, drunk-to-hell version. For the first hour in bed she twisted and kicked and headed to the toilet every ten minutes, smashed her pillow around, sighed, lay on her back audibly awake. I asked her to move to another bedroom (there were three more on the corridor we were on, all done out in tiny variations on dove grey, cream and white, the beds silent and pristine), and she got hostile and self-pitying:

'Oh, go away please. I was fine. I didn't know it was so strong, that's all. I need some affection for once.'

'What do you mean, "for once"?'

'Instead of just fucking and then you playing your fucking piano for days, or just leaving me somewhere.'

'I had no idea I was like that.'

'You're kidding. That's amazing to me.'

She smelled of Merry's perfume, sweat, wine and cigarette ash. I reached out and placed my hand on her forearm, and she repositioned so we were hand in hand. I took the path of least resistance.

'I'm sorry.'

'I don't know if I should go home.'

'I understand. Let's talk about it tomorrow.'

She did her best to stay still, and I was asleep shortly after, desperately wanting her to stay with me.

Three days until Kozar, so much work to do and nowhere to be, the fact that I have no apartment, adrift out here, frankly, how is it possible to get this far and just be this? I suppose I now have a piano to sleep in.

Elise gets up from her chair in a rush and heads back to the bathroom. She vomits, an animal dry retching. I get up to open the curtains.

I go to the window and see Tom at the pool trailing a net around, still dressed in his white pyjamas. He drags the net for a while, lifts it slowly, then moves it over the patio in one movement and tips the detritus into the bushes, all in a trance-like rhythm. He stops for a second and looks towards the house, before moving along the pool edge and recommencing. Merry appears on the opposite side of the pool, small, head bowed, wrapped in a red robe, already smoking. He stays in his task as she talks to him. Then she tosses her cigarette into the grass, gets out of her robe and, naked, takes a run and dives in a perfect arc into the deep end of the pool. Tom stops his trawling and apparently says something to her, but she doesn't seem to respond, just starts to swim a lap, her brown body with its scrawny untanned rump making her look like some striped water creature. Tom watches her for a while, leans his net carefully against a tree, then disrobes himself until, also naked, he takes a run, emitting a faintly audible yodel, and cannonballs with huge force into the middle of the bright blue water. He disappears for a few seconds, then surfaces powerfully below his wife, wrestling her into his arms. She kicks and I hear a squeal, but it's fake, and she gives in rapidly. He stands, cradling her tightly, his head bowed into her small body, and moves her gently from side to side. He kisses her sleek, wet head, then in a brawny contortion throws her and himself backwards into a huge heavy splash, and after a moment of chaos they emerge entwined, tumbling in their own surf.

Elise joins me and we watch them for a few moments. Then she says: 'Let's keep going.'

NEW ENGLAND

We're at a different motel, by water somewhere in central Mass. I'm in the room thinking about practising. Elise is visible if I lean back from the Clav, on a towel on the pontoon that reaches twenty yards into the lake. She's wearing Merry's pink bikini. A book, rarely consulted, is splayed next to her. She takes a dip every half hour or so, smokes, checks her phone, replaces it face down, picks it up again. It's ninety degrees out, and the AC in the room isn't up to the last movement of the *Hammerklavier*. I'm in my underwear, the last day or so an intensive alternation between Elise and Beethoven, in a bittersweet fug of music and sex.

I learned she's from Oregon, came to Quine because it was close to New York and the Literary Life. Her father made some money in lumber, and left her mother, who's a 'healer', as soon as it was forgivable. Dad now lives in a condo in the Pearl District of Portland and spends his money on hunting, golf, and girls he meets online. Her mother lives in a saltbox cottage near the coast and thinks Cheney did 9/11. Elise is not in regular contact with either of her parents. Her brother's 'in finance or something' in Orange County, California, and they don't speak either.

So if love starts off as involuntary, then proceeds as a series of choices, have I chosen to love her? She's a beautiful, clever, soft-edged girl upon whom I can't get any purchase. She says she thinks I'm going to abandon her, which is funny. I said she didn't read much for a doctoral student, and she said nobody does, and that she can no longer read for more than a minute or two, because her phone is more interesting than any book ('fact'). I said I thought this might have affected her ability to finish a doctorate, and she said I was damn right. Her professors don't read much either. She knows it's time to change things, though, and she's using this summer to figure out precisely what things and how precisely to change them.

'What do you think I should do next? If I quit college. When I quit.'

'Europe, surely. Isn't that supposed to be what you do in such circumstances?'

'I went to Paris once. It was so beautiful.'

No conviction in that. I nearly told her about Bolzano, but was instantly horrified at this instinct and made a noise of suppressed shame and amazement that I pretended was me accidentally biting my tongue.

The Boston concert is in three days' time. The day before I have to keep clear because part of the contract is that I spend time with Kozar at his house, maybe play something. So I have two days' practice, and I still haven't looked at the slow movement of *Hammerklavier*. I'm not anxious about it: it hovers just beyond the limits of my immediate consciousness like an unloved place to which, at some point, I have to return.

I'm drifting at the piano, just playing around. I look out of the window again: she's standing up, plucking her bikini pants into place. She does a slow forward bend, which is proof of God's glorious beneficence, then takes a little gangly run-up and does a star jump into the lake. I watch her head emerge, an otter. I can't see her face because she's looking out to the farther shore.

—

I talked to Elise about *Hammerklavier* at dinner last night. I need ideas, and quickly. We were in a roadside diner; the menu was burgers or chicken fingers with dipping sauce, onion rings, meatloaf and cheesecake. We sat at the bar, with some ball game on, picking at each other's red plastic baskets of fries.

'This is weird.'

'What is?'

'It's so coupley.'

'That's fine though, right?'

'Yeah, I guess.'

But an upbeat little 'I guess'. Her phone is nowhere to be seen: I think she made a decision to keep it stowed, which was almost touching. The mad system of power relations those things establish.

I did the short-version intro to the *Hammerklavier* and said I was having all these interpretive struggles, and she made it into a game: Compare The Great Piano Sonata to The Great Book.

Her first bid: 'So, it's big, serious, difficult. *Paradise Lost*?'

'Nope. Not entirely wrong, but still wrong.'

'*Hamlet*?'

'Let me think.' The ill-laid-out labyrinths of meaning, the overlongness, the variousness, it being a parody of itself and everything else. 'Yes, a bit. But I don't know. Something more *disciplined*?'

'*Paradise Regained*?'

'Nobody's read that.'

'I read eight pages? Three maybe?'

The literary comparisons petered out, my references highly limited in number, hers too abstruse. But then, with her apparently now interested, the barriers of intimidation demolished, I wanted to keep playing games, which was turning out to be pretty sexy and she knew it. She was sun-kissed and juicy, and by the third Jack and Coke almost relaxed, and I was going to get to take her home.

'Come on, what the hell is this thing? Free-associate. Give me something to work with.'

'Oh God, all right, so it's sort of repulsive and seductive at the same time, there's something kind of mangled about it. It's like a big sort of steampunk exhibit, with weird bits randomly bolted on to it, and there are gargoyles, but they're all right next to incredibly beautiful carvings or something.'

'Cathedral!'

'Too obvious. Sorry. Not quite. More alive in a way. So, it doesn't look like it at first, but when you get close up it's absolutely *teeming* with life.'

'It's a coral reef.'

I was momentarily astounded, and had to ask her to say it again.

'A coral reef.'

'That's brilliant.'

'See!'

I turn the thought over, something sprawling, slowly dying under the sun.

'Uh-huh. And why can't you play it? This reef?'

'I can play most of it, just not the slow movement. And I can play that too, I just don't. Actually, at this point I have to mention my wife.'

'OK.'

'It was the only task I gave my wife, and she never did it. What I mean is, I asked her quite often to listen to the slow movement and see if she could reach just *some* appreciation of it. Maybe even come to see why I valued it so much, but she didn't have to get that far. I had this slightly sweaty-young-man intensity about me: 'It's the greatest single movement in the entire canon of Western art music,' that kind of thing. Surely it meant something to her? That it meant so much to *me*, so could she just try? But she never did. She never, ever did. Which is strange, right? Isn't it strange? She never, ever listened to it. I mean, she apparently made no attempt whatsoever. I never understood it. It's got a tune, it's beautiful, it's less than twenty minutes long. I wasn't asking for much. Am I crazy?'

She looked at me painedly. 'I'm sorry, I just realized I don't want to hear about your wife.'

'But you said at Tom's you wanted something back.'

'I know. But this isn't the same as me talking about my doctorate. I don't want to be unkind. I just don't think I'm ready for it.'

I thought about her elsewheres: the constant texting, the phone face down, but now's not the time, and anyway she's right: it's in no way equivalent.

'I totally understand. It's OK.'

—

And today it is OK. I'm still watching her little silent comedy. She struggles up out of the water, splats on to the pontoon and rests her cheek on the wood for a moment. Then she stands and looks back out over the lake, smoothing her hair, shining all over. I can see the faint shadows of her lower back, the bikini pants on the cusp of revealing her butt cleft. She sits down cross-legged, dries her hands childishly on her towel and takes up her phone, lights a cigarette. I think she's probably writing a message: she looks up to survey the treeline every so often then goes back into her huddle, a little gleaming child against the blue-black of the lake, the deep green beyond.

I now have a vague sense of the people with whom she's

always in contact: her 'best friend' Marta, a fellow student at Quine who's from Moscow but lives in Brooklyn. She sends emoji-heavy texts of jokey blackmail to me via Elise's phone: *Look after her, piano dude, or I will set the dogs of hell loose on you!* Then there's Lulu, an actress friend from Oregon who lives in Los Angeles and Snapchats Elise several times a day. When they come in Elise always says 'it's just Lulu' then pulls a weird face and types out a series of seemingly random letters and gently berates herself for the dumbness of what she's just done. Elise mentions a summer they spent in Miami where 'it was awesome, we got laid *a lot*', and I feel unmerited but inevitable pain and she realizes she probably spoke too easily, and that her statement was meant for someone else, but the pain fades over the course of the day.

Then there's Gregory Carlson. They met when Elise spent a year at Reed before she transferred East. He doesn't seem to live anywhere. She's mentioned Jackson Hole, Santa Cruz. He's in Provincetown for the summer, doing a pop-up bar, which I sort of understand. He does all these new new things that feel simultaneously laughable and impressive: 'app development'; some charity start-up she says is 'philanthro-capitalism', to do with growing plants in the African rainforest to make into perfumes. He writes on entrepreneurship and environmentalism websites: all this stuff that's way out of my reach and in which I pretend I have no interest. He's from money and is gravely handsome. They clearly dated for a while, because she's defensive about it. I have started to dislike Gregory intensely, of course. It goes like this:

'Who's that?'

'Just Gregory.'

'Is he OK?'

'He's fine. Just texting me.'

'Right.'

But her face is bright: she holds the phone in front of her face like a communion host, thumbs gleefully knitting away at her response. Sometimes she laughs to herself, or even exclaims something outraged and affectionate, suddenly teenaged: 'Carlson, you absolute *dick*!'

He called her yesterday and she immediately took the phone outside the room and wandered around our little terrace smoking, sat on the white bucket chair, laughed too much, acted differently in every way from the way she acts to me, with whom she rarely laughs, if at all. I may be asking for too much from her, but I have no control over it and it's alarming. The first appearance of sexual jealousy since Esther; I can't get Greg or her summer in Miami out of my mind. This harsh, acidic feeling, some obstruction in the throat like a goitre, I can't think straight.

I pull the curtains on Elise, still hunched over her electronic amulet, and try to get back to the piano. I think about *Hammerklavier*, the coral reef extending palely into the distance, its infinity of details, shivering plant life, imperceptible growth, slow-moving nervous-faced animals, the cool, alien flow beneath... I don't know, it seems absurd in this clothes-strewn motel room, amidst all the sweat and jealousy, so I dress and go to the lake. As I walk down the pontoon she turns to wave, her hair messed up and filled with sun, and she greets me with a broadening look of joy and every other thought is cancelled.

—

We're on a trail in the hills above the motel. A walk neither of us wanted to go on but felt obliged to; to get away from the bed, the lake, the piano, for decency's sake.

'How come you've read Milton? If you didn't go to college.'

'My teacher, Tal. He told me I should only read the very best of things, poetry preferably. That if I read garbage it'd show in my playing. And I liked it. T. S. Eliot sounded great but didn't mean anything, like music. The Shakespeare sonnets, like music too. Then this guy George Herbert, do you know him?'

'I'm practically a doctor of literature, of course I know him.'

'"My comforts drop and melt away like snow: / I shake my head, and all the thoughts and ends, / Which my fierce youth did bandy, fall and flow"... I preferred the old-school things. Keats, those odes, I still read them. They're all free on my iPad. Amazing, really, to be alive right now.'

'Yeah, life is *so great* now.'

The path narrows and becomes more overgrown. We can't walk side by side anymore, so she drops behind.

'Wait, Declan!'

I turn around and she's taking a rest on a tree stump. She's out of breath because of all the cigarettes.

'I need to tell you. I'm going to this thing. Electric Daydream. You should come.'

'What is it?'

'It's a music festival. Bands and DJs, people. It's a party.'

'I know what a festival is.'

She's red-faced and still a little breathless, but she lights another cigarette anyway.

'Also, we get special access because Greg knows the guys.'

'What does "special access" mean?'

'We get backstage, in the VIP area, free shit.'

'OK. I just feel I'll be holding you back.'

'No! Please. I'd love it. You'll love it.'

'I'm scared. I'll be completely out of place.'

'No! It's the most harmless kind of goofy vibe.'

'I'm so old.'

'It's OK. Everyone's totally chill.'

'No denial of the fact that I'm old, I notice.'

'You're old. I'm old. It doesn't matter, nobody cares any more.' She looks up at me pleadingly, moving her shoulders around in a little fun dance of encouragement. 'Come on. It'll be awesome.'

'Why do you smoke?'

'Oh, for Christ's sake, can you fucking stop? You really think you have the *right*? You do way too much of this.'

I'm shocked at this realization of how she sees me, or maybe how I'm seen more generally.

'I don't have any right. I'm sorry.'

She softens at the sight of my immediate retreat. 'Listen, it's two hours' drive, then we can stay the full day and overnight tomorrow and we get to Boston the day before your show, easy.'

The fact that she's planned on being in Boston with me comes as a sudden, gorgeous surprise. Who else? Barlow, the Klains maybe, Tom and Merry (not so much now), Clara, Kazan perhaps? Who am I kidding.

'Where do we stay at this festival?'

'In a tent.'

'I can't practise in a tent.'

'Take one day off!'

'I'll take you up there, drop you off. This concert is a very big deal for me.'

'I'll persuade you. I will.'

We carry on walking, expecting a vista over the lake to provide some reward for the exertion, but we just get lost and hot. Then Elise sees a warning sign nailed to the trunk of a pine tree: a drawing of an unscary cute bear with a scary uncute BEWARE BEARS!! in 128-point emblazoned above it. She's spooked.

'They could have told us at the bottom of the trail.'

'It's OK, no one gets eaten by bears.'

'People get *mauled* by bears.'

'You're not going to get mauled by a bear. That's not how this ends. This ends with a standing ovation in Boston, and us deciding where to head next.'

'What's your playing gonna be like with one less arm?'

'Bears don't rip your arms off. They run away into the forest, because they're fundamentally peaceful creatures.'

'You stumble over a baby bear, then momma bear gets a lot less peaceful, I can tell you.'

'There are no baby bears.'

'That doesn't make any sense at all.'

'Yes, I know. I meant "don't worry".'

Now we're deprived of our climactic overlook, highly sensitized to our surroundings and completely lost. Every sound is a bear approaching, every silence a bear lying in wait. But I have this other feeling: once again in the hills with a girl I love and a sense of things going wrong. It can't be. There's too much irony, too much pattern, coincidence, whatever you want to call it. And then instead of thinking how terrible it would be, how absurd and grotesque if something did happen to her, I wonder instead what they would say. Two women separated by a few years, the common links: a remote spot in the mountainous north, a gloomy pianist, two dead female bodies.

I walk ahead of Elise, impersonating leadership. We're following a path where every so often there's a white splodge on a tree trunk. Follow those, I think that's how it works. There are no people. I can't tell if we're climbing or descending; the woods seem to thicken, the forest floor now ferns and high grass: is it getting wilder? Are we going into the wild? How can this be?

146

We go down towards a stream and splash ourselves.

'Let's leave the food here.'

'What?'

'Let's leave our sandwiches here. I can kind of smell them, I think, so I'm guessing a bear can.'

'Are you serious?'

'What do I do? Do we leave them or throw them into the water?'

'*I* don't fucking know.'

I take off my backpack and throw the sandwiches into the stream.

'Declan, what the fuck is this?'

'We're frightening each other. No one gets killed by bears. We only went two miles from the road.'

'But bears don't know about the road. It's just a bit of where they live to them, isn't it?'

'You're from Oregon. There are bears there: so what do we do?'

'I don't know. I don't fucking know.'

We're steaming hot and afraid. I look at her, the grubby, flushed face, the T-shirt plastered to her body by sweat and stream water, the jean shorts, the sneakers we got her from Walmart this morning. There is no possibility that anything bad can happen to us. It can't happen again. It's not mathematically possible: 'The first time the couple hiked in the woods together they were killed by a bear.' It's nonsense, there's too much life here, too much possibility, too many complications. This is not the end of anything. This is different.

'We're fine. We're scaring ourselves. We're absolutely fine.'

'OK.'

'Follow me.'

Not one in a thousand, not even one in a *million*. We set off with some amount of serenity restored by the favourable arithmetic. Then, after a tense, brisk mile or so which destroys her breathing, things start to open out: I can see farmland through the trees now, and then we're on a broad track. Still, by the time we're back at the road, we somehow recover our high state of bear panic and embrace each other like crash survivors.

She pulls her head back and looks at me with worrying seriousness. 'What was that?'

'What was what?'

'What just happened.'

'I don't know.'

'It's your wife again, isn't it?'

'You googled me?'

'Why shouldn't I? Tell me what just happened.'

'Look, I told you, I don't know.'

The first big lie.

She releases herself from me and walks ahead. Back at the motel she stays on the porch, and I leave her be.

2

We're driving again, the new mood of awkwardness dissolved by her excitement at what lies ahead. Elise shows me an ad for the festival on her phone. The artists appearing include Sound Haven, Memori, Bauke van Wely, Fantome, Ga$$$$$, Headspace, Dassarra: a stream of disconnected words hinting maybe at some state of druggy bliss or just pleasant meaninglessness with little intention; I don't know, my information is old and scanty, I freely have to surrender that I know nothing.

'Do you like any of these people?'

'It's not the individual acts so much as the *experience*.'

'I'm feeling nervous and defensive.'

'That's OK, that'll go. It's easy as hell.'

'I'm going to go for three hours, then I have to practise.'

'No, you have to stay overnight, that's the point.'

We stop at a strip mall doughnut shop outside some small Massachusetts town. She's trying to fix the meeting point for us. It'll be Greg Carlson and 'a bunch of other people: Gretchen, Samara, Levy, maybe Carew...' She comes out of the place with a soda the size of a bongo drum and sits on a bench under the narrow awning gurning into her phone, smoking and waiting for news. There is no mistaking her slight giddiness, nor my dread. Even dread may not be right: the sense that I'm going to see yet another aspect of her I haven't seen before, and that this will, of course, be closer to her true self, and the version she conjures up when she's with me – the erotic muse, the screen-gazer, the New Friend – will be revealed as a fad she was into for about a week. I also hear conversations that I presume are about drugs and plans for their transportation and deployment. Then there's the heat: I'm an indoorsman, seeker of temperate zones. This heat is in-your-face.

Right now I'm in the car with the AC running, eating a clammy turkey roll listening to Cortot play Chopin, watching Elise on the bench, fixated on the way her tan has deepened in just the last few days, the fabulous promise of the evenings, her diaphanous, pale blue halter top against the caramel skin, her transformation from a secretive campus cat into this fully realized American summer goddess. How much longer will I have with her?

She jumps up with a squeal and comes to the car window, cigarette smoke, hair, sexy snow-white teeth.

'Let me in, bucko. Rendezvous point established.'

We drive five miles, her sensing my unease perhaps, her hand frequently reaching for some part of me, her body turned towards me, legs pulled up onto her seat, arranging and rearranging her hair and saying nice things to me, even putting up with Chopin.

'I'm going to look after you.'

'Why would I need looking after?'

'You don't really: it's all just a big fuckball of love and affirmation.'

'Why don't you tell me more about Augusta Webster?'

'Must I?'

'I think I'll find it comforting.'

'Well, I'm done with her now.'

'Since when?'

'About a week ago.'

'What happened?'

'I just finally figured it out. Me and Augusta. She was cool, she was so intelligent, she was accomplished, she was elected to office, she campaigned for women's suffrage, she was a scholar, she spoke about five languages. She was a mother. And she was a writer too. Poems, plays, translations from actual Ancient Greek. Totally original, totally herself. I adored her. I thought maybe studying her would make me more like her. I wanted to *be* her in some way. But now I realize I can't be, and actually I don't care. Well, I do care, but I care more about figuring out how I made such a dumb mistake.'

'What mistake?'

'I don't know. Something to do with wasting a lot of time.'

We're quiet for a moment.

'That wasn't as comforting as I'd hoped.' She laughs, thank God. 'Are you using my coral reef thing?'

'Kind of. Not really. Beautiful idea, but useless in the end.'

'Well, thank you. Just what I needed at this point.'

She withdraws her hand and I think sighs through her nose,

almost resentfully. A quick change. This is her style: if not immediately persuasive she withdraws and feels wounded, but it never lasts long. She'd rather things were fine. Although I'm no expert, I think this has something to do with her phone. Everyone wants *likes*, so everyone's super-sweet to each other. There's no motivation to bear grudges if you can have this other thing, can be borne along on this cloud of constant low-level applause. No hostility or bigotries, everyone a combination of neuroticism, gentleness and an ardent desire for frictionless pleasure and ethical perfection. Alien to me.

'It wasn't useless at all. Sorry, that was unnecessary. It's just hard to apply, is what I meant. I get this panic if I can't play, so I get a bit tetchy. I'm not in control of it, but it's OK, it never ends up hurting anyone.'

'Greg'll fix something. He's one of those people. He'll know some guy and find you a place.'

'You talk about him like he's some kind of shaman.'

'Oh, that's funny! We used to call him The Shaman. Years ago: Carlson the Shaman, for he is wise in all things.'

She's said nothing about Merry's outburst other than that she felt sorry for her, that she was obviously very unhappy. This was a Tal idea. He thought anti-Semitism was an illness that visits the soul when its immunity is reduced. The host deserves pity as well as contempt. In no other way is she like Tal. My life has been governed by a benign gerontocracy, all vestiges of previous eras: Tom and Merry are the *Mayflower*, Tal the Kindertransport, my mum and dad the Irish Question. Elise, despite being less than five years younger than me, is something new, exists only in the present and the future, and maybe in that summer in Miami. And this is the substance of my fear of Greg Carlson: that he will quickly identify and expose my obsolete European soul.

What about practice? It's noon, none so far, and no imminent prospect. Elise says all the motels will be full of festivalgoers. I have a building anxiety that somehow there will be no space with an outlet in the whole of central Massachusetts or wherever the hell we are. In addition, my animosity towards the Boston audience has begun to surface early, and with surprising virulence, no doubt hastened into being and intensified by a range of other factors that don't need listing.

And finally, I haven't started to practise the slow movement really at all. Astonishing recklessness. I've played it through in my head many times: yesterday afternoon Elise left me on the lake in a supine dead man's float to get wine and smokes. I hung in the soundless meniscus between water and air and felt an idea emerge: something distinct but yet subtle, the small cool wavelets filling and refilling my ears, an amount of breeze cooling my surfacing skin, not necessarily verbal nor really even sensed in the fingers, just a thought. I played through the entire thing in my mind, the thought being to de-emphasize all contrast or drama and instead concentrate on an almost meditative expression, as if the music was resolved before it began, its end present in its beginning, so any sense of narrative or struggle would be needless and in truth some grave embarrassing error. Suspended in this thought for seemingly aeons after I heard the last note in my mind, adrift like a doll on the black water, I seemed to have it, the whole thing right there: simple, playable, original, *correct*: 'Byrnie's vision of the music is…'

Then I heard Elise dive in. She emerged alongside me, her cold, wet face, cigarette breath and pale blue eyes instantly inundating my senses, her cool limbs gently bumping me around, demanding the buoyant awkwardness of a water cuddle.

Then, later, in the room, wrapped tight in a towel, I couldn't recover the thought, it seemed like something that worked only in that moment of almost-stillness, a symptom of the day, the lake, the heat, nothing more, nothing, just beautiful and thousands of miles away, like a coral reef.

Upshot: still *nothing* on the Adagio.

—

We pull up in the lot of a long shack-like building, desultory neon beer brands and ball game schedules in the windows: Carla's Roadhouse and Grill. There are a few other cars already there, two pickups, a dirt-caked Rabbit and an old red Cadillac convertible, the super-duper hipness of which surely marks it out as Greg's.

The bar is cold, A/C, and black inside, smells strongly of stale beer and bleach. The bartender's thick white arms and face are luminescent in the afternoon dark. She's talking to two dusty guys in overalls, one greying, thin and lousy with rosacea, the other both fat and muscular the way only Americans and Germans can be. The bartender looks at us for an instant and says: 'They're in back.'

Three people arranged around a picnic table: a light-skinned black girl with a big Afro and a thick-lashed Seventies face, a thin guy dressed all in white, including a small white fedora, and someone who is clearly Greg.

Without saying anything, he gets up to greet Elise by hugging her, forcing her face into his chest, his eyes tight closed in some kind of rapture. He whispers something to her, and she nuzzles in more. He looks at me with what feels like kindly indifference: 'Hi, you're Declan.'

The two other people are Samara and Lee, and they fold Elise into their conversation with friendly ease and offer her what I presume is a joint. She takes it naturally and I feel as if I'm spectating on some tribal greeting ritual.

Greg sits on the tabletop, his feet on the bench, elbows on knees, comfortable. 'I'm so pleased you're here with us.'

'Thank you.'

Greg is slender and beautiful, blonde and tan, his blue linen shirt open to near the belly, his body smooth, brown and ribbed. 'It's truly an honour, though. Elise has told us about your work. It's very impressive and awesome.'

'Thank you. It's just my job.'

'I'm a writer, so expressed artists are always amazing to me.' His pale eyes gaze at me with embarrassing candour; his affect is almost priestly.

'I didn't realize. Elise said you were an entrepreneur, is that the word?'

'Sure. But writing's where I centre.'

'I was going to buy drinks.'

'That's so kind. Lee and Samara may have something. I don't drink.'

'And I have to ask, sorry: I need to practise today. Elise said you could find somewhere for me. With an outlet for my keyboard.'

'Of course. When we get to the place, I'll see some people there and we can fix it, sure.'

No one apart from Elise wants a drink, which I interpret as hostility. I go inside and the barmaid takes some time finishing her lewd-sounding chat with the drunks. Unwanted thoughts: too far from home, then 'You're a fraud.' What did he mean? My playing? It wasn't, though, that night. No more than is permissible, anyway. OK, sometimes a bit too much sweetness here and there, trying too hard to express compassion or vulnerability, but then I rowed back quickly. Only fascists portray themselves as tender-hearted.

Maybe I overdid the inner voices, a thing I do when I'm

playing well and feel capable of anything. Something to do with Esther, maybe? Did he read something about me at the time? Or has he just made some ethical judgement about me playing again after her death? My wife is dead. Did you know that? I was with her the day she died. Some people blame me. Some even tried to imply that I killed her. Her brother still believes it. Ridiculous, isn't it? Absurd. If they only knew. I was there. I discovered her body. Leave me alone.

Back in the little yard, the sun is out, which is way too much for me and my night-time eyes. Samara and Lee continue to monopolize Elise, who has apparently decided that I don't exist apart from to stroke my hand when I deliver her vodka soda.

Greg is lying down, resting his head on his elbow on the small grass knoll that provides the yard's boundary, and pats the ground next to him.

'Be gentle with her, Declan.'

'I think I am being.'

'There's a lot you don't understand.'

'Like what?'

'Did she tell you she and Samara were dating?'

'No? When?'

'They pick it up and drop it again. It's just that kind of thing, you know?'

'Maybe she should have told me that.'

'You just have to let it happen. If she wants to tell you, she will. She told me she likes you a lot. She thinks you're very brilliant. She's so smart herself, she needs to be challenged.'

'Does she though?'

No reaction.

'She told me you don't drink. That's good. Alcohol is bullshit. It's amazing to me that it's so central to our culture. I've seen so many people ruined by it.'

'I do drink a little, actually. I have two Scotch whiskies. Then that's it.'

'Why do that?'

'It's a game I play. There's a lot of alcohol in my family. My dad in particular. So I want to prove I'm different, and that I can control it.'

'Almost like you're blaming him. I get it.'

I don't like this person.

'Is it that? I think I'm honouring him in a way. In fact, I don't know how it relates to him. It's just what I do. Two Scotches, then that's it.'

'It's OK. It's an addiction. It's just a drug. It distorts the mind – everything to do with it. Even abstention means that it's won. That the drug has.'

'You're probably right. But then what's the alternative?'

'Elise drinks too much. Too many drugs. Lee and Samara, the same. All these people you meet tonight: they think they're happy because they're on MDMA and ketamine. All of them, literally every one, will be smoking weed or drinking or something. It's insane: all the music, the thought of all these thousands of people being together, the friendship, the dancing, the *people* – not enough for them. So sad, honestly.'

'Why are you here?'

'For me, it's the music, the people, what you might call the broader community of affection. You been to a festival before?'

'Not really. Not this kind, anyway.'

'It's straight religion. Nature too, I forgot to mention: twilight, sunset, the stars above, the air at midnight in midsummer, Declan.'

There's something unsettling about the way Greg uses his body, and it's taken me a while to realize what it is: he has no tics or fidgets. On occasion, he looks at the back of his flawless brown hand and turns it slightly this way and that, but he doesn't scratch, or play with his hair, or move his feet back and forth. He doesn't check his phone or even pull at the grass.

'I'm sorry to mention it again, but I really need to find a place to practise.'

'Yeah.'

'Are Elise and Samara still having a thing now?'

'Hey, don't worry about it.' He gets to his feet and stretches. 'OK, folks. It's time, I think.'

Elise stands and goes to hug Greg again, hangs from his neck like a needy teenager. She speaks to me without looking.

'I need to drive with these guys, Dec. Is that OK? Not seen them in so long.'

'That's fine. I'll just follow.'

Greg's car is the Rabbit. Instead of getting in Lee's Caddy, Elise gets in with Greg, as I knew she would.

Ten miles on, they stop for gas and snacks. I sit in the car.

—

Berkeley, CA
May 24th 2014

Hey You

So orderly, so picturesque, so wealthy and yet so neo-Marxist! I had dinner last night with the dean of the music faculty and eight or nine profs, dons and beaks, and it wasn't always easy, I can tell you. For instance: what is 'intersectionality'? It sounds like something from trigonometry but is, I sensed, in some way related to me being a terrible person without understanding why. Strangely familiar! Then someone told me he was interested in Bach's exostructures. What? Isn't 'exo-' something that goes outside something and a structure is inside something? So it's something that's inside out, like a sock in the tumble dryer? This was a musicologist doing his doctorate, by the way. About 'exostructures'. In Bach. Again, sounds like maths to me, or when I say 'maths' I mean a raging bonfire of total balls. I just said, 'Hmmmm, in...ter...est...ing.'

They were all very nice, even if trapped in lives of exointersectional mumbo-jumbo. And they warmed up nicely: I did my performing poodle thing, where they play a song off their phones and I do a riff on it. They thought it was an absolutely tremendous joke – such a wry comment on the wherefores and whatsits of modernity! – and were teetering around in glee, especially when I played 'Single Ladies' as a mad, hurdy-gurdy-like fugue, and one of the single ladies looked at me in non-theoretical ways and *maybe* shimmied the top of her caftan down a little? Anyway, despite the enormous pressures being brought to bear, I remained faithful.

Everyone left at around ten, and the dean drove me back to the hotel, lecturing me about Mozart's key relations – a subject about which I knew zero before the trip and now, after twenty minutes' earnest elucidation, I know much less.

How contrasting the musical parties in Bolzano! Right? Where the guests are literate and voluble, where everyone brings their own home-made tiramisu in a viciously competitive but ultimately good-natured sugar war, the grapes for the wine are grown in a vineyard visible from the balcony of the house in which the party is held, which is a white-walled, parquet-floored chamber of charm and civilization, and everyone plays a woodwind to a high level of finish, and by happy accident we have assembled exactly the forces required to play the Mozart 'Gran Partita', and our former wine- and cake-fuelled exuberance is quelled by the work's youthful interpenetrating mastery and our leave-taking is hushed and has a solemn, almost spiritual character...

Is it real, by the way? It seems so absurd, the thought of us living some other life in Bolzano (the joke is wearing thin, right?) or wherever (where else could it be? It's up to you. Or maybe it's up to me, once I stop being away so much?). A place where I'm home a lot, and we're together, and I don't worry about what you do in the evenings, and I wouldn't be concerned that you don't write to me even half as much as I write to you (if that). And why is this the case? I really need to know, Esther.

I'm beginning to find *everything* unbearable. The paradox of touring and being surrounded by these serial outpourings of approbation and *actively hating it*. People who like me and admire me and fear me as well (the privilege of being a bully allowed to artists, a privilege I occasionally abuse), so I feel like some combination of demonic child and benevolent father, demand unquestioning love, simultaneously withhold my anger (my audience doesn't live up to my expectations) and judgement (they can sense their lack of comprehension so offer their opinions with preadolescent timidity, and showily I choose not to point out how little they know).

Why would this set of circumstances which sounds so ideal, and that I've spent my life pursuing, why would it leave me feeling so *lonely*? I'm here in this gorgeous beige, olive, cream and midnight blue mini-suite in the Grand Hyatt, Berkeley, California, paid for by someone else. Exquisite really, and I'm miserable as hell. I can think of many reasons, but chiefly *why don't you write back to me*? Do I make it difficult in some way? Or is it more that you don't want to write because there's something on your mind? Is this (I'm typing this quickly as I don't want to write it at all; the implications are too vast and horrifying) not working for you any more? What am I doing wrong? This is what Bolzano is about, isn't it? A place where we're absolved, or a place that returns us to innocence, those first few months, at least, they were all right, weren't they?

Pimlico – at least *that* time was what it seems to me now, please tell me that? Bliss, right? Surely you remember the strange, grey radiance of it, in that shabby, tiny flat we came to love, the late spring, the tree outside the bedroom window, the sound of the hard little buds pattering on the glass, the brisk London showers, it rained every day for weeks, *but only in the mornings*, and then in the afternoons it would brighten up just a little, but the light was shades of grey the whole time. March till June, wasn't it? Then I went off to Switzerland for the festivals.

Enter: The Schedule, I suppose.

Was that it? Did I mess it up that early?

It's late here: I'm sitting at the desk in the hotel room

and I have to practise. I only managed a couple of hours before dinner, and I was slow and weak. I'm sorry. Don't even reply. I'm home soon – although admittedly I'm now very nervous about that. Should I be? Don't bother answering. Why do I keep asking questions and then simultaneously ask you not to reply?

Saves time.

At least I'm practising Bach, so that'll help. Then I think about our trip to the Lakes, and that helps too. You'll love it. We have five days and it'll be just the two of us. We can walk up into the hills, or round a lake, or we don't even have to go outside if you don't want to. Or we could drive up to Carlisle or somewhere and you can take pictures. Or one of those tiny bleak little towns they have up there. Barrow-in-Furness, that sounds as if it'll be truly revolting: smoking old women in headscarves being attacked by three-legged dogs so the Spam falls out of their shopping trolleys. You'll love it.

Anyway, as I say: must work, on the exostructure I call the Sixth English Suite. The one with the mad finale, remember? Don't worry, I know you don't.

Los Angeles tomorrow, then home: you do realize?

Write? Please?
Declan

The last letter I wrote to her. No response.

3

What is this place? We're pulling into a vast meadow already containing hundreds of pickups, Jeeps, florally painted vans and fourth-hand undergraduate hatchbacks. I park alongside Greg and Lee. Elise gets out and stretches, her midriff outside my window. She's sharing some in-joke with Greg. I long for her, but sense that, incredibly, I've lost her. But I can't leave without proving it to myself, plus I need Greg to find me a place to practise. I'm stuck here. It's 3 p.m. and my anxiety is building. I have to start by five, otherwise I'll not even easily get to four hours. Or maybe I can skip the concert, head for Yukon Territory. I could do that, couldn't I?

I don't understand what's happening in this place at all. I look around the variously clad groups of partiers traipsing peacefully from their vehicles towards the sound of distant drumbeats as if towards some war spectacle.

'You'll be hot like that.'

I'm wearing black jeans, blue Oxford button-down, maroon New Balance sneakers. The universal uniform that works in every situation outside of a funeral. And, it appears, whatever this thing is.

'I don't really have anything else. My swimming trunks are small and they don't have pockets.'

Greg laughs at this for some reason, whereas Samara scoffs. She's sitting on the bonnet of her car shaking out another joint and has changed into a foil-silver halter top and white shorts and reapplied kohl to her sci-fi eyes. Despite her extreme beauty and the friendliness she displays to Elise and Greg, I sense in her the embodiment of antipathy.

'Should I bring my Clav?'

'What's that?'

'My keyboard. Are we going to a place where I can plug it in?'

'It's OK, D. You just need to relax about that. When we get settled, I'll fix you up. I know folks here, really.'

'So I'll bring it then?'

'Whatever you like.'

How Greg has attained this mastery over me I have no idea. My rapidly emerging hatred is obviously related to my dependence on him – but did he establish this consciously? Some deep strategy that was unclear to me as we lay on the knoll? Here I am, powerless without him. His acolytes seem to revere this aspect of him most. They don't move until he moves. Maybe they *can't* move until he moves. Could I not find an electrical outlet myself? I look around the meadow and have no confidence I could even find my way out now, as it fills up, dust clouds rolling through it in the summer wind.

'Hey.'

Elise turns around.

'I came with you.'

'I knew you would. Are you seriously bringing that thing in?'

I have the Clav over one shoulder and my hopeless little backpack, in which I've stuffed some overnight gear, over the other.

'Yep.'

Greg is leading off, not carrying anything other than a tiny tan suede shoulder bag. Samara and Elise follow behind. Lee is looking sympathetically upon me.

'Hey, boy.'

'Hi.'

'First music festival, I'm guessing.'

'Not necessarily.'

'You'll be good. It'll be so good. Wanna pill?'

'What?'

'I got some pills. E. MDMA. Want a pill? Half a pill? Or you can dab.'

'I'm sorry, I don't know what "dab" is.'

'Just take a dab. I got powder too.'

'Thank you, but I don't think I want a pill.'

'That's OK.'

'What the hell is this thing I'm at, Lee?'

'It's the good stuff, boy. Just come with us.'

—

They've taken me to an RV parked in the VIP lot, right by one of the stages. It has a generator attached, and so notionally has electricity, but inside it has the dimensions of a large doll's house: I can't stand up, nor can the two other people in there with me: Lee, who's seated at the bench-like table in the cabin, dividing a mound of powder into tiny sealable bags; and the wretched thing's owner, a man in his sixties called Topper, who has the furred, muscular frame of a silver chimp and a sheet of white hair. He wears only frayed jean shorts and bangles made of coloured string or leather or turquoise shells. Topper has a piccolo that he plays short, warbling phrases on while he talks, and every so often he reaches over to Lee's pile of powder with the tip of his little finger, dips it in, rubs the fingertip around his gums. He has the toothless battered concave face of a Disney crone.

'Yeah I'm a musician, man, I played with everyone, Dylan, the Dead, Crosby, Stills, Nash, Joni, Tull, I was on sessions with Quincy and Stevie Wonder, man. I feel ya, I practised that shit, man, I played every fucking thing, tenor sax, I played trumpet, I fuckin' played bassooooon man, I played fucking bassooooon when they asked me, for this crazy-ass shit Quince was doing, man. They said, "Tops, Quince wants a fucking bassoon on this arrangement, man, can you play bassoon?" I'm like, yeah I can play that shit, they gave me a day to learn the bit and I fucking nailed that shit, never played bassoon in my life before. Never since! I play piano, I play the drums, it's all I ever did, man, just played music.'

There's a little speaker next to Lee playing some feature-less beepy boopy electronica, and Lee and Topper have almost imperceptibly worked a sympathetic dance into all their move-ments, both their bodies gently flickering with the pulse of the music.

'That's very talented. I can only really play piano, and a little cello, but hardly.'

'That's why I feel you so bad, dude.'

'I can't play here, though, it's too small.'

'Yeah, when Lee finishes up, we'll put the rig over on the table there, man, you can stand up and pound it.'

'I can't really do that. I need to sit down somewhere quiet.'

'No, man, that's bullshit. I've played every fuckin' place: fuck-in' you name it, man, I played there, boats, cars and fucking every place.'

His head twitches and he stands hunched, arched across me, smiling, his mouth half full of teeth, his hair swishing across his face as he starts to dance, his arms outstretched, slowly tipping back and forth as if he's a tightrope walker, eyes closed now, clenching and re-clenching his jaw.

'Turn it up.'

Lee does something on his phone that takes the volume up, and the bass resounds in my gut as Topper waves in front of me, his movements making his stench eddy through the tiny space.

Without opening his eyes he reaches for another dab, frosting three or four fingers this time, which he then crams into his mouth.

'Muuuuuusssic, man, fuckin' muuuuuuuuusssssiiiicc.'

'I need to find Elise.'

Lee turns his sleepy gaze on me and nods slowly as I leave.

—

I wander, feeling like an abandoned child. There are walkways and rest areas and stalls and people everywhere in a slow amble of sedated pleasure, a constant juddering ostinato, just as you walk away from one bassline you walk into another. The sun is starting to set; I have to squint or lift my arm to shade my eyes, and the dust and the pollen rises and everything is in some weird Seventies Technicolor. I've never felt so alone, partly because I always wanted something like this and now I realize I can't take part: you can't miss the sense of love and kinship, even if, as Greg says, it's narcotic and maybe the symptom of some kind of universal disease.

And also I've lost her. When did it happen? How?

It's dark, my phone says 8.33 p.m., but there's no time here. I'm walking invisibly through the people in their stupefied bliss, the smell of weed, fat from the food trucks, incense, Boston barely two days away, always this soundtrack, the quasi-celestial combination of deep bass and spangling high notes, and I see Elise with Carlson and Samara entering a huge circular black tent which has NIGHTBASEALPHA projected onto it.

'Hey, Greg!'

He lifts his head in greeting. 'Come dance, Declan.'

Elise sees me and reaches her slender arms out, her eyes tight shut. 'Declaaaan, I missed you.' She almost seems to mean it, and draws me in and kisses me, her mouth dry and sour but her lips still with their soft, leafy magic. 'Did you do your practice?'

'No. I can't do anything at Topper's.'

'Awww, sweet. C'mon. Forget about it tonight. Just for tonight.' She tries to pull me into the tent after Carlson and Samara.

'I hate it here.'

'It's because you're not doing it right. Come in with me.'

'I shouldn't be here.'

'Then go.'

'But I want you, too.'

'Then stay and come in with me. Come and dance with me.'

'I can't.'

'Come in.' She takes my hand and pulls me into the tent, through some kind of pitch-black antechamber and then into the main space itself, still substantially black but now exploding with a murderous bass beat, the black air overhead illuminated with splinters of strobing light which move at the panicked pace of the music.

As soon as we're in the room, the beat starts to speed up and I see Elise start to spin towards Samara and Carlson, who look as if they're trying to enter some different state, both with their eyes closed, trying to merge with the vast black rhythm, their faces and bodies flashing in and out of view as the lights spin around them. I'm almost still, frozen with doubt and fear, they no longer look at me or each other, and I can just keep myself sane by faintly moving my arms as I walk round, eyes half-closed, as the beat is joined now by the sound of a synthesizer playing some deep slow-rising chords which sound like a series of great collisions happening way out in space and which keep ascending. The bass slows again, getting louder, until there is an unbearable sense of suspension, until my entire body is screaming for some kind of resolution, then, just at the point at which my desire for release is a kind of agony, the room plummets into absolute silence, absolute darkness, nothing at all for a passage of time which seems emptier than any time I've ever known until, until, I stand alone, my fists clenched at my temples, all thoughts gone except for the desire for something to break this hideous void and everything hits at once, bass, lights, melody, at supersonic volume and speed, and the humans around me are visibly delivered into elemental bliss, faces upturned in rapture, arms lifted in worship and surrender to the Big Bang, and I see her, this girl I almost love, look towards me and not see me at all, because she's consumed by something higher altogether than love, or different anyway, and nothing, *nothing* like anything I could give her. I have to leave. I struggle through the blissed-out dancers, leave through the disaster of light and sound, a thought of Esther instantly blown to smithereens by the light and drums, until I'm finally in the field outside, where I have to instantly shy away from the low sun.

It's somehow raining, but the people are embracing it. Many are now naked to the waist, some explicitly rain-worshipping, faces tipped back to the clouds, arms reaching up to heaven. I keep my head down, feel the rain on my back, the Manchester walk. I never knew a Mancunian who had an umbrella, nor one who looked up into the rain as if it was anything other than a hard fact.

I'm going to get my music bag and Clav and get the hell out. There are two people I don't know in Topper's van, one asleep face down on the grimy lino floor, the other a young girl, maybe nineteen, sitting at Lee's bench table writing on a laptop.

'Hi.'

'I came to get my keyboard.'

'Sure.'

'And my music. These are mine. I'm not stealing them.'

'I bet.'

'Is he OK?'

'Yeah. He's napping. Recharging, for the dawn session.'

I look at the Clav and must seem desperate. The bass with its hungry insistence thrums through the van.

'I just need a quiet room with an electrical outlet. This might be the only place I can't do it in America.'

'I'm sorry, I don't understand.'

'I'm in the wrong place.'

'No. Explain to me. Are you a performer?'

'In a sense.'

———

She woke her boyfriend, and they're driving me to their motel. They're both at university somewhere in Vermont: she's a language student and event organizer and writes for music sites, he's a philosophy major. They took me without hesitation.

She's talkative: 'I already do promoting, so I come to these big shows for ideas. I'm helping promote a show in Italy in August. I speak Italian, they've got a great scene there. I mean it's not *so* different, honestly? But I was at a show last year they did in the square of this hill town, the whole town. It was literally beautiful. You know, like, *really* beautiful. The Italians lead the world in the illumination of ancient buildings, trust me. The whole place was lit up, the buildings in the piazza were all gold, dark red, yellow, pink, lilac, it was so fucking utterly amazing, like Disney couldn't even *dream* of it. And we had bands and DJs, and everyone was in on it, even the mayor. He was awesome. Like, twenty-eight years old this guy and the actual *mayor*, and his family were a big noise in the town and he'd brought the place back to life, I don't remember exactly. This walled town at the top of a hill with a castle at one end, and this insane church and this piazza beyond belief. The piazzas are *made* so people can hang out there, you know? It's this old, obvious idea to them. We gotta have a big space for all the people – rich folks, poor folks, visitors, we don't give a shit. Come to the piazza, boys! Eat, drink, talk, check each other out. Fuck it, go to church, just lounge around whatever you want to do. America never got anything like that. You know, you've got Union Square and they put a whole load of landscaping in it, or jungle gyms, shit like that. In Italy they just give you the square and say, "Come on, people, it's up to you." And we did just a great, great, *great* party.'

'I've played in Italy a bit. In churches and halls though.'

This sounds so lame after her speech. Her name is Belinda, which is somehow fantastic.

'Well, yeah, get out of the hall and into the piazza, baby. This is us.'

Jacky, the boyfriend, still drowsy to say the least, stops the car outside their motel room, exhales with elaborate animal noisiness and lazily pats all his pockets.

Belinda looks at me with a 'look at this guy, will ya?' deal.

'The ignition, Jacky.'

'I knew that.'

She gets a little hausfrau-ish: 'The place is probably like a crack house.'

Jacky helps me get the Clav out of the boot of their tiny station wagon.

'I'm sure it won't be. And I won't care at all. I'm so grateful for this.'

Even here, miles away, a slight disturbance in the air brings an intimation of The Bass. Jacky's not up to operating door keys, so Belinda lets us in. Their room could be currently occupied by two sixty-year-old Mormons, shoes lined up neatly against the wall. Each, I notice, has a book splayed on their respective bedside tables.

'Wow, this is so perfect. Can I set up here?'

'Anywhere.'

'Trust me, I won't steal anything. I'll just play and taxi back to get my car, and I'll go back to my friends.'

Jacky's sucking down a can of Coke, seems finally to be emerging from his nap: 'No, shit, man, this is great. Your friends seem like a fucking bag of assorted assholes, tbh.'

'Jacky!'

'Seriously.'

'It's fine, they're not my friends. Thank you so much for this. Honestly, I'm all set now. You can go back.'

'No, we want to listen. You gotta prove this isn't an elaborate scam and you're not here just to steal our priceless trove of Goodwill clothing. Come on, what you got, British man?'

We have to slide a bit of furniture around, but in the end I have a great space at the foot of the bed, which they sprawl on while I noodle for a bit with my headphones on, relishing the sound after so ridiculously long without it.

I flip my headphones off. 'Sorry, I'm ready, just getting my head straight. Do you want something fast or slow?'

'Slow.'

'The Copper Penny Motel is an intimate and charming venue, best suited to chamber pieces and sonatas and whatever else the hell little bits of music for piano are called, said the Chaucer Times of Old London Town.'

I think a bit, feel a tedious stiffness in my left hand, probably from carrying the Clav, and Belinda gets an idea and tumbles off the bed to go to her bag.

'Hold on, I've got a candle somewhere, let's do that.' She finds it in her backpack and holds it aloft like a trophy. 'Aha!'

Belinda turns off the room lights and the two of them settle into an attentive pose, propped up on their pillows. Jacky reaches out discreetly and holds her hand, as I would, as any man would, oh Belinda, the two of them sweetly romanticized by the candle's yellow glow. It should feel weird, but it doesn't. I go with my first thought, the G minor Chopin nocturne. I don't have to think at all. I disappear almost instantly, slowly braiding this golden sequence of music into the air. I close my eyes, which I rarely do, and feel the sound dissolve Elise, and Boston and the future and the distant bass, the night, Esther even, into almost nothing and hear myself emit a low groan, the meaning of which is unclear to me.

I finish the piece and look at them on the bed: they seem to have entered the mild trance from which I have just emerged.

After a little while, Belinda holds her finger up in the motel gloaming. 'OK, you're definitely legit.'

This allows Jacky to sit up straight. I notice that he has short arms, and he scratches his chubby face like some woodland creature. 'Fuck, dude, that was the absolute balls.'

'Thanks. I wish more people would say that instead of clapping like crazed sea lions.'

A squall of bass from the forest; Belinda is getting herself together.

'Stay here as long as you like, really. We're going right the way through past dawn, so you've got six or seven hours at least. When's your concert?'

'I don't know, I've lost track. I think it's the day after tomorrow.'

Belinda is chivvying Jacky a little, which I imagine is a recurring motif.

'OK, well, whatever, stay the whole time, whatever you want.

And I want to thank you. That was beautiful. I don't even have any words.'

'Thank you too, obviously.'

She reaches out for a hug, which I give with honesty, and Jacky does the same. As we end the embrace he doesn't quite look me in the eye and says: 'Ooh shit! Forgot my…' and goes to the bathroom in search. Belinda shakes her head in loving reproach. We're a little awkward now, Jacky having thrown his little wrench into the naturalness of our parting.

'Whereabouts in Italy is that town? With the party?'

'Oh, it's called Castelnuovo di San Felice. Emilia-Romagna. You know it?'

'No, I don't. I'm trying to find somewhere to go. Maybe I should go there.'

'It's great.'

I want to take her with me, Boston rising above me giving me the fugitive impulse.

They both wave as they leave – how come such kindness? I watch them gingerly reverse from their space before they putter off, then I strip to my underwear, select the exercise I want. I'm breathing well, headed (surely) towards the *Hammerklavier* Adagio, the bass gone from the forest for now. Elise too is fading, just the faint question as to why women won't ever write back to me, the drugs, the dancing, some other boy. Ah well.

The o'clock, and we know what that means.

—

Tal wondered how I could be so unfussy when it came to pianos – 'Eat junk food, you become junk, Declan' – but I just play the piano nearest to me. If Tal knew I practised on the Clav he would feign mocking astonishment and feel genuine disgust. He hated all electronic sounds to the point of affectation. He kept a rotary phone in his study, his doorbell was an actual bell, he claimed sirens inflicted physical torment on him, which is, he claimed, why he stopped visiting New York in the Nineties. He didn't like clocks, birdsong, the glitches on vinyl records, stereo hiss, the sound of fizzy drinks. The piano room at his house was soundproofed, the acoustic dry and clear yet strangely dead. He played quietly, not just because of his physical decline but because he was looking for something: 'You play this music loudly, you can't hear a thing.' He did let me play loudly: he taught me how to use my entire body to achieve extra volume, especially in concerto parts. When he played for himself, or for me, though, everything was very quiet and very personal.

And I bring this to the Adagio tonight. I play it as if it were being spoken quietly, not sung aloud. It transpires that I don't need to disappear at all: I am incontrovertibly present throughout, and the music can sense that I'm there. It unfolds like an improvisation, asks me to follow and in I go, hearing almost everything for once. I pass through it with total awareness and zero thought.

My God, what a thing it is.

After it stops, I realize I'll never play it better. Might not play it ever again. We're done with each other.

What was I afraid of?

I need to rest for a while, so I lie on the floor, not wanting to despoil Belinda and Jacky's bed.

A little bit of peace.

—

I wake suddenly and check my phone. 5 a.m. Nothing from Elise, and no feeling from me in response. I sleep for an hour, shower, dress, zip up the Clav, pack my music bag and call a taxi back towards The Bass.

In the cab it's OK; I have a plan. I'll go back to the car and drive away. I don't know what I did, and maybe I did nothing, but I'll never see Elise again. What is it? It's a version of what I've done so many times. Why would I think she can't do this? It's been five days or whatever, she's had her fun, and it turns out it wasn't so fun after all. That's just the way it goes.

At the entrance to the festival I get out of the taxi with my jumble of gear and text Elise again: *I'm leaving now. Thank you for everything, I'm sorry if I did something wrong. I understand. I like you very much. Declan.*

The bass is slower and sweeter now, joined by some higher notes that sound like they're sung by some electronic choir. There's still a bit of coolness in the air, but you can sense the heat arriving from the east, and there is unmistakably some kind of sacredness going on, a thin white glow of sunlight behind the hilltops, the humid sweet scent of the earth. America suddenly seems vast.

A few people are scattered amongst the cars in the parking lot, quietly reassembling their lives, dipping into bags, staring into the open trunks of their vehicles, rubbing their faces in the half-light. I find the Volvo with amazing ease and pack up.

Before I drive away, I check my phone again. Nothing.

BOSTON

'We have sold all seven hundred seats, as we always do.'

I'm with Semyon Kozar on the stage at the church he's converted to a recital hall. He's on the piano stool, I'm standing around awkwardly. St Barnabas is a pristine white clapboard box in the middle of the tedious commercial towers of downtown Boston.

'You see the posters? We have them all over town. Not tacky: the same design every time to build the brand recognition – this place, the artist and then the programme, me. It's beautiful. If I might say, you look the same as your picture, which is good because it was when you were younger, I think.'

'Yes. Ten years ago.'

A swooping feeling.

The acoustic is good, the space has its New World purity: clear blue sky is visible through the windows that run the length of the nave. The chairs are blonde oak, there is no altar, just a perfectly sized stage, a Hamburg Steinway upon it, another gallery of high, clear windows above.

'Do you like the space?'

'It's idyllic.'

'Yes. A lot of money for idyllic, but worth it. The idea was to make the best possible performance area for piano. This was always my thinking. I went to the people at Harvard and said: I will give you a lot of money to do this, make perfect space for piano and chamber music, maybe even small orchestra, but they didn't want my money.'

'Why not?'

Semyon is dressed in a dark navy English-cut suit, a white shirt with an old-fashioned high collar and a black tie with tiny polka dots. His head is large and square, shaved to a silver stubble and he wears big, black-framed glasses. I'm not sure exactly what look he's going for, but he seems to have achieved it.

'There was a campaign. I don't want to say too much. They snooped around a bit. I think many people say, "How can he be rich and this old, so even under the old regime he was rich and now he is even richer, so he must have done bad things." Which has some truth! But not now. I live in London, I have this place, my house in Switzerland. Music only now, everything else is behind me. And my family. Frankly, I hoped giving Harvard many millions of dollars would get my family in to study. But no. Anyway, this is done.'

He stands with surprising quickness.

'Play me something, a scale even. Just very quick, ten seconds or something.'

'OK.'

I sit down and give him the first twelve bars of a Liszt exercise, Scales in Double Sixths. The piano has a beautiful action, the sound choral and bright.

'It's almost in tune.'

'Oh, that is so beautiful! I am *thrilled* already. Now we have lunch. I put in contract, you read it? This is what I have to do to speak to musicians, I pay them to have lunch with me. My assistant says this is really really sad, but it makes me happy, so fuck off, you know. Like in England? "Fuck off", so much better I think than "fuck you".'

He laughs, a gleeful hee-hee noise that sounds ancient and slightly mad.

'I don't know why this is funny, but I find it funny. Saying "fuck off" in church. Hah. But it is my church, I own it, so shoot me.'

He waves at his driver, who's sitting on a pew looking dull and boyish.

'We're going home, Masha, look lively.'

The driver leaps up and semi-trots out to get the car.

'We eat at my house. We email you to ask what you like, but you never reply. So, you eat what I eat today. Like it or lump it.'

—

Semyon's house is in the middle of Beacon Hill, a double-fronted eighteenth-century affair, only the facade of which remains as it was when built. He's left me alone in his library on the first floor, which is maybe fifty feet square, furnished like a Belgravia townhouse from 1908: Chesterfields, swag curtains, oil paintings of English landscapes and racehorses, dark Persian rugs, another Steinway. Three of the walls consist of shelves of CDs, alphabetical by composer, and from my brief survey almost all piano music.

I hear the clotted, Gothic sound of Russian: Semyon is standing in the door of the library talking quietly but irritably to a young woman, who is giving as good as she gets. He seems to relent, while she nods and walks off into the depths of the house.

'Ooosh, these young women. Anyway, I make my bed, I lie in it. Listen, I have a trick. I sit, you stay there.'

He sits on a deep red couch and holds a unicorn-emblazoned cushion over his tummy. Semyon is apparently pushing ninety, but he still has exquisite energy.

'Here. So choose any CD to play and I will tell you the piece, of course, all the details, and also the pianist too. Yes.'

'Surely not.'

'Yes, yes. I can do this. Watch, I close my eyes. Go.'

There are thousands of discs. I pick almost at random:

Chopin *Nocturnes*, still on my mind. I want to be with Jacky and Belinda, that would be fun.

I skip to a random track number, and the track plays for less than twenty seconds.

'Chopin's Nocturne Opus 15, No. 2 in F sharp major. Moravec. This is very easy for me. I knew him. Nice man.'

'That's very impressive.'

'It's a trick, nothing more. I could not play, so I learned this trick.'

'Did you try playing?'

'Oh yes. Many years. I play a lot. But I was not good, with technical element. Not fast enough, also no ideas. Just *dum-di-dum* play the notes. Not terrible, but not any good. And then business, and other things, you know. One more.'

This time I look for my own name. I put on the Adagio from *Hammerklavier*.

'Ha! Very good. You'd be surprised how many of you people do that.'

'I'm sorry.'

'No, it's funny.'

'Do you like the way I played this? Be honest, it's a while ago, I'm not attached to it.'

'Well, honestly, no. But it's not an easy piece for young men. They think it is beautiful, which it is, but my theory is that it is an unbearable farewell. You know this when you are my age. It is beautiful of course, but it is no consolation for what it speaks of. This farewell. I have had it now many times in my life. A funeral is beautiful, the feelings are beautiful, and the speeches and the music, but all the beauty is not enough, not by a long chalk.'

We both listen to a bit of my playing. It sounds neither young nor old to me, just a little insincere. It wasn't a farewell for me, it was a big, jazz-hands 'well, hello there'. And that's probably the issue.

Our lunch arrives on a pre-set table, room service-style. Semyon is inspecting the salad with a critical squint. The waiter looks anxious.

'This is spinach?'

'It's arugula, sir.'

'Huh, I doubt it. Come sit, Mister Byrnie. This is what I paid for: a conversational lunch with a piano player. Do you know the phrase "wanker"?'

'Yes, I do.'

I turn off the Beethoven and go to sit opposite him at the table that's been wheeled in. We're oddly close; I feel if we ducked to our forks at the same time our foreheads would bump. His skin is an even shade of pale beige, presumably lent some youthfulness by medical intervention. He's still looking at the salad.

'Too much oil. Like Russia! Ha! It's funny. It's why I live in London: the English people give no fucks. They're funny people. The fancy people fuck this fuck that fuck my Uncle Harry, everybody the same. Don't care I am rich, no sycophant. Not so much as here, you know? More fun, is what I'm saying, less bullshit. I use these phrases, English phrases, because they're funny, and to make a connection with you. Which is American phrase, this "make a connection". Horrible.'

'Thank you. I already feel at home.'

'You went to school. Royal College? Guildhall?'

'No. I skipped. Because of that record, partly. I had a career.'

'This is terrible for you. Here am I, many experiences in my life, but the most powerful to me are my teenage years, as they say now, but then university. Friends, of course. My partner in business, Dubov, I met in Moscow at university. We spoke every day for next fifty years. Before phones and things, and internet. Every day, Declan. And then he fucking dies on me. The wanker. I'm sorry.'

He kisses his fingers and flings them up to the sky, a blessing on Dubov, I guess.

'I think I'd have liked university.'

'I assume everyone from England goes to Oxford.'

'Not me. Completely uneducated. Didn't even try. I had a record deal at seventeen, you know. I think my parents would have liked me to have gone. It would have been a big deal for them to say they had a son at university. Particularly Dad.'

'A poor man, then?'

'Well, not quite "poor", maybe. He worked on the buses, collecting fares. I never felt poor. But yes, we certainly weren't rich.'

'Interesting. Usually the kids are middle class, in Russia mum and dad is teacher or engineer. Or pianist.'

'I don't think my dad ever touched a piano.'

'All these great artists lost to the class system. You see, I'm still a Commie underneath it all. A rich Commie.'

Semyon has an arugula leaf hanging out of the corner of his mouth, and looks like a billionaire diplodocus.

'Declan Byrnie – Irish?'

'Yes.'

'Drinking?'

'Yes.'

'Hah! Sorry. Irish and Russians, such a shame. I never drank. I never drank a drop. In Russia this makes you weirdo, but also I don't care because it put me ahead of everyone in school. No hangover. Never one.' He holds up a fist in confirmation of his triumph.

'I don't drink either. Well, I sometimes have two Scotches.'

'Your father raised a very good boy.'

'I don't know about that.'

'I never did it. Fathering, I mean. Six children by three women, two, two, two. I was busy. What did I do? They are charming, four of them anyway, but trivial, empty, you know, sex and clothing, and working in these bullshit things – "venture capital", and "start-up incubator". With my money. And this shit they do, which means you do nothing all day but sit around waiting for cocktail hour. And drugs. Three of them. Three!'

'Money's not my subject.'

'This is a good idea. I set precedent with first because I was guilty I never see my first boy because I'm working all time, so I give him too much. Also, I thought: he is Semyon's son, so he will be good, hard-working, no-drinking man with respect and tough as well, you know? And he turn into spoiled brat – seriously. I look at this fellow I'm like, who the fuck is this? This little fellow, strutting around, "I want this, I want that" as if he earned it! So incredible. And then I have to do same with other five. The two girls are OK, but the youngest boy, oy! They got worse not better! He's the worst! But the others not so good either. It's the money, yes, I think. Not me! Ha! Couldn't be me, could it?' He looks at me as if he's seriously asking the question.

'No, of course not.'

'No. I'm kidding. Probably is me. And they're all right, you know.'

'I'm sure they are. Not many people are truly bad, I don't think?'

He sinks into his suit a little and looks at me with the sincerity of the lifelong salesman. 'Come to Switzerland.'

'Why would I do that?'

'My youngest son's wedding. In a fortnight. On Lake Lucerne. Very beautiful area. Too many Russians, but you know, everywhere the same now. London, New York. Who can blame them? I haven't been to Russia in ten years. They'd arrest me or poison me is Point One, but still, I wouldn't.'

'What am I doing at the wedding? I don't know anyone.'

'Play! We will get you playing. Play for me even.' He's tilted his head and looks kind and helpless.

'I don't know. It's a long way to go for a private party.'

'I have a guest house. It's big. No piano, but I can get one moved over there if you like. Tal said you're practice-crazy. I'll move over a piano from the main house. Stay for a while. Study. Think about where to go next. Seriously. Come. If you say yes, it will be done in an instant. We pay money, clearly. It's a long way for you. Let's say one hundred thousand Euros to have you for a week.'

Jesus. And a flight out: that sounds good right now.

'Do you like Hofmann's playing?'

'Of course. They tell me he was a drunk by the time he recorded anything, but still I like it. And then of course I like the *idea* of him very much.'

'OK, so would you like to buy his piano? From me. I could accept a deal like that, maybe. I come to Switzerland, you pay me for that, but you also get Hofmann's piano. There's no way of pricing it, it's up to you. But I don't want it. I just need some money, because I need some time. So OK, here's the deal: I'll come, you get the piano. Three hundred thousand euros.'

'Of course.'

A pause. I'm dumbfounded.

He nods and leans forward. 'I knew Tal a little, you know. He told me you were the most talented boy he ever taught.'

'Did he?' I try not to react to this, which is difficult because I am absolutely elated by it.

Semyon nods. 'I wouldn't take it seriously.'

Although how can I not?

'We talked about you several times.' He smiles at me for a little while, and then snaps out of it. 'By the way, Declan, that was a terrible negotiation. Regarding the piano.'

'I don't know, was it? I got what I wanted. I don't need any more.'

'This is fair! Now, tea and a sticky bun, I think.'

———

I cab to the church for 5 p.m. A slight, sixtyish woman called Sylvia, who I guess volunteers at St Barnabas to get close to the artists, takes me down to the basement and makes it clear she's at my command: 'I'll be outside in the hall. Anything you want, just let me know. I'm just reading my book.'

The rehearsal room is a low-ceilinged chamber, quaintly decorated: bouquets of flowers in kitsch ceramic vases, paintings of bonneted shepherdesses in flowery nooks, children in naval gear, many spaniels. There's a mahogany writing desk mocked up with pens and paper, a side table upon which there is a glass water jug, two tumblers, simultaneously stale and fresh, a wooden bowl with three green apples. The place is like a funeral parlour, someone's idea of serious and fancy. Even Semyon money can't keep out the smell of damp.

The subterranean instrument is a New York Steinway, clearly inferior to the Hamburg upstairs, which the tech and I agreed produced an offensively rich sound.

My anxiety ebbs and flows: I can finally see through to the other side of all this, but I do have to get there.

There's a list of attendees on the table: scores of unknown Mr and Mrs This and Thats, and down amongst them Peter Barlow, but no one else I know. No Melissa Gore, no Tom and Merry

Gilpin. No Elise. No Jacky and Belinda. No Klains: that hurts. No Clara McLellan, of course. I'm not sure yet whether Esther is here. Then, highlighted in yellow, the man from the *Times*.

Was it him or some other know-nothing? 'A robotic and un-involved performer' because I don't pant and writhe and fake orgasm. I'm still and quiet precisely *because* I'm so involved. Or did he mean 'uninvolving'? In which case, he's illiterate, and also: fuck him.

How dare they? 'The extreme drama, imagination, and pow-er of his playing are surprising bearing in mind the robotic posture' (robotic, robotic over and again), whereas the drama and power, such as they are, are a *direct consequence* of my pos-ture, which is the result of years of intense self-discipline. It's something they would never understand, because it's a huge, exhausting, endless struggle to make sure my playing is as much as possible my genuine expression of the music, not six hun-dred words by 11 p.m. How *dare* they? And Tal is wrong, about this, about everything: there is truth, not merely beauty. I know when I'm telling the truth and when I'm lying. Everybody does. When you tell the truth you look at yourself with a sense of peace, and when you lie, especially about something as im-portant as music, you feel disgraced.

One thing I know for certain, after that *Hammerklavier* in the motel: I'm not a fraud, at least not always.

I stop my steady pacing around the basement and find myself transfixed on the jug, half full, the cloudy ice gathered at water level, its stillness, and I seem to hear the fractional slow melting happening within it, feel an increasing sense of dread, and say out loud: 'I'm not a fraud.'

And suddenly Sylvia is in the room. 'Do you need anything?'

'No.'

'Oh, I'm sorry. I thought I heard you say something.'

'No. I probably did. But I'm OK.'

'And is everything OK – with the piano?'

'Yes, it's lovely. I don't really play much before a concert. Usually.'

'Perfect.'

'I'll play something if you like?'

'No, no, of course not.' She hesitates to leave. 'Can I just say that we're so proud of you. My friends and I, that is. We've followed you closely for many years. And we're very happy you're back, and to have you here.'

'That's very nice of you.' The sense of obligation freezes me, and I close my eyes and exhale loudly.

'I'll leave you alone.'

'What shall I play tonight?'

'I saw the programme, and it looks…'

'I'm not going to do that. Tell me what to play.'

She starts to look panicky. 'I really wouldn't know. I think you should play what you want, maybe?'

'OK, thank you. I'll try to do that.'

Another hour of this, without even the fury to keep me company.

—

Barlow is standing in the door of the green room: 'What the hell, Declan?'

'What?'

'Answer my emails.'

'Why?'

He wants to conceal his anger but can't, which is making him more angry. 'So *infuriating*. You were supposed to do an interview today.'

189

'I honestly didn't know. And I didn't answer your emails because I didn't read them.'

'I am very angry with you.'

'Oh, I know that. This isn't helpful, twenty minutes before a concert.'

'We need to talk to you. We need to talk about where to go next. Can we sit down after?'

'I'm not sure.'

He just shakes his head briefly, slips four fingers of his left hand into a pocket of his suit, leaves the thumb out. It wriggles around as he talks.

'Are you OK, Declan?'

'I think so.'

'Look, here's what I'm here for: there's no programme. I mean, there'd better be one, but there's nothing printed. So what's happening?'

'I decided to scrap it this afternoon.'

'Why?'

'Because I didn't want to play it.'

'"It"? Oh, please don't tell me.' He's becoming increasingly agitated.

'I spoke to Semyon. He's fine with my programme.'

'You're not playing the *Hammerklavier*?'

'I am not.'

He tries to restrain himself, but can't. 'You fucking idiot. If you knew what we had to do to get this fixed for you.'

Stiff with fury now. I've never seen him like this.

'It's OK, Peter, really it is. The concert will be good. It's what I want to play, and people will enjoy it, Semyon will be happy, and I'm happy and you should be too.'

He shakes his head.

Then a stage pause.

'Declan, we really can't carry on like this.'

'Oh I know. I thought you might say that. I'm sorry. But there's no way I could have played it. It would have been very bad. Actually, it wouldn't have been bad, it would have been wrong.'

He looks at me for a long time, and his anger visibly abates. 'Oh, Declan. I really don't understand, but I'll pretend I do.'

'Thanks. I honestly think you'll like tonight.'

He calms himself, then walks over to embrace me. I stand and let him cling on for a bit. He steps back with a parental sigh. 'I'm sorry for calling you a fucking idiot.'

'It's OK. I probably am. But this is the right thing to do.'

'And there's not much point meeting afterwards then? To talk future plans?'

'None whatsoever.'

'OK. Play well. We still love you. Just!'

He leaves, and suddenly I can't wait to go onstage.

SWITZERLAND

I'm on one of Semyon's balconies. It turns out that Lake Lucerne looks like a high-definition rendering of Lake Lucerne: clean Swiss blue, one pure white yacht. I become aware that he's calling me from somewhere in the house.

I go down. The Hofmann is turning up today.

Semyon greets me cheerily from a downstairs gallery: 'Come see where she'll live.'

The room he's set aside for it is a dark gallery on the second floor.

'Is this a good space for a piano?'

'Yes, it's out of the way, which is always good.'

'Oh, I forgot to ask: did you ever read the Boston reviews?'

'I never did.'

'They were very good, excellent in fact. Exactly what we needed. The *Times* was very complimentary. Effusive even.'

'That's good. I thought I'd blown it with them.'

Having missed the interview, then a modest Mozart and Bach programme, all rather subdued, no encore. Was there something hostile about it all, maybe? Pretentious?

'And what do you think of this?' He pauses, then slowly blocks out the words into the air with his free hand: '"He used the French Suite as a screen upon which to project the finery of his musical intelligence."'

'A little overwrought.'

'Yes, fools, these people.'

He is dressed in a baby blue cashmere sweater and jeans. I've been here a week now, and this is my last day. No one ever visits.

'This was my last wife's dressing room at one point. When she was my wife. These are the pictures she wanted.'

There is a series of portraits of women on the walls: some look Renaissance, some more recent, one or two are clearly twentieth-century.

'Courtesans. That was her thing. A joke. She liked pictures of courtesans. She would tell me that she was my very own. Is that funny? Not really. What do you think of them?'

'I don't know. I'm not a good judge.'

The women are beautiful and sad and look into the far distance, as if they're being painted against their will. Maybe feminine mystique is just women wanting to be elsewhere.

Semyon polishes his glasses on his sweater. His head looks shrunken and naked without the giant black frames. We walk out of the gallery into a corridor lined with musical memorabilia, old programmes, photographs of himself with conductors, a framed morning coat to which Semyon gestures ('Horowitz, Carnegie, sixty-five'). Then, towards the end, me: the *Boy with Piano* painting.

'My God.'

'Ah, I bought it a few years ago. It's rather charming, I think.'

Just look at me: barely formed, the mournful, pale face, the jester clothing, the laughable symbolism of that big old piano wedged between me and my parents.

'What's that look on my face, Semyon?'

He gazes at the picture for a moment. 'Ah well, I don't know. Hmm. Impatience?'

'I think it's bafflement.'

'At what?'

'I don't know. What did I do to deserve this? Something like that.'

Semyon laughs. 'Yes, I see.'

I look at the painting again and manage to find some compassion for the little weirdo portrayed therein.

Semyon snaps me out of it: 'Ah, don't dwell on it. You'll be fine. Come on.'

We walk on for a few moments and find ourselves looking down on the lobby. The big windows look off towards the house's front gate, which looks like Checkpoint Charlie. Below us, people are moving out the last of the trappings of the wedding party.

'Did you enjoy the wedding?'

Five hundred people, glistening with money and pleasure. I played in the summer room as people drank champagne and ate caviar: fully expressive of the complete imaginative void. They'd ordered a white piano. It sounded fine but a white piano is just wrong, a complete misconception. I tinkered through some Mozart and stole away after half an hour. Not one person noticed. I spoke to one of his daughters, in from New York. She was appalled, almost offended for some reason that I'd lived on the Upper West Side, and was bored with me before she began: I had nothing to offer her – and vice versa, to be honest. I left her without making an excuse, got a driver to take me into the nearby village, and booked into a hotel for the night.

'It wasn't my toughest gig.'

'And did you meet my children?'

'Not really.'

'Maybe you should have met Michael. The one who got married. Michael is not so bad. My one good one. But then, you may have been bored. He has a good character, but little personality.'

197

'That's from Tal.'

Semyon looks puzzled. 'I don't think so.'

'He said to me once, "You have a personality but no character."'

'Frankly? He never knew what to do with you. You know he wants to see you again.'

'That will never happen.'

We look down into the lobby as two young men argue about how best to carry a large round table top.

'So where are you going now?'

'Italy.'

'Ah, yes. Rome: I once was in Rome very often, had many good friends in what we might call a previous administration.'

'I've never been. Not sure they have too much of a piano scene.'

'They have other things on their mind. More inner sanctums than anywhere on earth, it seems. There's always some courtyard beyond which you are not allowed to go. And everyone is trying to do that: get to the courtyard that's just beyond them. They kept me out of all of them.'

'Do you mind me asking what you actually *do*?'

'Many things. I export aluminium – very much to Italy, in fact. I had some mining interests but sold them. Russia's biggest glassmaker, or was. I'm a blue-collar kind of guy. I'm still very happy around mines, in my factories. Now I can't go back to see them, that's most of my pain.'

'I can't even begin to understand what it's like to have a factory.'

'Once you have one, you want more. Beautiful things, if you understand them. And they are very big, which is pleasant, and you are impressed by yourself when you think that they are yours. They have your name on them also, as big as you can paint it.'

'I can imagine.'

We're now facing each other at the top of the staircase. He looks suddenly ardent: 'Come and work for me.'

'What?'

'I can make a job for you. London, New York, wherever you want to be.'

'I'm sorry, I can't do that.'

'No, of course you can't.' He nods quickly and looks almost shy. 'Where in Italy?'

'Bolzano. Just over there, I think.' I gesture in the general direction of an Alp. We hear a rumble, some gravel scrunching.

'Ah, this is the truck with my new piano.'

We go to the window and watch the movers' van pull up.

'Will you ever play it?'

'Yes, Declan, I will play it very often.'

He goes to say something, then stops himself, then goes ahead anyway: 'You know the quotation from before, the "finery of the intelligence" and all that?'

'Yes.'

'That was me. I wrote it down after the performance and didn't know what to do with it.'

'Oh, I'm sorry.'

'No. It's OK. I was trying to say something clever, I suppose. Maybe it's too bloody clever, right?'

'I don't know. Thank you. It's a really kind thing to say.'

He looks at me with gentle scepticism, then brightens up. 'Now, fuck it all! Before you go, we must talk money: I'm good at that, at least.'

And as we head down to meet the piano men, he outlines to me the basic principles of tax avoidance.

ITALY

1

Bolzano
May 30th 2019

Dear Esther

I think you'd like it here. I suppose you need to know how I broke our pledge and decided to come. There isn't much of a reason. I wasn't that far away, so really thought I should stop by.

First off, it's not a hill town. I don't know why I thought it was. In fact, it has no defences at all. I guess all those hill towns were war towns, right? Building them high up made it harder for a Guelph to wander in and throw you into a pit, or a Ghibelline to loot the church and deflower all the nuns. But Bolzano is in a valley, and the mountains rise all around. It's well-to-do, civilized and peaceful. We chose right.

At least I live in the hills: my room is in a huge house, five hundred feet up, overlooking the whole city. My landlady is called Frau Weber, and she looks after me well. The area used to be Germanic, but after World War I Italy got it as part of the settlement, and has slowly worked its magic. The town's a perfect blend of the stereotypes: everything's very clean and 'efficient' (the buses are devastatingly punctual), but the people gather in the main square in the late afternoons and talk, smoke and drink

Aperol spritz. Some of the girls have blue eyes, and the wine is very deep red.

I could afford a bigger place (I sold a piano that wasn't mine, and now I'm set for a while), but I like it here. Frau Weber is a gnarly, industrious little widow with cropped silver hair and a fine set of those northern blue eyes. Once her husband died, she realized quickly that she couldn't bear to be alone and so lets out rooms – exclusively, it would seem, to itinerant young men.

The house is up at the end of a passeggiata that leads up out of the city. My room is on the third floor, looking back across town. I have a little balcony where I can watch the sun set over the entire show. It's a perfect urban diorama: the city's circled with mountains, Dolomites off to the east, the foothills extending westward off to God knows where. Way out of town you can see the airstrip, then the industrial zone on the other side of the river with its new warehouses, glass commercial encampments, an arc-lit running track, the funiculars sliding up to the hill villages, the river cutting through the valley. Then the density of the old centre, the roofs jumbled round the spire of the Duomo, which they illuminate from sundown till midnight. Then away to the left, beyond the city, there's the traffic moving up and down the highway, headed north into the Alps and Europe in general, or south into the heart of the Bel Paese.

My room is like that Van Gogh painting: a thin, high-ended bed, an old wooden chair and a tiny desk, barely big enough for this laptop upon which I'm writing this. There's a portrait of Mozart on the wall above my bed, another of Goethe next to the door. There's a 'library' for the renters on the floor below, but it feels a bit like an old people's home, so I usually stay here in my room, or go down to be with Frau Weber. Franka, as I'm now permitted to call her.

The house is arranged round a cobbled courtyard, and if she's home this is where you find her. She has four dogs, of deeply contrasting styles, which lollop and wriggle around her, tails a gogo, as she moves around the compound, tending the hanging baskets, taking coffee and fruit with her renters, overseeing the work of her son, Jan, who has a workshop at the end of the yard. He spends hours on end in there soldering and sawing in a scary welder's helmet. All the bigwigs from around and about come up the hill to pay their respects to Franka, bringing baskets of wine, biscotti, cheese and pastries, and talking about the provincial ups and downs, often related to issues to do with the border, or infrastructure, a local obsession: they're building a train up into the mountains and nobody's really sure about it. There are migrants here, most of whom want to go north, but they can't get into Austria any more so they're stuck here: no one knows what to do about that either.

Franka gives everyone her 'famous' *Hochzeitssuppe*, a giant tin pot of which she always has simmering on the industrial-scale range in the kitchen. There's a long picnic table under an awning outside the kitchen, and there's always someone there, smoking, reading the paper or murmuring to the dogs. I'm there a lot, pretending to read but actually waiting for a conversation to start up. The renters come and go – hikers, postgraduate students, other lonely young European males who don't say much, quiet, motherless, bookish types.

She takes a complicated interest in the African migrants. They hang around in the streets of the old centre in off-brand ball caps and tracksuits, begging, selling cheap leather goods and plastic doodads. She doesn't like the fact that they're here, let's be honest. But this doesn't stop her from housing a group of them, for no rent, at a townhouse she has over in the newer part of the city. The neighbours over there are appalled and cause her a good deal of her daily *tsuris*. That's fine by her: she's built for *tsuris*. Franka is clearly someone about town and I love her, despite the fact that she's a little cool towards me. To be fair, she's cool towards everyone who isn't a dog. Anyway, it's clear that somewhere in her person she's instinctively and unquestioningly kind.

The library I mentioned has a solid upright in it. She lets me practise until 11 p.m., which is curfew across the compound. My practising is a bit desultory at the moment. I play what I want, which is usually Bach. I still don't play him that well. And the crazy practice routine has gone completely. I miss it, but only in the way you miss some awful old relative who never stopped going on about your faults.

There's a classy old Blüthner grand in the parlour downstairs. I do little salon recitals for Franka and her friends. Bach is part of Frau Weber in some quite profound way: the only time she can really be still is when she listens to old vinyl records of the cantatas and masses, sitting with her hands intertwined in her lap, lips a little pursed, immersed in that awesome, processional wall of sound. For her music is about humility in the face of the serious: joy is for kids. She asked if I knew a piano transcription of 'Where Sheep May Safely Graze'. I did, and played it through for her. She asked me to repeat it and then said: 'Thank you, Declan, but you must play it like a Christian, not like a pianist.'

Seventeen years now of doing this job and only one thing remains true: everyone's a critic. But I've found my ideal listener. She doesn't applaud or exclaim when I play to her. When I finish there's a little silence, and then 'Thank you.' That's it. It's more than enough.

OK, so. It's taking me a while to get to what I'm doing here. I wonder what you'll think? Here goes: I play twice a week at the bar in the Streicher, the town's 'grand hotel'. On Thursdays I do kind of smooth jazz standards, full of ripples and runs. Then, for shame, on Sunday I do my thing: people give me songs to listen to and I play crazy piano versions for them. It's a circus trick, I know, but I like it, Esther, I really do. It's *fun* for me. I even have a little patter going as they play the song for me over the PA: I'm an act. My face is on flyers all over town, and middle-aged women stop me and want a word, if not yet too many selfies (some though!).

The hotel bar is the centre of the life of the city: all the businessmen and government folks gather here every night on the couches, round the tables, pretend to talk about the serious world for ten minutes, then get stuck into the Lagrein and *stuzzichini* and start on what they're really interested in: who's up, who's down, what diet they're on, cars, the rent, who's left who for whom. The young professional types stand at the bar, throwing back salted almonds and mojitos, doing their businessy dance of love, the girls in sharp office outfits a bit sexed-up for the evening, the boys with precise tie knots and arrogant why-am-I-here aspects, everyone primping their hair and checking their phones like mad.

Is it wrong to quietly dig the hell out of it all?

I've been working on my schtick. I've figured out that the key is not to be too sarcastic: these people are Germano-Italians or Italo-Germans or whatever – it's not their thing and I'm not going to change them. So here it is: with audience interactions, I blend self-deprecation with a bit of ribbing, (especially if the audience member is French or, better yet, Swiss). Everybody's there for the fun. But then ultimately you have to show that you respect the gift, that there is in some small way something serious happening here, because even to do something slightly silly well you need to know some important things. This means I always end my shows with something beautiful, often an American country ballad, or a standard. Nothing to be ashamed of.

These borderland places seemed to be obsessed with national differences, maybe understandably when they've been invading each other for centuries. But as far as I can see, everyone here believes in exactly the same thing: earn a little money, have a little fun, raise good children, put something back. I'm about half the way there.

Then the rest of the time I teach a little. Bolzano has a conservatory. It's on its uppers, so I work pretty much for nothing. The head of piano is a magnificent entity named Donatella who glides through the cloisters trailing sails of chiffon like some perfumed galleon and wears her hair and make-up Sophia Loren-style. She is, I am afraid to relate, no pianist. Her favourite composer for piano is Mozart, which is certainly convenient for her skill level. Miaow. She is terrifying, has a fine ear and a very good soul.

There are some accomplished students, but none of them is really, truly first-rate. In fact, this is the cause of my greatest difficulty. I have a friend, Esther. When was the last time I could say that? Didn't you always say I should make an effort on this front? I didn't really understand what you meant: I had you, I had The Schedule, I had the music, I went from one to the next, and it seemed like a perfectly adequate triangular life, even though it obviously was far from that.

But now I can say with confidence that I have a friend, and this friend has a daughter. He actually has three daughters and two sons, and he has one daughter in particular. Her name is Marilena and she's Eritrean. Carlo and his wife adopted her when she was a newborn, partly because they're baby crazy but also because they're religious in this reassuring, almost invisible way.

All their children play a little piano, but they think Marilena may be something different. She's twelve and has that compulsive element: they can't drag her away from the damn thing. She practises with commitment, her temperament seems good. There's no doubt she's beyond the talents of the local teachers, and so they've asked me whether I think it's worth sending her away to study.

What to say, Esther? I'm not sure she has it: she's good, but is she good *enough*? The line is fine, but also very distinct: all the expense and all the disruption it would cause would probably be wasted. *Probably. Most* probably. It's hard to tell. She has musicality, not enough technique. If offered the choice I'd take the former, but the way the world is going, it's the lack of the latter that will rule her out. She has so much ground to make up. She started a bit late, then her teachers let her survive on tone and phrasing when she had that anyway; they should have tried to crush her spirit with exercises. 'Pianists are forged in misery.' That's not Tal, but it might as well be.

So, all very difficult, because Carlo's love for Marilena and his pride in her beauty and talent and dignity is one of my favourite things about him. We go walking together, staying overnight, setting our tent in the peaks. We also go to the movies and then have a coffee in town, where I practise my Italian. He and his wife have me over on Sundays for lunch and Napoli on TV: the house is pretty snug and is always teeming with well-dressed Christian children, helping out with the food preparation, asking me politely about how my life's going and offering savage critiques of the state of the English national team. I'm sure I seem weird to them: the near-silent loner who's shown up from nowhere. But I'm tolerated.

Carlo's wife is Laura. You'd love her. She's apparently trying to exceed the Platonic ideal of an Italian wife: she cooks and bakes *all day long*, and the only times she gets in a bad mood is when you try to do a single thing in her kitchen or say *basta*. She has this coterie of six or seven pals who hang out at the kitchen table or on their terrace, glugging Prosecco, smoking like billy-o and laughing their backs off. I always want to be with them rather than with the men watching football, but the segregation is brutally enforced. These men, by the way, took me a while. I've never been part of a group of any sort for so long: maybe football at school, though even then I was thought to be a bit of a freak – and left wingers have their own loneliness, part of the team but also not really, pelting along that rail when asked but more often just standing around toeing the daisies, waiting to be let loose. The thing is, though, it's perfectly OK to sit with the guys and say nothing. Everything is unspoken, so when you don't speak you're just demonstrating kinship. There's usually about five or six of us gathered on Carlo's big L-shaped settee, fidgeting and casting occasional aspersions on the athletes, Laura coming in on a regular basis to ply us with snacks and to insult us as a gender. Carlo sits me next to his dad, who speaks mainly in Neapolitan dialect, which means that he sounds as if he's spending his whole life trying to cough up a furball. He drinks tiny goblets of what smells like old-time medicine, or poison.

I see them midweek too: I play seven-a-side on Tuesday night: I'm not much of a winger any more, but I can stroke it around a bit in the middle of the park. We get a drink afterwards (I'm down to one Scotch), or make lame excuses and traipse home. I could almost be in England.

I don't know what to say now. I'm trying to give an impression of my life here and I don't know if I'm really getting it across. Honestly, I don't think I ever mourned you. The life stoved in, how would 'mourning' help? What even is it? What would the practice of it look like? But say it *is* a real thing, say there *is* a way of doing it, then it's not hard to see that it's the opposite of what I had been doing: the attempt to sequester myself, the elaborate lie of my practice routine (that it was headed somewhere rather than being its own reward, perpetual motion, spinning the wheel, running in place), the lousy sex. And Carlo saw the same thing in me, but didn't just rudely interject and is giving me time and space to work my way through it. He's made an effort to help me out because he thought it was the right thing to do and I barely even noticed.

Here's the thing, Esther: the day you died I died too, I did. But now, between my nights at the Streicher, Carlo and the mountains, my teaching, between arriving at Frau Weber's house longing to hear her news, and the seven-a-side games, between the sun going down over the city and the astonishing Alpine mornings, I feel like something good is happening to me.

I hope you don't mind.
Your husband

2

We're going up to Castelnuovo di San Felice, Belinda's beautifully lit festival town. We've done these trips many times now: Carlo chooses the destination, picks out some hikes. We leave town

Friday night, stay in the cheapest place available then head off on our walk at dawn on Saturday, camp somewhere in the hills for the night in his beloved blue pup tent. On Sunday we have to find a church. Sometimes I go in with him, usually I use the hour to enjoy being away from him: two days with any person provides a little too much intimacy – for me anyway.

Then off we go again, usually a gentler walk, hop in the car at threeish and we're back in Bolzano by early evening. Carlo drops me at Frau Weber's and I get spruced up and head down the *passeggiata* to the Streicher, slowly turning my mind to music.

This Friday, we meet at the coffee kiosk off the main square, get a couple of *caffè corretti*, and once the traffic's died down head off into the dark blue hills.

Carlo drives an ageing cuboid Fiat people carrier that's always strewn with empty bottles, curled-up drawing pads, food wrappers, crumbs and dust. A wooden crucifix and a little stuffed lion hang from the rear-view mirror, forever jostling for primacy. He's in a good mood this evening, which is painful, as I know that this weekend I promised to tell him my thoughts on Marilena.

'I read about this San Felice place, Declan. Very beautiful idea, no? Oh, I nearly forget.' He reaches into the back seat and finds a heavy little package. 'From Laura. Panettone.'

I break some off for him and have a chunk myself: so dark and sweet, lots of booze in it too. Carlo scarfs it with erotic enthusiasm. There's something generally erotic about him. He's burly but solid, grows a beard in seconds flat, his voice is a quiet, musical baritone. There's a suppleness to him, his interactions with the world are rhythmical and gentle: he even drives a Fiat well, resting his wrist on the wheel, hand hanging languidly, completely in control.

'So let me tell you then about this place. Claudio, the son apparently, has now got the money from the regional government because he did this deal. And this is the deal: so there was no baby born in the whole town for twenty-five years, OK? And that baby was Claudio's little sister. So Claudio decides he has to go back and that he will be the father of a new baby, right?

'Claudio works in Milan, something like digital things with advertising and so on. He's done very nice, he's worked in America a year or two and he was in London but then he decides, "I have to go back, my village is dead, I have to fix it," and to have the first baby in twenty-five years.'

'I had no idea.'

'Yes, it's beautiful. He also needs money for the town, because it is dead, so he thinks, "Do a festival!" But no one gives him money for a festival in a dead village. So he says to the government that he found a law: even if one baby is born in the village then they are allowed money, OK? He finds this law in an old book in the castle up there, in the library, very old book.'

'But why would that have force?'

'I don't know; it doesn't maybe. But maybe also the government guys are too lazy to check, OK? I don't like to say it's Italy, but it's Italy, beh. So they see this law, he has a copy of it, and say "OK, if there's a baby we give you the money." But Claudio is a gay man and there are no girls in the village anyway, the youngest women is four hundred years old. So he runs some adverts on the internet and offers this thing: the girls can come and have the baby in San Felice in exchange for his family's palazzo. They can start family there. And he interviews a hundred pregnant women and their husbands, you know? And suddenly every baby in the whole of Italy is wanting to be born in the village, so Claudio changes his rule and they can put the palazzo into smaller apartments, right? And everyone is

OK with it, because anyway this palazzo is too big for one family, of course, it's where some old duke lived or something, and Claudio's family got it somehow many years ago. So Claudio pays for this and four apartments are made in his father's house, and these babies are born one after the other and the next and now the palazzo is back to life. They have the pictures in the paper: very funny, very nice pictures, these young women with their babies in the palazzo, and the government people now have to give the money to the town and Claudio makes the festival happen, and two of the husbands of the babies now work with him on the festival, and now there are two or three a year and it's a beautiful thing.'

'Husbands of the mothers.'

Carlo laughs. 'Yes, husbands of the babies would not be such a nice story, probably, right? Oh dear.'

'Are we staying in the village?'

'No, but it's perfect, we stay over the hill in the next valley, and we walk up tomorrow, then along the ridge, then we can go down and we get to the village for the evening and they have a big Easter concert with Handel *Messiah*, which maybe is wrong kind of Jesus because it's English Jesus but it's still Jesus so I'm OK with it.'

'I like the sound of Claudio.'

'Little tiny guy, and his grandfather too, there in a video on the website, and says he prays that Claudio is not gay forever and one of the babies can be his, and Claudio gives a laugh, but it's a little sad, maybe. A shame.'

We drive up into the mountains in silence for a while; they're all around us now, you could reach out of the window and touch them. Carlo is quiet, his thoughts, no doubt, in his work.

He deals with the Brits and Americans for his business, a wine and spirits exporter. The only thing he truly hates is 'the fucking Euro', which he thinks has impoverished his country and has certainly screwed his business. The wine from around here is expensive and hardly known in London and New York, and that's a tricky combination. He's explained to me how they've already whittled the profit margin down to nothing, all the staff have taken pay cuts or gone part-time. I wonder how he does for money: he wears unbranded clothes, and on our trips he always books the cheapest hotel and buys the cheapest sandwich, fills his water bottle from the stream. But then his children are always perfectly dressed and the food in the house is prodigal. I don't know, it seems to me that money is a problem and I hope they don't think Marilena will fix it for them, because, it occurs to me again, at a petrol stop as I watch Carlo in my side mirror filling up the car and happily murmuring to himself, that in all likelihood she will not.

He gets back in the car. 'Music?'

He gives me a case of CDs. I slide one at random into the machine and we wind up into the Apennines listening to Sinatra.

—

The campsite we're staying at is twenty-odd kilometres from San Felice, and Carlo's idea is to walk there and hitch-hike back.

'Long one, what's that, fifteen miles?'

'Beautiful though, look at my plan.'

It could feel patronizing, the way he takes complete control of the route planning, but I take it as an act of kindness, and also as an expression of his creativity. He researches and builds these fabulous and perfectly judged excursions for us, and what they really are is little stories, and today the final scene is an arrival in a medieval square just in time to watch the *Messiah*, a good thing to have playing over the end credits of anything.

As usual, the plan is printed out onto a large piece of blueprint paper: the route is inked in red, with little crosses for rest stops, circles for potentially good overlooks. We're going along the valley, then up into the hills, along the ridge, further up a steep section to the top of a mountain he wants to scale, and then we have a long slow descent through the pine forest, and into San Felice. He reckons at about six. Then the concert starts at seven.

'They're having food stalls all around the square, in fact I know some of the people. Some from Alto-Adige, some from Romagna, some from Marches, even a couple guys from Abruzzo. Abruzzo, I hate to say it, the food is good. The people? I don't know about that, but the food is good. For peasant food, obviously.'

'I'm looking forward to meeting the babies' husbands.'

'This is two times now, and that's enough.'

Off we go.

It'll be cool on the ridges but the weather's set fair, and Carlo leads us up into the woods at his even, slightly testing pace. Laura has no problem telling him that he's getting tubby, so there's an aerobic element to these weekends. We never talk much as we walk, just little touristic moments: 'This lake is such and such, that city over in the distance is what have you.' Today we're especially silent, and I know it's because of the Marilena question, which is flitting about in the trees. We climb for an hour or so, and make a stop at a clearing. Carlo's map indicates a view, but there isn't one, the greyish hills across the valley barely visible through the pines. He's a little peeved.

'Too much forest.'

'Damn forest.'

'Let's keep going.'

No woman for a year now. I haven't even put myself in harm's way. There's a violin teacher at the school who is clearly interested, but compared to Carlo and the football crowd or the scene at Frau Weber's, the thought of a relationship still seems arduous. She's too keen. I'm worried she's on the baby clock. She plays beautifully, she could have gone further, but she has this compact, satisfying life – teaching, leading the local orchestra, playing in a couple of chamber groups around the Südtirol. She's a Bolzanina, and it's a hard place to leave, but there aren't many men for her. Not me either. I'm sorry.

Barlow tried again. He pleaded over email to get me on the phone, and when I finally agreed he said they could fly me to London and we could talk about a schedule I could live with. He wasn't interested in the money, but he truly believes, as someone who loves pianos and pianists, that I should be playing and recording, even if only a little. He's probably right. If this is what you're capable of, then maybe some kind of debt is owed. You shouldn't hide from it or not do it justice. Isn't there something childish about all this withholding? But then that was my old ethos, and that was a different era, and the thing I took a decision to react against. Quitting was the first decision I ever made – that I acted on, at least. Amazing. You can live your life entirely without agency and still kid yourself that you're in control of exactly what you're doing.

He suggested twenty concerts a year, a deal at a smaller label. I thought it over, and the prospect felt quite luxurious: every few weeks a trip to Munich, Bern or Toulouse, a programme of my choosing. But then, the promise of half-empty halls, the drab attendant duties, the tepid wine in plastic cups, the drowsy, impatient audience. At the high level everything feels taut and adversarial: you fight flight delays, agents, promoters, fatigue, stage fright, piano stools, the lights, your mind and hands, your wife (should you have one), then, finally, the fearsome ton of unyielding machinery onstage. A sense of the gleaming bloody struggle of battle. I've given concerts where I felt that something quite titanic has been achieved. Once you move down a level, though, it's all too inconsequential, easy victories that feel more like defeat.

I'd like to record again. Unfinished business for one thing, something to give to the children for another. I've already rehearsed the line that would accompany the ceremonial hand-over of the CD: 'This was the best I could do.' The likelihood of this is currently low, but it's something to aim for.

We're at an overlook now, a knoll off to the west of the main path, and we can look all the way back down to the town where we're staying and across to Monte Fornati, which rises over San Felice.

'Snack time. Laura was in a hurry, but there's some stuff.' He gives me my box: olives, ciabatta, soft cheese, hard cheese, blood sausage, a couple of her tomato pastries, some more of the panettone, a flask of apricot iced tea.

There's a rock each to sit on and, of course, he offers me the bigger, more comfortable-looking one.

'This is the time my father would say, "This is how we know, Carlo, that there is a God. Why else would there be so much beauty in the world?"'

'OK, I get that, but then how do you get to Jesus?'

'I know, you've said this before.'

'Why if one guy dies, can I, Declan Byrnie, go to heaven? What's the mechanism? How does it *work*?'

'People expect it to be easy. A simple explanation. Why should it be simple like that? I don't think it would be. If it really is the most important thing, then why should you understand this "mechanism"?'

I yawn for no reason, then say in a placatory tone, 'You could well be right.'

'I hope I am.' And he continues eating.

I've been to his church a few times with him and with Frau Weber: the only Protestant church in Bolzano. The services are tranquil and austere, the building itself spartan but lofty. There are clear glass windows all around, like Semyon's church in Boston. Everything feels simplified. The congregants have a quietness or a naturalness in the presence of their God, no boredom or fear.

Carlo has explained to me before how a boy from Naples whose brother is now at a seminary in Rome ended up a Lutheran: I didn't understand the theology but I get the aesthetic, especially on a cool morning as we're settling in for their Mass, the well-dressed, rational crowd neatly arrayed beneath the streaming mountain light, looking forward to getting this over with and commencing the serious business of Sunday lunch.

My friend is perched on his rock: his beard is thick this week and he spreads his fingers into the dense black growth while he looks out over the valley.

'We're going to have lots of time, we can take it slow.'

'This is just perfect.'

'Italians are mountain people. People don't know this.'

Then he adopts an uncharacteristic posture, hunched over, looking down at his fingernails like a nervous schoolboy. I hesitate then say, too loudly: 'OK, Marilena.'

'Yes.'

I look at him, the proud yet kind face, the faint perplexity it often expresses, evidence of the constant serious engagement with his conscience, and it's instantly clear: he doesn't want this for himself. Of course he doesn't. There's no selfish desire that his daughter would enhance the glory of his family or release him from near-poverty or any hope in any way that the benefit would redound to his favour. He's seen something within his daughter and he's amazed by it, and it's something I'm not entitled to extinguish. From the depths of this realization, I astonish myself:

'Don't send her away. Let me teach her.'

He seems almost to flinch. 'No.'

'Really, Carlo. I've thought about it a lot. There's no one here good enough. But then London or wherever would be tough. She may not be ready yet. She's so lovely and there's real talent there. There's nothing certain, obviously. But I want to help us all find out.'

He drops his head and closes his eyes tight. I need to say something.

'I'm going to work her half to death, you know that?'

'You know I was not asking for this?'

'I do. It's fine. It's what I want to do.'

He looks at me, baffled and inexpressibly grateful, and bows his head a little.

'No payment, obviously. Pay me in Italian lessons and food.'

'Some payment. Definitely. We'll find some money.'

I am a little relieved at this; it could have got awkward rather quickly. 'That's up to you.'

He knows he doesn't need to say thank you right now: I have stored up gratitude that he and Laura will spend months and years dispensing. He makes a sound of uncertain provenance and complex meaning, something like 'Hoohoaah'.

Then he recovers himself and gestures across the view. 'You see this town here?'

He's pointing out a greyish reef of buildings on a low hill across the valley, marked out by a tall white campanile.

'This is an interesting town. Vernazzo. They have this church, you see the tower? And next to it a convent, which is now closed I think. The town was left alone, because no one wanted it really – small town, low on the hill, nothing much there. But sometimes they wouldn't, all through the centuries, you know how it went here for so long. They live in peace for some time, then there is trouble, people are killed. It's crazy now, you think? So it goes on, the peace, and then the guys come in and take over and kill a few people, sometimes many people. It's Italy, you know, it's not a country, it's many many cities and towns and the guys in Bergamo hate the guys in Ferrara, and the guys in Ferrara hate the guys from Bologna and everybody hates the guys from the South and the guys from the South hate themselves. This is how it goes. Then, anyway, in World War Two the convent was hiding some Jewish girls, three of them, who came from Rome, they were smuggled here by some people, because no one looks here, right? And they dressed the Jewish girls like the nuns sometimes, and everyone knew, but no one talked about it. In fact, two of the girls became Catholic after a little while. Converts. Maybe too frightened not to, who knows. And then there was one day when some German soldiers were coming through and stayed, and no one knows why, but it goes that they were tired from fighting somewhere, who knows really. But they arrived late at night and knocked on doors and stayed at a house on the piazza, near the convent. And in the morning they are leaving and they have some breakfast outside the house and a girl comes to them and says there are Jews in the town who escaped from Rome. Some say the German soldiers had an argument and most of them did not want to do anything, just leave, and they did not want to wreck the convent, you know. Probably Catholic boys from Bavaria or something, or maybe the thought of it was too difficult even for a German soldier. But, of course, there was one of them who want-

222

ed to stay and find the girls. This one, always there is one. And always he is the one people listen to. And they did; they stayed and asked the girl who told them about this how they would know which were the Jewish girls. And the girl said, "They will come out of the convent at noon, because then they take food to the poor down in the part of the town near the gates. When they come out I will run and embrace them. The first three I embrace will be the Jewish girls." So they waited in town, went to church, sat in the piazza and waited, and yes, of course, the nuns came out to give their food, and the little girl ran and gave the embraces to show the soldiers who are the Jewish girls. So the soldiers stopped the girls and asked for their papers, which of course they do not have. Then they make them kneel on steps of the church and ask them to recite the Mass. And the girls who converted can recite the Mass perfectly, but the other girl cannot. I will not say what happens then, because you can imagine. But anyway, why do I tell this story? The small girl, the one who betrayed the young Jewish women, is still in Bolzano. You see her walking around still. Very refined. Fur coats, expensive shoes. People know, but she doesn't care. And the reason I tell you this is that it is the reason why we have Marilena. Does it make sense?'

'I think so.'

'Maybe, maybe not. It does to us anyway, to me and Laura. Come on, let's keep going.'

—

We get to San Felice at dusk. There are cars parked all the way up the road to the city walls, and by the time we get up to the ancient gatehouse we're part of a crowd. We have to amble slowly behind everyone as we move towards the piazza. The streets are more like alleyways, and every building is shuttered and worn out, like a medieval shanty, or a plague town. Then we get to the square. The lights are coming on and it's a festival: food stalls, musicians (a guitarist wearing a bandanna on the church steps playing soft rock, an ocarina player under the porticos offering something folky and getting no takers), the black-clad techies slowly getting the stage ready, which is good because as yet it's not in any kind of shape. Carlo is doing the rounds of his foodie pals. The piazza is a thin rectangle, the church at one end, a large, crumbling civic-looking building with the porticos along one side, the square sloping up a little to where the stage is, then along the fourth side a row of three-storey townhouses and then a solid, ornate palazzo which I guess is where all the new babies live with their husbands.

Carlo finds me watching the ocarina man, who is now doing a Sergio Leone medley.

'This, Declan, try this, from my friend Javinder, the only beef-eating, homosexual Sikh in Pescara, as far as we know.' He offers me a little pot of spicy ragu that badly needs a rethink.

Carlo looks around: they're doing a lighting check, the old *palazzo pubblico* across the way being lit in lavender, pale blue, soft green, the church pure white, overhead strings of lanterns criss-crossing the square. They come on at once and blank out the black sky. Belinda was right, of course, about this skill they have for beautification. Carlo has quietly set aside his curry bolognese and is looking around the square.

'It's not real, is it?'

'What?'

'All this stuff.'

'Why do you say that?'

'I don't know, it's fine now when it's the new thing, but I don't think it stays.'

'Seems pretty nice to me.'

'This is the problem. We can make it all look good, and taste good, but we're ignoring the real problem.'

'The fucking euro.'

'*Essatto*, Declan, finally you are getting it.'

—

Around seven thirty, a mere half-hour late, the orchestra and choir have assembled on the stage, and I have my familiar feeling of envy at players and singers. I watch as they chat and joke: a tenor waves to a cellist, who waves back with his bow, two mezzos pluck lint off each other's clothing, a violinist is doing a little bop in her chair as she flicks through the score. When a pianist plays with an orchestra he is an interloper, somehow in cahoots with the conductor against the interests of the many. This lot are in it together, for tonight at any rate.

A man who must be Claudio comes on to the stage, dressed in an iridescent skinny suit, white shirt, white pocket square, his tiny little body a twist of energy. He's not audible from where we are, but his body movements express pride, gratitude and recently abated extreme stress. He gives a deep bow and is cheered powerfully by audience and musicians alike. Although he tries to deflect it with embarrassed hand gestures, he makes sure to stick around until it's absolutely over, then jogs backstage.

The orchestra is from Florence and is conducted by a harassed-looking young woman wearing a white tunic. The impromptu choir, named after the town it's currently appearing in: Il Coro di Castelnuovo di San Felice, which, let's be clear, is a ravishing array of sounds. Everything starts a bit lumpy – there are a lot of moving parts – but once they get going, the music binds them together.

It quickly becomes apparent that they're doing highlights from the *Messiah* rather than the whole thing: they miss out the bass arias, the recitatives and even a chorus here and there. I immediately imagine what Tal would say, but surprisingly turn up nothing. Here, on this warm and generous night, haughty, malicious voices are unwanted. No good person can have contempt for the heroism of this: the sincere if ramshackle orchestra, the crazy, semi-comic diction of the choir, the frantic gestures of the conductor as she tries to keep the whole rickety contraption from hurtling into a ditch; it's tremendous, and satirical observations are not welcome. Then, the small, pale mezzo sings 'He was despised,' swaying softly, her finger planted on the score, her absolute purity of tone sending the crowd into a state of grace signified by a deeper level of silence. And by the time we reach 'Hallelujah' all thoughts are obliterated in the music's refining fire, which is presumably why they decide to end it there. I turn to Carlo, and there are tears in his beard, his eyes closed in earnest rapture.

—

Later, by the stream at the foot of our guest house garden, we lie next to each other on the grass like young boys.

'I'm going to ask again: are you sure about Marilena?'

'I'm sure I want to be her teacher. I'm not sure about what happens then.'

'I just thank you so much.'

I have to say something true, and all I can come up with is: 'It's fine. I'm really excited about it.'

'Me too.'

Then: 'Hey, Carlo, I need to tell you something.'

And I begin to talk.

3

'I've been nursing this for five years now. I've tried writing it down a hundred times, and I never get anywhere. I've rehearsed it over and over again. For whatever reason, I never felt like it was ready for someone else, for me to tell someone else. But now it does.

'I knew before we set out on our last trip. I'd already found the letter – this email she'd printed out. We'll get to that. It hurt so much that she'd printed it out. She folded it neatly and stored it carefully so I wouldn't find it. The whole thing was so laden with pain. His pet name for her, the second word on this neatly folded email, a pet name I'd never have used, someone else's pet name for my wife, for God's sake. It was as if she was an entirely different person to him, so the one I knew was incomplete and possibly entirely false. But I'm getting miles ahead.

'When she stopped responding to my emails. That last tour I did in America I wrote to her nearly every day – what was it, seventeen, eighteen days? – and she stopped writing back after Berkeley. Three or four days without a response. What else could it be? I can't stress how bad and unusual this was. She was always pretty terse, never much of a writer, but I'd always get something.

'I phoned her when I was on my way home. I had a few hours in Los Angeles. I thought hearing her voice might make me say something, or at least ask something, but it didn't. The call was a complete non-event. I asked if she'd bought the stuff she needed for our trip. She hadn't. She didn't really take many actions in life. She'd occasionally get these panics that she was mooning away her entire life and resolve to do something about it: enrol in a course or enter some abstruse and respectable field, librarianship or something. She wanted to work at an art gallery, or said she did, but I don't think she ever applied to one.

'We were in West London at the time. We had a small but nice flat, and a matrimonial routine to go with it. Or I thought so. I'd go off to practise and leave her at her "spot", which was at the little kitchen table we had, and she had her small amount of stuff arrayed around her: her cigarettes, a big blue mug with a sunflower on it for her fruit tea. Sometimes I'd come back hours later and there was no evidence she'd moved at all, or maybe she'd be on the balcony smoking. The balcony was right by the table, like two steps, slide the door, then you were on the balcony. She was always online. That was one of the only things I ever got irritated about – how immersed she was in her computer. She never shared what she was doing on there. She wasn't political or involved in some online community or whatever. I sometimes thought she was writing something. It would be like her to have something going and then tell me about it later. Not that – I don't mean a lover. No, I just mean I had this idea that she was secretly working on something but wouldn't tell me about it until it was complete.

'She went out doing her photography a couple of days a week. Then she would go and use the darkroom at a studio nearby, but only for a couple of hours at a time. She had her best friend, and they'd meet in the evenings, or the friend would come to our flat and I'd be expected to go out. I never minded. I wanted her to have more friends. Sometimes I even pestered her about it. She was so self-contained.'

I look at Carlo, who's adopted an air of indulgent studiousness, his hands knitted on his chest, stargazing. I'm trying to be honest, but that's somehow making me sell Esther short, which I don't want at all.

'I'm making her sound very different from how she was. For a long time, what happened at the end affected my impression of her. Even what I'm saying now, it sounds as if we had this arid, static little relationship. But that's just not true. Not until the last month or so. And not even then: before I went on that American tour we were doing well. I'd promised – again – to go away less, and she'd promised to maybe come with me, even for a few days. If I did Europe she could come out and I'd rent a car and we could do long drives between concerts. Practically, this was impossible. Maybe two or three times a year when I had dates grouped together in Switzerland and Austria, or maybe Scandinavia: Stockholm to Oslo, I don't know. Not doable, clearly. Even if the travel had been doable then it just wouldn't have worked. I'm unbearable on days I perform. Imagine her trapped in a car with me in fucking Gothenburg or somewhere five hours before a concert. Instant divorce. But maybe the conversation was worth something, though: at least we acknowledged that we needed to change some things. As I've told you before, I wanted a child. But with me away so much, how would it work for her? The Schedule. It takes so much blame. Maybe because it *was* to blame, you know, or maybe because it stood in for what was really going wrong. She never said anything about it. I'm making her sound like something of a dead loss, which is completely wrong. She just liked not making too much of an impression. Part of it was a kind of timidity, but also I thought she didn't need much to be happy. The photography thing: she would do print after print after print of the same image, sometimes over the course of several weeks. I'm not joking. Then she would go to a studio in the

West End and lay them all out and she'd pore over them with this guy who worked there who was the only person she'd take judgements from. Then after she'd done twenty prints or whatever it was, more maybe, she'd choose one and then just store it in this file in the studio and never look at it again. But the day she'd settled on a certain print she was certainly happy, as far as I could tell.

'I never had many girlfriends. Even when I first got to London and had some money and freedom and met lots of people. For two years I lived in a flat in a mansion block in Marylebone where some other musicians lived. Another pianist called Dmitri Kazan, who's quite famous now, and a violinist, Mary Torres, who became very successful but then left soloing and is now the leader of an orchestra in Cologne. These odd little musical lives. I never really understood how we ended up there, but it was some rich guy who had these apartments for young musicians and my agent got me one. I was busy. I practised a lot, performed a lot around England, and in Europe quite a bit, and I was in the Far East, Korea and Japan. They have this fetish for what they call "super-virtuosos", and I somehow qualified, so I was there a lot. Christ, I'm back on The Schedule, sorry. But somehow, the point being, I never had girlfriends. Mary Torres and I had a fling, but I preferred playing with her than sleeping with her, to be honest. Then I met a singer, a lovely, slightly older Irish girl called Colette. That went south when she had some health problems. You know, singers are difficult. I think it's because they carry their talent around in their throats, like a little pilot light. Such a fragile thing. When it goes out, it's gone forever, nothing you can do. She had polyps on her vocal cords, and frankly had a very difficult time, and our relationship, if that's what it was, was an early casualty. Two girlfriends, if you could even call them that.

'Then one afternoon I was in Regent's Park. There's this place where you can watch the giraffes without paying to get in the zoo. It's weird, you can only see their top halves, completely mesmerizing. I was watching them parade by, three or four of them, all in contrary motion, uselessly traipsing around, these bodiless necks and heads. Animals never look at each other, isn't that right? These giraffes didn't seem to. Just these crazy-necked oddities serenely drifting by one another, each in its own world, pretending they haven't seen anything untoward. I often watched for ages, would almost go into a trance. I remember clearly: one of them licked its own eyeball and then batted its lashes at me like Clara Bow. And at some point Esther drew up alongside me and was doing this thing which I came to know as utterly characteristic, this puzzled squint. It was her look: the knitted brow, her mouth kind of bunched up. Childlike, obviously. It had many different variations. For instance, when she had to do any kind of administration, say her tax statement – which shouldn't have taken her long at all, trust me – the same brow, the same bunched-up mouth, and then also a slight but distinct look of panic. Do you know what I'm talking about? When you love someone most is maybe when they look serious and vulnerable at the same time. Maybe it's all just a long way round of saying "cute", I don't know. Not American "cute", which can mean anything, but English "cute", which is specifically something that provokes a powerful desire to cherish and protect. I don't know. We had a coffee at the little place in the park, and she had tangerines in her bag which she ate one after the other, which was surely nervousness, and when she became aware of just how many tangerines she was scarfing, she sort of slowed down and tried to eat them in a sophisticated fashion, and I spoke with excessive vehemence, and tried too hard and all the rest of it because I was already in love with her, you'd have to say.

'I found out quickly that she knew nothing about music. My kind, anyway. I don't think she even had a folk memory of what a concert pianist should be like. You know, even my parents who were from very working-class origins, their generation had some idea. I don't know, I may be wrong, but I imagine they knew who Horowitz or André Previn was. The "piano recital" was this very fancy thing, tuxedos and flourishes and the Royal Albert Hall, something the posh Londoners did and which sometimes showed up on TV, when even the commentator wore a tuxedo – and, probably, you imagined, even the cameraman. But my parents had no class resentment. It was "how the other half live", or "it's a different world": just a fact, unalterable, almost reassuring. And when it became clear I had a chance of entering this "other half" they had nothing but slow-dawning amazement and pride. And then they were both dead before I played the Albert Hall. I did a prom a month after my mum died. I never usually wore a tux: I was a Young Lion – sharp suits, dark open-necked shirts and so on. But I did that night. I just thought it would complete this idealized picture, dressed how I thought she would most want me to dress. It was a TV thing, and I had this reputation for appearing cool and distant. Well, that night the cameraman saw something in me early in the concert and the entire broadcast was close-ups, me trying desperately to hold myself together, this constant unstoppable river of tears on my expressionless face. I played the second Chopin Piano Concerto, and played it badly because I pretty much played underwater. It was probably the night that made my career. I even did some TV interview shows afterwards where I had to tell the story of why I was in such a state, and they'd show the Albert Hall video while I sat on the couch trying to look aw-shucks and then make a joke of it. It was definitely helpful in some ways, career-wise. You wouldn't believe some of the fan mail I got. Women sent me naked pictures of themselves. Some of them were quite scary, actually. The assumption that the man crying over the death of his mother must need sex. Is that odd? To console me, I suppose. Still, it was all totally unwanted, inappropriate, grotesque. But I need to get back to Esther.

'She didn't even like the concerts I did in London. She said they made her too nervous, and that she didn't like all the phoney glad-handing and awkward adoration afterwards, everyone frightened of saying the wrong thing: "I loved the Schubert." "Really? Because I thought I completely cocked it up."

'And then there was this thing with the music. It started off small, mainly about the slow movement of the *Hammerklavier*. I asked her to listen to it, and she never did. What was it? I'd put too much on it? Why was it a deal at all for her? Then it became an issue between us, and every so often I'd ask her in a kind of jokey way – that was obviously aggressively passive-aggressive – if she'd managed to find twenty minutes, and she would get irritable or sometimes just not answer me at all. The whole thing became very odd, and obviously affected me quite severely for some reason, and it all resurfaced on that tour in New England. I never understood it.

'Sorry, I'm losing the thread, where were we? OK, fast-forward to near the end again. I was in the States on this tour and the idea was that I had a solid ten-day gap when I got back before I had to go to Germany to do a recording. We'd not had such a large amount of time in years, so I thought to hell with it, once I'm back, I won't even practise for a week, I'll just dedicate that time to Esther, and we'll go to the Lake District. I wanted to show it off, really – even though by that point I couldn't remember much about it. It's very English: finite but insanely intricate. Knowable in some ways, and completely mysterious in others. Domestic and sublime. Even on the highest peaks you're never more than an hour or so's descent from a pint and a sandwich. And the *design*'s so good, you know. Whoever thought of putting the lakes and the hills right next to each other like that really knew what they were doing. It's exquisitely done. Lakeland.

'Esther always preferred city vacations. She was a Francophile, but not Paris so much. I think her favourite place was Lyon. That region of France. Her family had this house near Chalon she went to when she was small. I forgot to mention: that was her other social life, hanging out with her mother. Gloria had this tiny flat in Chelsea and they'd go off for the day together and do the V & A and Harvey Nicks and all that. Mostly they just mooned around together, though. A pair of happy aimless wanderers. Her mum was pretty upper-middle-class, but no cash whatsoever. She had the flat on the King's Road and there was a small cottage in Oxfordshire that may or may not have been entirely hers, it was hard to tell. Esther's father was a career adulterer, and when her parents divorced she discovered that he'd spent it all. He was a small, muscly little man, very vain. He held his arms out at his sides when he walked, like a powerlifter. His speech at our wedding was almost entirely devoid of affection or detail. It was as if she'd lived in the same house as him for all those years and he'd not noticed a single identifying thing about her. He kissed her on the lips once when she was twelve or so, and tried to force her to, you know, make it a sexual kiss, whatever you call it. She hated him to some extent, of course, but had to go through the "but I still love him" motions, like people do.'

Carlo gets up to stretch and looks around at the darkness. He sits down a little way away. Facing me now, not alongside. This isn't ideal, so I try harder to peer up into the stars, of which there are seemingly trillions visible tonight.

'So I came back from California on the Tuesday, the overnight flight. I was absolutely raw by the time I got to the apartment, no sleep on the plane, very nervous, nauseous with anxiety. And when I got in she wasn't there. It was ten o'clock or around that, and she knew I was coming back at some point. I was back in the flat, which smelled smoky, and was untidy, which was unusual: as I said, she didn't make many ripples. But there was a plate of half-eaten toast on the coffee table, and the cushions were on the floor, her laptop oddly placed on the love seat by the window. She *never* sat on the love seat, it was my spot. It felt as if someone else had been living there. To my already disordered mind it was pretty frightening. The toast with the bite taken out of it. The size of the bite seemed a little too big, of course, some famished post-sex masculine mouth. Her mug was there, and there was a glass of orange juice too. She had orange juice sometimes, but not really if she had her tea, you know? That was the kind of thought I was having: everything was evidence for my suspicions being correct.

'I went to lie on the bed, paralysed really, thinking I was losing my wife and my talent. I didn't sleep, just lay there very still for an hour or two with these two dreadful thoughts chasing each other's tails in my mind. No talent, no wife.

'She finally came in quietly, around lunchtime, and made a little exclamation. I guess she saw my case and music bag. She came into the bedroom slowly and stood for a moment without saying anything. My mind heard: "I'm leaving you." But what she actually said was: "Oh, I thought it was ten o'clock tonight. Are you asleep?"

'And after a while we made love, and it was very sweet, even though I was so fragile, and she clung on to me afterwards, slightly odd. And I said: "Why didn't you write back?"

'And she said: "I did."

'And I said: "No you didn't."'

'And she said, hardening suddenly: "I wrote to you three or four days ago. Leave it."'

'"Six days."'

'"God, so I'm useless. I'm sorry. Don't I often leave it a few days? What's the difference?"'

'"I have to practise today. I'm really worried."'

'And at that point she repositioned herself, slackened her hold on me. "What are you worried about?"'

'"My playing is going. I felt it in Los Angeles. I can't play any more."'

'"I read the review."'

'"They don't know anything. Who ate the toast?"'

'"What?"'

'"The toast in the room."'

'"I had it this morning before I went out."'

'Then there was this weird dust-filled pause, some creak somewhere in the floorboards, and I temporarily saw sense and said, "I know."'

'"I met Mum for coffee. I got you a panforte from Totti's."'

'That was the conversation, to within three words I'd say. And then I went to a practice room in town and practised six hours straight, all focused on a rhythmical issue I'd had in LA, and after half an hour the issue was gone. I needed for it not just to be gone but for it to be obliterated, ended for all time, and so I set about doing that, and was entirely successful.'

I take a breath and play the Schumann sequence through in my mind, finger it out on the grass. Even now, that mad afternoon five years ago has it locked with certainty in my brain and hands.

'We were in the flat together for two days before we set off for the Lakes. The atmosphere was awful. There was no escaping it, I felt that the only thought available to me was "she's been cheating on me", so everything I said felt like a deflection or a subtitle. And she was very quiet and pretended she wanted to finish the book she was reading, which was *Mrs Dalloway*. I'll remember that forever. That first night I got back, she was stretched out on the sofa asleep and the book was in our bedroom, which was just not like her in some way, so little things like that, any tiny mismatch in what she said versus what she did became more conclusive proof. I tried to watch this Fellini film about a prostitute, but I just couldn't, my mind was in this awful racing animal panic.

'It was part of our Bolzano plan. It was a joke gift. She got me a set of his films on DVD so when we went to Bolzano we would "be able to converse with fluency and intelligence with the better class of local". That mock-fancy way of speaking was one of the tropes we had around the whole thing: "We will take our morning stroll and stop in at one of the many fine pasticcerias that line the porticoed streets of that fair city," and so on. It was fun when we started, and was fun to maintain. I mean, eventually I used it more, and maybe she got to the point where she thought it was silly. She would never say that out loud, but it was a feeling I got. The comedy was stale. When the old joke doesn't work any more you have to stop with it, but I didn't want to because, frankly, there was no new joke to replace it. So anyway, that night she went to bed before me, which wasn't unusual. I quit the film and read through a score, trying to immerse myself in something to chase away the spinning craziness. I had two Scotches, not even any bigger than usual, and they helped a little, and it was a Bach score, which helped a lot. There is a religious element, no question, in that music. In fact it *is* religion: you know, a view of the cosmos as explicable and morally correct, constellations turning in rhythm over the imperfect world, a presiding power observing and forgiving, it's all there. I don't know whether this is Lutheran, or even if it's true, but when people say Bach is perfect I think what they're trying to describe is completeness. Each piece is a complete vision of itself.

'I never had a piano in the apartment. It sounds like some pretentious or eccentric quirk, but it was more to do with habit. I always lived in small places, so got used to going to the Royal College or Guildhall, or a piano studio to practise. Also, it had the beneficial side effect of keeping me away from the music, at least for a little while. I've always practised a lot, maybe sometimes too much. I don't think it meant I lost spontaneity when I performed, or anything like that, but it was obsessive behaviour, no doubt. It verged on being something unhealthy: I was fairly unavailable to those around me. The truth is, I could never think of anything to do. I don't like going to the theatre, or eating out, or going to the pub, or even going to the cinema. I'm at home doing not much, I read thrillers and Graham Greene and Anthony Powell, Muriel Spark, C. P. Snow for God's sake: nostalgia, but for what? Then, as you know, the poetry, at Tal's behest. *Four Quartets*, of my own accord, longing to be older and cleverer so I could understand it. But even then I'd rather be playing the piano. There's this secret that pianists have: this idea that you have a relationship with the composers. You never get jaded with them, and they never disappoint like real live people, and I'm convinced this is why people carry on doing it despite the absurdity, mental torture and so on: you spend your life in communion with these vast, fantastic minds. This is what I want to give Marilena, I think, when I get down to it.

'She's got some of it already. Watch the next time you see her with a score, the reverence she has for them. The painstaking way she marks them. The space she gives them. She knows what's going on.'

I exhale and feel the pain quickening inside me, which only makes me want to keep going.

'The next day was perfect London weather: cool, a little overcast. The kind of day she would go off and do her photography. She was always fascinated with shades of grey in her pictures, lots of clouds, grey council flats and the puddles in deserted playgrounds. I suppose it was a way of not saying anything. Not just that black-and-white photography is "classy" or confers instant artistic status. She was beyond that. People who knew much more than me always commented on her technical skill, the beauty of her prints, things beyond my ability to see.

'I think the monochrome thing was an enactment of her perfectionism: there's less to control, so she had a better chance at arriving at something flawless. Colour to her was like an almost physical affront: too much visual information, too much noise. Maybe she thought that doing tiny variations on her one idea would get her closer to God or something. It's also related to this need she had not to make a ripple. Small, but flawless.

'I've thought subsequently that her photography was a bit like Bach. Parts of him anyway. The obsessiveness and lucidity of it.'

I take a moment to concentrate on the night sky. No music though, just what happened next, clearer and clearer as I proceed.

'That morning, after we had sex again in this very brief and frankly hideously fake way, and she deliberately made toast as if to make the point that she always made toast, she went out with her camera. And that was the last time we ever made love.

'And I thought about where to practise that day, but the racing thoughts were back and I was simultaneously exhausted and filled with this fearful adrenaline. I crashed around the flat for a bit, you know, lying down, getting up again, turning on the radio, turning it off again. I even played a CD or two, or started to, and I never listen to music unless I'm driving. I had a bath, intending to wallow for hours, but I got out after three minutes. The behaviour of someone on the verge of losing it completely.

'I knew where to look, if I wanted to find something. There was a leather box in her wardrobe. This was where she kept her old boyfriend stuff. Early on, when we'd been married a few months, I came home and she had it open on the kitchen table with its contents all around her. She talked me through them: letters, postcards, photos of boys from one of her summers in the States. All these tanned and physical Americans, on boats and jetties, on motorbikes, and in meadows with the mountains behind, and at fancy parties in parodies of English black tie. She was in most of the pictures, I guess, but all I remember is the boys. These landscapes she had without me. They were these sexy, outdoorsy, optimistic boys. And I tried to be funny for a while, but she could tell I was having a horrible time with it, and after a while she packed it all up quietly and we never mentioned it again. But I knew where the box was, and so, after all my skittering around, I took it out of the wardrobe. It had a padlock, but you could easily unscrew the metal plate that fixed the lock to the box. We had no screwdriver, though. Of course we didn't. I replaced the box and walked to the hardware store and bought a full set of screwdrivers to make sure I had the right one. My mind was just this pulsing morass, some hectoring demon that had me completely in its grip. And then on my way back to the flat this calmness came over me. I was still highly anxious and nauseous, but I was morally calm, if you like. I knew what I was about to do was justified.

'I'm just going to take a minute.'

I walk down to the stream and hear its trickle for the first time all night. I bend down and scoop out a bit of water and splash it on my face. I look back at Carlo, who's now reclining on one elbow. He summons me with a head gesture, and I go back to my former spot and start again, a bit quieter than when I'd left off, at a steady pace:

'I got the box open, and there was the email. It was on the top. Printed out and neatly folded. The name was "JayHawk83@ gmail.com", it was dated 27 May, two days before, and the first line was "Hey Essie, don't worry", so there was no room for doubt. I remember precisely the sequence of his argument: of course she was worried, because she was falling in love with him, and she was married. Of course he understood that they might have to end their affair, but this thought was unbearable to him. Yes, she should go to the Lake District with me. But if she decided she wanted to stay married, he would have to end the affair himself, because he couldn't cope with it continuing as it was. There was a paragraph about some time they'd spent together in her mother's cottage, which I could barely read, because it was clear that the trip was very recent, in fact when I'd been in California, so three or four days before. And then a sentence I had to go over a couple of times before I understood it, which implied that she'd missed her period, but it was OK because it was almost certainly stress-related. I didn't read the rest, just skimmed it. It was made up entirely of more professions of this fresh new love, and I refolded it, placed it back in the box, screwed the panel back on. She would never know. I was obviously demolished.

'Then north the next day. We stayed in this slightly battered old hotel in a place called Borrowdale, which is, amongst other things, the rainiest part of the entire United Kingdom. Two hundred and fifty days with some rain or something like that. Also, the place smelled of full English breakfast. It was in the carpets, the curtains, the bedding. The staff were all young Romanians or Serbians or what have you, and were barely keeping things afloat. But Borrowdale's the most beautiful place, you don't even have to get five hundred feet up and you get these views up, down and across the valley. And the weather, the clouds, the movement of the clouds, it's an intrinsic part of it. The sunlight breaking on the hillside across the valley, the peaks drifting in and out of view, the way the colour of the water changes, it's constantly shifting, this permanence, and the mountains are a billion years old, and the clouds are three minutes old, and so you get this collision of massiveness and insubstantialness, the now and the ancient, and the constant shifts between green, grey, white, blue, brown and silver, zero visibility and infinite.

'The contrast of the sublimity with this fusty, camp English hotel: under any other circumstance we'd have had a great time making fun of the whole thing. For instance, we found two dirty socks in the sink when we checked in, and when I plugged in the kettle it kind of exploded. Just a little *pfizz*-type noise, but definitely an explosion. And of course the atmosphere was murderous.

'We'd driven up late and not really spoken. She was a sleeper, especially in the car at night, so probably wasn't even faking it. We got there at midnight and the entire journey had been, I have to say, close to hell for me. I was continuously in the act of forming and reforming these ways in which I could break it all open, a range of different approaches and the best way to express the oddly shifting balances between anger and grief. This was the main debate I was having, in this terrible oppressive state: how to give one way primacy when none was going

242

to end up at all good. I had this form of words: "OK, look, I really need to say something now, and I think you know what it is." What is that sentence? I don't even understand why this was, in my mind, the permanent precursor to anything else, but also why I had nothing else. Do I provoke the confession in some way? Do I force the whole thing? "Who is Jay? What did I do wrong? It's over, right? How could you do this to me?" All these urgent questions, all of them prefaced by: "OK, look, I really need to say something now, and I think you know what it is." God, what a dreadful night.

'Once we got there she went straight up to the room, but I asked them to get me a Scotch and went to sit in the garden. They had an arboretum at the back and heavy white wrought-iron furniture dotted about. I was on a bench looking up into the hill behind the hotel. It was clearish and windy. I sipped at my Scotch, though I didn't want it. I was cold but I didn't want to move. At one point I got up and walked into the trees, feeling that the wind would clear me out in some way. I was just caked in this filth of fear and guilt. The wind was smashing through the trees, and this animal roar and the confluence of dreadful feelings was almost transporting. The grotesqueness of it all made me feel not quite real, like it couldn't be happening to me. How come I was the monster in the garden? Why should I feel like this when it was her fault? Or this other unknown person's? Anyone, surely, but me? But I turned at some point and was facing the hotel and I could see Esther at our window gazing into her phone and texting with the tip of her middle finger like she did, and I immediately knew that she was writing to Jay, figuring out with him when and how to end her marriage.

'I couldn't bear to be with her again that night, so I waited an hour or so in the bar, pretending to the night manager that I had work to do. I sat at the bar, a score in front of me, looking at the pages without absorbing the slightest thing about them. He served me another Scotch. I'd tipped most of the first one away, but it seemed somehow validating for me to order the second: I'm the guy who turned up late with his beautiful wife and needed to do some work and have a drink or two before he could start his holiday in peace. So plausible yet so completely untrue.

'I'm sorry, this is very difficult for me,' I say to Carlo. 'I'm just going to walk around again for a little while, just a minute or so. Thanks.'

But all I do is stand and keep talking.

'She was up before me in the morning. She woke me up with the news that she'd found a pork pie in the wardrobe, and she was keen to get this incident in front of me. It was something that was made for me, in a way. I can't describe exactly why, it's to do with pork pies being intrinsically funny, and me being this low-born northerner who's an international concert pianist, and many other things chiefly to do with England and sadness or something. But it wasn't at all funny. And then she put the kettle on before remembering last night's little self-immolation, and I just said, "It doesn't work." And it was at this point: I was still in bed and she was in her T-shirt, sitting on her side of the bed with the suicidal kettle in her hand, and she had suppressed her laugh about it because when she looked around at me to share this laugh she saw that I knew.

'That wasn't the right time, though. I wasn't ready. I'd managed to sleep a little but was still very on edge.

'We went down for breakfast. I brought a map of where we were walking that day, up into Langdale and then Glaramara. We were in the dining room, and she was at the large central table with the stewed pears and muesli and tomato juice and cereal packets. I watched her make a tentative, overly serious assessment of what to take and what she was allowed to take without being accused of theft or at least taking advantage of the system. She was dressed as close as she would let herself get to hiking gear; her lovely skinny tan legs were horribly traduced by the bulky socks and hiking boots, and her black shorts were much too short, so she looked a little like the image of a sexy hiker from a photo shoot. And she wore this lopsided oatmeal sweater which looked like some fashion person's idea of what you wear halfway up a mountain and was completely inadequate for its intended purpose, and her hair was partly contained under a red wool cap. So beautiful. She was always unaware of her sexual power. You might think she was faking it, and using the unawareness as part of the thing itself, but I really don't think so. I know this is true. She would have been amazed to discover that this Jay person found her life-changingly attractive.

'I never met him. He wasn't at the funeral or memorial service, that I knew. He was a graduate student at King's College London. I googled him last year, after I'd moved here: he's a literary journalist in New York. "Culture" journalist, anyway. He writes fine, but ponderously. Everything's a thesis. No sense of humour – earnest, conscientious. A version of me? I don't know. There was an email address on the magazine's site too, and I hovered my cursor over it for a second or two but then got out. I looked at his headshot for a while. No clues to anything, obviously, though you try to read things into it. He looks a bit like me. He's got the same colouring, the same shape face, curly hair like this. It turns out she had a type. Ledesma, Jay Ledesma. Spanish or something, I guess. Her other man.

'So anyway, the hotel. The thing is, when she came back to the table with this nervously chosen amount of breakfast foods, the cute earnest expression, I almost forgave her right there. I was on the verge of saying, "I know about Jay, and I don't care. I want to keep you, that's all I want to do." And this internal vocalization caused this vast wave of relief inside me. This thought that I should tell her and forgive her at the same moment almost came as a shock to me. I wasn't sure if I meant it at all, which is probably why I just couldn't get it out. It was like having a stammer. I tried for an instant, my mouth opened, but nothing came out. I must have looked so strange. I think she sensed that I was about to say I knew. She kind of shied away, lifted her hand in reaction, almost up to her neck, and dodged her head to the side, and maybe because of this the sequence of events changed completely. Whatever it was, I ended up saying nothing.

'But again, internally, I resolved before we set out that I was going to tell her today: that I knew everything, and that I was going to forgive her. Anyway, we drove to the foot of the trail and set off.

'It was more of a climb than a walk. We went on pretty much in silence, me ahead, constantly going back to the map, as there was one tricky little set of instructions – "Over the stile, immediately left, along the stone wall, then right up the field and right again at the place where the paths fork." I memorized it. I didn't know this area at all. In fact, I didn't really know the Lakes at all. My uncle had always taken me out.

'She went to get her small camera. She had this little digital thing she used for holidays and things like that: she could just take snaps with it, took the pressure off. She hardly ever took pictures with her phone, and that day she made a point of ~~taking it back to the room. I guessed she was sending Jay~~ a *Here we go, wish me luck* text. Or maybe she didn't want to take the phone on the walk in case I demanded it as evidence.

'So we're climbing. She was in much better shape than me,

despite the cigarettes. She ran every day on the treadmill at the poky little gym in our apartment building. This was typical of her. Down to the basement in the lift, punch in the code and she was on the machine, four or five miles a day. She said it helped with her anxiety. This was another aspect of my dismay: in order to enact her betrayal she would have had to get over this awful anxiety problem which was a major part of her. She must have felt something approaching terror, some high level of self-loathing, to go ahead and betray me, but she went ahead and did it anyway. Whether this was possible because she loved him so much, or whether she never loved me much at all, each conclusion was equally unbearable.

'Even though she was quite physically fit, she was tentative on the rocky paths, so she slowed us down a lot. We climbed a thousand feet in about an hour and a half, in pretty much total silence. At one point I remember I started to feel a new sense of relief, and the forgiveness idea came back to me, or nearly did: I don't know, it's hard to separate what happened then from what I thought about it later.

'The weather was still OK at this point. It was occasionally overcast, but mostly cloud banks drifting by, and we'd get these fabulous breaks and you could see all the way down Langdale, and the river was blue-black ink then bright silver and the slopes across the valley looked like they were shot in time-lapse, with the light wheeling across. You really see up there that being in a cloud is really just being in shadow. I still think of myself as a northerner, and we spend most of our lives in this watery shade, and the light brings out these colours and it's like looking up at a cathedral window when the sun strikes through and the colour and brilliance is too much, and you have to avert your eyes from the whole kaleidoscope. At one point she sat on a rock by the side of the path, and I stood beside her and we watched the valley suddenly illuminate and she looked at me and made an appropriate sound of awe and I was vindicated. The earth made my case for me: he can't give you this, Esther. You never wanted the music, but surely you want this?

'We took a drink and moved on, up into the craggier region at twelve hundred feet. If I'd known where to look, off towards the west and Ireland, we probably could have seen the weather coming in, these enormous shoals of cloud, getting heavier and darker.

'Then before we started to crawl up the scree below the last ascent to the peak, we put on wind jackets from my backpack. Hers was cerise, mine black. It wasn't cold yet, but there was damp in the air, and sometimes you'd get a little hit of rain in the face. Rain is the worst thing up there: once you get cold and wet you're done. There's no point waiting for the sun to warm you up again: it's not coming back.

'As yet, on the hill, the rain was light. I asked her if she wanted to go down, because she was very red-faced. "Just hot. It's beautiful," she said, but I felt uneasy. Another hour and a half to the top, probably. Then the descent could easily be as much again. Glaramara only has rocky paths down from the summit. It's the price it makes you pay for the time you spend up there. So I thought it best to head back. Also, bizarrely, I needed a piano. It's a feeling I get – a craving, a palpable buzz in the system. Once it sets in, it doesn't go away. It makes me irritable and impatient and everything else seems like an obstacle or even an aggression. Anyway, this feeling of suddenly wanting to be at a piano, needing to be off the mountain, made me take a turn off the path marked on the guide, to what I thought would be a gentler way down. I didn't want to tell her in case she figured out I was worried. And I got another sense of relief at the idea that we'd be back down in the valley soon. But I couldn't stop feeling this piano craving and obviously, every step of the way, thinking about her naked body next to his, her face reflected in his eyes as they lay in bed, their gentleness with one another, their private language, the utter sickened feeling, the knowledge that there was no way out, that every road led to misery. The only person I'd ever loved was now lost to me forever.

'It was definitely raining by now. And after we started out on what I thought was this descending path, I stopped under the protection of this big boulder on a sharp turn down and she stopped too. Her flushed, wet face looked up at me with such clarity and healthiness, and yet she must have seen something in my eyes and her mouth opened and her face became this pure mask of fear, but even then I saw that "cuteness", the wild angelic prettiness in its purest form: absolute vulnerability. And before I even said some version of my prepared thought, I knew none of this could make me unlove her. I also know I couldn't be stopped. All my thoughts of forgiveness were completely gone. Something that was me and not me had to bring the whole thing down: "OK, look, I really need to say something now, and I think you know what it is: I know about Jay."

'The boulder, and the turn in the path, created this odd sense of stillness, as if we were in a small room, no echo, just this dead acoustic, and this extreme intimacy on this vast imper-sonal mountainside, the only sound the rain spattering on our rain jackets. Maybe I thought that saying it there would calm me, would organize this horrific mess of feelings or at least provide some single feeling out of all the others. I had to speak, I have no idea whether I had control over it, but I had to speak. She said nothing in return. Are people supposed to look down when they're shamed in this way? Isn't that the learned behaviour? She didn't. She looked at me, her mask of fear now relaxed into grief, and she looked towards the boulder, then up at the sky, then said out over the valley: "You can't know."

"'Your mother's house in Oxfordshire. Last weekend."

"'You can't."

"'The letter. The email you printed out. Jayhawk183. In the box. I opened the box and found it."

'Now she did drop her head, and her whole body started to shake in this terrifying way. There was no forgiveness in my body, not possible, even seeing her destroyed like this. I just said: "We have to get off the mountain."

'I watched her in misery, with no reduction in the sickened feeling. In fact it spread around my body, along with a strange muscular weakness, which at least displaced the piano craving but had no merit whatsoever other than that.

'I couldn't bear to look at her any more. We had one more exchange of words, and I turned and set off. The weather was really coming in, and I was panicking because it was clear the path we were on wasn't headed down to the valley but up into the clouds. There was a steady wind now, we were in mist, and the path was getting rougher. And so I thought, "A few more minutes, we can turn back." I still believed that this path, marked on the map, would eventually get us down to the valley. There wasn't another, so it *must* take us down, and so I stuck to it and got to another steep turn, and when I turned around she was gone. I must have lost her in a second. Not a second, maybe, but much less than a minute. It was just mist after all. I had no doubt she was going to emerge, so I stood there looking back into the cloud waiting for it to blow through, but it never did, and she never came out of it. I ran back up a few hundred yards, I could hardly see the path ahead of me. It was so dreadful. I was in a black panic, calling her name. And then off to the left through the mist again, way, way down a steep slope in a ravine, I saw her cerise jacket. And then her arms splayed out, the red cap still on her head, her legs twisted at impossible angles. I don't know what I thought in that moment: that she must still be alive, she had to be alive. There was no way this could be happening. Totally impossible. I somehow managed to get down to her. But I was already too late. I imagine – I hope and pray – it had been instant.'

I wait for my breathing to slow a bit.

'Anyway, I suppose that's it.'

Silence for a while. Carlo inhales deeply. 'What was this "one more exchange of words"?'

'What do you mean?'

'You said there was "one more exchange of words", but didn't say what they were.'

'I don't think I remember exactly.'

'No?'

He's right, of course.

'She said: "I'm so sorry." And I said: "I don't care." And I turned my back and walked away. I could have said nothing. I could have forgiven her, as I knew I should have done. I could have told her at breakfast. I could have told her on the drive up. I could have told her in London before we even set off. I could have not looked in the box. I could have been around for her more. I could have asked her more questions. I could have asked her why she liked Lyon so much. I could have done any number of things, and any one of them would have been better than what I did. Any one of them and she wouldn't have lost her footing in the mist because of the tears in her eyes, or the confusion in her heart, or whatever it was that made her fall. In fact, what I did was the only possible thing that would have caused her to fall. And I think that's beyond doubt.'

Carlo seems to hum to himself before he turns to face me.

'Can I ask you, when you left her there, after she said sorry, before you knew she hadn't followed you, what was in your mind?'

'That she'd follow, of course. That she *was* following, that I'd get over my anger and start to feel pity and remorse. And forgive her. What I'd not been able to show there and then. She'd catch me up at some point lower down the mountain and we'd walk home together. And later on I'd say, "It's tough for me, but it's obviously best that we get a divorce" – because I really believe, after thinking about it all this time, and had begun to understand even then that, from the tone of his letter and all it implied, she would be better off with Jay. Why didn't I say sorry before she did? I knew even in the moment that that was what I should say, but I was too weak to say it and said something else instead, and this weakness cost me and the world an entire person.'

'OK. I see. This was all terrible, I realize. But you said you write to her?'

'Yes.'

'And talk to her?'

'All the time.'

'And you see her too?'

'Sometimes. When I walk up to Frau Weber's after a night at the Streicher. It's pitch-black on the *passeggiata* and I see her. Not her ghost or something like that. I see Esther herself, and she walks with me for a while.'

'What's she like?'

'She's quiet. A little out of breath. It's steep up there. Her face has that look of hers: a bit baffled by everything, but fine as long as I'm around. She loves Bolzano. She's proud that, in her way, she's given me my life here, but doesn't say it in so many words. We were always good at being quiet around one another. At our best, we were completely at ease: me in a score, her in a book. We had these peaceful, equal silences. We walk on together in the dark for a bit, and then at some point she needs to be elsewhere and says "Goodnight, Declan," and she's gone.'

'How does she feel about you?'

'I think she's pleased. It could have been much worse.'

'I meant, do you think she's forgiven you?'

I'd never thought of that.

'I really don't know.'

It's cold now and we're both done. Carlo gets up and yawns like a bear.

'Come on, Declan. Let's get some sleep.'

4

OK, so it's a big night: Marilena's playing in the hall at the Conservatory for the first time, and everyone but her is in pieces. In the year I've taught her, the only time she's ever got flustered was the one time she forgot to bring a score to her lesson. She is a maniac for tedious, arduous, repetitive, ugly work. In other words, she has a chance.

I'm at Carlo's place stupidly early, in the kitchen, where I'm least wanted, Laura in a culinary fugue state.

'Declan, go somewhere, please, I'm trying to work.'

'I'll go if you make me a sandwich.' I don't want a sandwich, I just want some fun.

'Sandwich? Now? Oh, you are such an idiot.'

She's got the oven stuffed and every burner going, pots and pans gurgling and fizzing; it's three hundred degrees in here and she's dolled up like Gina Lollobrigida. Inevitably, after the show it's everyone back here for pig and duck and *paccheri* ragu and pie and cake and ice cream, and then the *real* eating will start.

Carlo leans into the steaming chamber, looking highly scrubbed, cheeks gleaming pink above his freshly clipped beard. He says something to Laura in filthy Neapolitan and she responds only with a grunt of matrimonial derision. He knows not to try a comeback so he addresses me instead: 'Declan, come choose a tie for me.'

In the sitting room the kids are laughing and slapping each other, the boys' hair gelled into lacquered black soft-serve, Marilena imperious and still amongst them, doing the little thing she does before a performance, playing everything through in her mind, picking out fingerings in the air with her long, amazing hands, the rhythms indicated in twitchy movements of her face, eyes and mouth wide open, head a little tilted for the super-difficult bits.

Carlo stands before me, bursting out of his new shiny blue suit, three ties, all bad, held aloft for me to choose from.

'Which?'

'I hate them all.'

'Bah.'

'Go with the red one. It's very nasty, but at least it's not an actual felony.'

He goes back up to his bedroom, muttering outrageous falsehoods about the English. I watch Marilena for a second, let her finish another tricky little rhythmical thought, then: 'Hey, Mari, come outside. Something just occurred to me.'

She gets up and follows me. Nothing whatsoever has occurred to me; I just want to be with her for a minute or two. We stand in the street outside the front door of the house. She looks pristine, hair scraped back, wearing her favourite pink-and-white gingham dress, silver ballet flats on her canoe-like feet.

'Listen, that thing we talked about in the Beethoven, the repeat.'

'I remember: no diminuendo.'

'But last night I was thinking: yes diminuendo.'

'Really?'

'Really. Just a little one. Listen…'

And I do a weird 'poppada poppada poppada' thing to demonstrate my idea. She looks at me doubtfully.

'Huh.'

Which means 'no chance'.

'Come here, you.' I give her a quick squeeze and she makes a highly disapproving noise. She's like a six-foot furled umbrella. 'How can you be so skinny living in this house?'

'Nonna says it makes me grow up' – her arm slowly climbs into the air, fingers pursed – 'like a plant.'

She's thirteen, but my height. I look at her, and she looks back at me as if to say 'What?' so I have to say something.

'Are you OK?'

'Yes, Declan, I'm perfectly OK. But you're not.'

I feel the need to be servile: 'I had the piano double-checked. It's great, but still a little bit dead down low—'

'So no pedal in the quiet bits of the Schumann?'

'I'm being repetitive, I realize.'

'It's OK. I'm really, really happy.'

'Wow, you don't hear that very often. From pianists, I mean.'

'Crazy people.'

I hear Laura from inside: 'Declan! Declan! I make him a sandwich and the idiot disappears?!'

'Coming!'

I turn to Marilena. 'Damn, Mari, I really don't want this sandwich.'

'You better eat it.'

'Oh yes. I'm not *that* much of an idiot.'

—

The hall at the Conservatory is a shabby memory of its original state: peeling barrel-vaulted ceiling, a deep, wide stage, backed by a disused organ, the seats in the auditorium are slightly tipped back, upholstered in beaten-up blue velvet: a perfect place, really, to listen to these magical antique sounds.

It takes two hundred or so, and tonight it's absolutely packed out: music students, Mari's school friends, folks from the church and Frau Weber's crew, all floral dresses and high seriousness. How many decades has it been around, this genteel hubbub, these fancy frocks and men pulling at their collars in slight discomfort, the anticipation of ennui but also a fair chance of a glimpse of sublimity, and all best wishes to and admiration for the exquisite performer.

My nerves are dreadful and I can't sit still, so I leave Laura and Carlo's circle, mother and father in full plumage, wordy with anxiety and pride, and hop up onto the stage to triple-check the piano. A quick few seconds of *Exercises for chords in sequential progressions with modulations through the circle of fifths* and I realize Liszt himself would gladly play this instrument. I get a few ironic, well-meaning bravos and make craven acknowledgements as I hustle back to the stalls.

The lights dim and we start to settle. Carlo asked me not to sit too close to him in case he ends up clinging to me in terror, so I'm a few rows behind, Frau Weber to my right. I had suggested introducing Marilena from the stage, but Franka persuaded me not to: 'She will speak for herself.'

And she's right.

Then all the lights go out. Complete blackness.

My eyes adjust and are barely able to pick out the form of the piano, and you're there. In the total shadow, on the stage, walking towards me. It's too dark to see your face, but I imagine it in sunlit clarity. No reproach, just calmness. You stand still, a black silhouette, edged with soft light. I close my eyes, dark upon dark, so I can see you better. I start to move through space. This will never end, nor should it. You're closer now. I try to reach out but can't. I open my eyes to look for you—

The lights snap back up, and there is a small hubbub of relief. This is swiftly quelled because here is Marilena, walking peacefully, straight-backed, into the light. She moves downstage in her rehearsed but easy way, clasps her hands in front of her and gives a little bow. The applause is bright but brief, because she's at the piano now, settling herself. Then a moment of total, absolute, unsustainable silence, and she's away.

THE GHOST VARIATIONS

DAMIAN LANIGAN

First published in 2022
by Weatherglass Books

001

Cover design by Luke Bird
Text design and typesetting by James Tookey
Printed in the U.K. by TJ Books, Padstow

A CIP record for this book is published by the British Library

ISBN: 9781739983321

www.weatherglassbooks.com

Weatherglass
Books